THE ASSOCIATION

Footlight Theater, Book 4

"Ryder"

Judy Kentrus

The Association

Footlight Theater, Book 4 - Ryder

Author: Judy Kentrus

www.judykentrus.com

Book Title: The Association by Judy Kentrus

they lose their scholarships to Ivy League schools; an unregistered hand gun shows up in Ryder Wayne's locker, killing his chances to go into the FBI.

Despite the threat hanging over their lives and being blackmailed by unknown forces to maintain their silence, they achieved success in their chosen professions. Everett Troy, Oscar and Tony Award Winner; Jackson Vance, High School Principal; Mason Trent, Publisher of the Beacon Pointe Gazette; Ryder Wayne, Lieutenant on Beacon Pointe Police Force.

Thirty four years after that fateful night, they've reached the middlescence of their lives and decide, as The Association, to fight back and look into the murder. During their investigation, they're shocked to learn how much influence the killers have made on their lives and the women they love.

Chapter 1

Lieutenant Ryder Wayne stood in front of his captain's desk. He'd been a cop for twenty-plus years and had never faced such a quandary in his career—no, his entire life. The heat coming from the legal document in his hand felt like he was holding the burning end of a lit torch.

"You actually expect me to do this?"

Paul Clark took off his gold-rimmed glasses and carelessly tossed them on his desk. "How do you think I felt when I got a call from the prosecutor asking me to handle an extremely delicate situation that involved your girlfriend? He's afraid of a media blitz and wants to keep it in-house as much as possible."

Ryder gripped the triple-folded piece of paper and pointedly thrust it in his captain's face. "This is complete bullshit!"

"You think I don't know that? But we have to follow through on procedure, or we'll be brought up on charges."

"This is going to destroy her and everything she's worked for." Ryder almost choked on his own words.

"Your choice. I thought it would be better coming from you, because she's going to need a lot of consoling. I could always send one of the young, rookie cops."

"I'd like to call you a piece of shit, but I can't because you're my superior."

Captain Clark glanced at the time on his watch. "I deliberately waited until after the court offices closed so we don't have a judge to hold a preliminary hearing. She's officially in your custody and has to be in court Monday morning, nine a.m. Make sure she has a couple of good defense attorneys, if you get my meaning."

"That won't be a problem. I'll deliver this piece of garbage, and then I'm off this weekend. Don't worry, she'll be in my custody the entire time."

He turned around to leave the office, but stopped when his boss called his name. "Ryder, you didn't hear this from your captain but a good friend. Inside, you're furious and you want to rip a few new assholes, but don't. There is so much more at stake. I want your promise that you won't go off half-cocked and seek revenge by yourself. We're getting close, so keep that in mind. Console your lady, because she's going to need your strength and support. The media are going to have a field day. As your friend, I'm suggesting you make her unavailable."

Ryder nodded, understanding his hidden meaning. "Thanks, Paul. We'll be going to my grandfather's cabin. Keep it to yourself, but I'll also let The Association know where we'll be."

"I'll call my wife at the restaurant. The Plumb Beach will be buzzing with the news. Hannah is aware of what's going on and will keep her ears open. She'll also be the first one to defend Jillianne."

"Tell her we both said thanks."

Ryder shoved the offensive piece of paper into his back pocket and walked past the closed doors of the court offices. That much was in her favor, he decided, and took his time going down the wide metal stairs to the first floor of police headquarters. His office was sandwiched between the one dedicated to the shift sergeant and the larger one used by the detectives. The hustle and bustle of a big modern department was missing, but there were very few dull moments. For a late Friday afternoon, it was relatively quiet, but he avoided the dispatch area, where he'd be drawn into a time-consuming conversation.

He debated contacting her best friends directly to let them know what was about to go down, but decided to wait. They'd hear about it from their husbands. The six of them would be livid. Once the news got out, it was going to cause a small riot throughout the seashore community. Jillianne was loved by everyone, but when it came to someone messing with other people's finances, they could turn on her like a vicious cat.

Grumbling snores greeted him when he walked into his office. Watson had a dog bed from LL Bean with his name embroidered on the soft cover, but preferred to sleep on the old brown leather couch that came with the office Ryder had been occupying for five years. The German shepherd was considered the station's mascot. Trained in drug and corpse detection, Watson seemed to consider himself human. The other problem was he liked to smell the flowers and run after squirrels and would work only for steak, hamburger and homemade dog cookies. He could tell the difference.

The reports on Ryder's desk that needed his signature weren't going anyplace, and he shut down his computer. For the first time since he was a teenager, he wished he wasn't a cop. He reached for his black leather jacket that hung on an old clothes tree, a gift from his dad when Dexter retired as head of the detective bureau. "Let's go, sleeping beauty. We're going to see your girlfriend."

A head covered in deep gold fur jerked up, instantly leaving doggie dreamland. Ryder swore the dog smiled at the mention of Jillianne. "Be extra nice, because we have to do something very unpleasant. It's going to hurt."

Watson's long sleek back stiffened, and his grin turned into a menacing growl.

"No. I'm not going to do bodily harm, jug head. Let's go. You're a cop, act like one."

Jillianne was anal about keeping a strict schedule and could be found working at her desk at the Footlight Theater on Friday afternoons. Lately, all she did was work. She'd put her friendships on the back burner ever since she'd taken on the Burrows real estate account for her CPA firm.

His temper vibrated with barely controlled fury. She'd just been stabbed in the back. His cop sense saw it coming a few months ago, but there had been no way to warn her without any proof. They were using her as an example to punish him.

To his unending frustration, their lives were controlled by her schedule and his shift work, but they had a standing dinner date two times a month. Then he'd take her home and they'd have what they jokingly called "reminiscent sex." Three times during the year they'd enjoy a week's vacation together, and they worked in occasional weekends for some much-needed alone time. They'd been best friends and lovers since high school. Jillianne was his first and only love.

Ten minutes later, he parked his motorcycle in the employee parking lot behind the theater. Watson knew enough to wait until Ryder removed his specially made dog goggles and the strap harness before trying to hop out of the sidecar. With the cool temperatures moving in, this would be one of the last few days he could use his motorcycle.

It was after five, so the lot was empty but for a champagne-colored Lexus. Jillianne Bennett was independently wealthy from inheritance and hard work. Her vanity license plate read JILLY. Only one person was allowed to use her nickname.

Since he was on the board of directors and oversaw security, he had a key to the administrative entrance and was familiar with the security code. Watson's nails tapping against the wooden steps filled the lighted stairwell to the second-floor administration area. The other offices were closed for the day, and he headed for the only one with a light showing through the top of the frosted pane. The gold lettering read, *Jillianne Bennett, Endowment Curator and Director of Funds.* With each step, dread hung on him like a death shroud. He didn't need a sword to know he was about to cut her to pieces.

He tapped lightly on the oak doorframe, but didn't wait for permission to enter. The moment he pushed open the door, Watson rushed in, offering up a happy bark. Jillianne's head of reddish-gold hair shot up, and she looked away from her laptop that occupied the center of her neat desk. She'd recently added lighter blond highlights to the sweeping length that brushed the underside of her chin. She had a beautiful smile, considering what her family had paid for her perfect white teeth. In high school, he used to throw her retainers away on purpose.

It was the end of the normal workday, but she was still perfectly groomed in silk and pearls. She was the only person he knew who actually lifted her pinky when she drank a cup of tea. It no longer bothered him that she felt she had to reapply lipstick and check her makeup after they finished dinner. His uptown girl was the perfect lady, and he enjoyed watching her walk into a room and immediately command attention. The public and her employees saw her as the ultimate professional woman.

His adolescent heart had gotten slammed the first time he saw her, standing in the guidance counselor's office. Jilly's family had just moved to Beacon Pointe, and she was starting eleventh grade in her first public school. She was wearing a demure white cashmere sweater with a pink and light blue plaid skirt that brushed her knees, white knee socks and these girlie pink ankle boots. A single pearl suspended on a real gold chain adorned the front of the sweater.

He eventually found out her grandmother had insisted a lady wasn't fully dressed without her pearls. His boots were black with silver chains, and he was wearing a worn leather motorcycle jacket. She was Ms. Prim and Proper versus his rebel without a cause, her good to his bad. It was the start of a beautiful, loving friendship.

He was one of the few who knew the real Jillianne Bennett. More important, he knew her better than she knew herself—the unselfish side that would do anything to help her friends; the strong, inner person who fought for the underdog;

the side that anonymously supported charities that focused on children; the take-a-chance, laugh-at-herself side.

The cop side of him was prepared to handle the kaleidoscope of emotional stages she would go through, but as the man who loved her, he was wavering on innate turmoil.

"Hi," she greeted and removed her reading glasses and set them on her neat desk. A faint blush of sky-blue eyeshadow called attention to her pretty hazel eyes. "Tell me we didn't have a date tonight. Not that I wouldn't love to spend the evening with my guy, no, both my guys."

She laughed when Watson hopped up and put two large paws on her desk so he could give her a tongue-lapping kiss on her cheek. "You're the only one I'll let get away with that, considering I'm a neat-freak prude." She pulled open her bottom drawer and took out a Ziploc container of special dog cookies she kept just for him. "Here, my sweet love."

Watson accepted the treat and gobbled the cookie in a couple of bites. The look he gave Ryder when he sat on the floor and leaned against Jillian's hip said, *I'll protect her.*

"To what do I owe this unexpected pleasure?" Jillianne asked, running a hand with perfectly manicured fingernails over the top of Watson's head. "You know I hate that you're a cop, but I love my guy in uniform."

He was being torn apart. One side wanted to take her into his arms, but the professional side won the battle. He kept the desk between them. *Do it. Get it over with.*

"Jilly, love, I'd give all that I own, no, my life, not to have to do this, but I don't have a choice." Ryder pulled the paper out of the pocket of his uniform trousers and placed it next to her laptop.

She picked it up, and her smile faded before her mouth dropped open. Her fiery-hot eyes shot to his. Phase one: questioning disbelief.

"What the hell is this?" she challenged.

"It's a warrant for your arrest. You're being charged with embezzlement of a hundred thousand dollars from the Burrows Real Estate Organization."

"Ryder, I know I've been working a lot lately, but this is a sick joke!"

"I wish I could say April Fool's, but wrong month."

"You're serious?"

The hitch in her voice said she still didn't believe him. "I'm deadly serious."

Jillianne shoved up from her seat, making the chair roll toward the window behind her. "You're saying Cornelius Burrows initiated these charges against me?"

Ryder only nodded and prepared for phase two: outrage

"That conceited, ego-driven son of a bitch! Embezzlement? In a pig's eye! Two of my top-notch accountants and I have worked our asses off the past six months to straighten out his financial mess that we tracked back to over thirty years ago. I've a meeting with him next week to show him the details of numerous discrepancies that I've brought to his attention."

Ryder momentarily closed his eyes, comprehending what Jillianne had just revealed. She had access to the accounts he and The Association needed to help prove their case the two generations of Burrows and Magellan's were up to no good. That also posed another problem. She was being charged with embezzlement and would no longer have access to the records. First thing they had to do was clear her name.

"What was his reaction when you spoke to him about the discrepancies?"

"Cornelius said I'd probably made a mistake, but would be glad to speak to me."

"Inferring you made a mistake was like waving a red flag in front of a bull." Jillianne never made mistakes when it came to her business and personally stood by her work. What Burrows was doing to her made too much sense. Burrows knew The Association was getting close in their investigation, and he couldn't take the chance that she'd help her friends. That was Burrows' plan all along. Let her straighten out his financial accounts and then damage her reputation and credibility.

Jillianne moved to her desk and reached for her phone. "I'm going to call that back-stabbing shit right now!"

Ryder quickly put his hand over the device. "Wrong move, Jilly. I'm sure he's expecting you to call, but the only call you're going to make is to your lawyers."

"But..."

Watson woofed when Ryder's phone gave off three short barks that sounded only when one of The Association was trying to reach him. The text was from Mason. *911. Call me right away re Jillianne's arrest.*

"This isn't good. Mason wants me to call him. Word about the warrant for your arrest has already gotten out."

"This is absolutely ridiculous! I haven't done anything!"

He turned his hand over and gave hers a gentle squeeze. Phase three: personal defense in the face of cold, hard reality.

"Let me call him." The phone barely rang before Mason answered.

"Put it on speakerphone!" Jillianne hurriedly demanded.

"What the hell is going on? Fred got a call from Liam Thompson's wife asking about Jillianne stealing from her clients and helping herself to Cornelius Burrows' money."

"I'm with Jillianne right now, and you're on speakerphone. He's accusing her of embezzlement of funds from his real estate corporation."

"That's a crock of horseshit! She wouldn't steal a penny from a blind person!"

"Thank you, Mason," Jillianne called out.

"I'm sure the masses will agree. I was given the unpleasant duty to serve her with the warrant for her arrest. She has to be in court Monday morning at nine, with counsel."

"Arrest! Burrows is out to ruin her, just like he tried to do to my wife."

"That entire scenario still bothers me," Jillianne added. "I don't know why he wanted to destroy Mollie's restaurant."

Ryder concentrated on running his hand over Watson's head. *Bite your tongue. This isn't the time to tell her what's going on. We need to save her reputation first.*

"Jillianne, I can get something out on the weekend edition," Mason said, "a personal message from you. I don't mean to scare you, but the cold hard reality is, people and their money don't want to be separated, even if these charges aren't true."

"Mason, you're one of the few people who knows how important it is for me to keep my reputation spotlessly clean. I've been running my business for twenty-four years and have never been questioned, about anything."

"I agree with you, but people panic and react without thinking," Mason said.

Jillianne reached for the string of pearls around her neck and gave them a nervous tug. "If I put out a note, I'm practically admitting I'm guilty."

Her voice wasn't quite steady. Phase four: apprehension and acceptance. Ryder needed to join the conversation. "Jilly, by keeping quiet, people will wonder if you have something to hide."

"So I'm damned if I do and damned if I don't. Okay, put out a message from me apologizing for the unpleasant situation. It's all a big misunderstanding, and their accounts are secure. It will be business as usual. They can contact the office, and we'll provide a full accounting of their financial records."

"That will work," Mason said. "I'll also let the others know what's happening. My suggestion is get out of Dodge for the weekend. Knowing that conniving asshole, he's going to start turning the tide in his favor, especially with the media. That doesn't mean they won't start harassing Jillianne to get her side."

"Paul gave me the same advice. We're heading for my grandfather's place and will be back Sunday. The cell service is spotty, but I'll try to check in to find out what's happening. Thanks, Mason."

Ryder shoved his phone into his pocket, and the extra pair of handcuffs he always carried fell out onto the floor. He picked them up, but didn't immediately put them away. "We need to leave, right now."

"My God!" Jillianne stepped back and put the dog between them. "You're actually arresting me." She held out her arms and pressed the insides of her wrists together. "I'm a hardened criminal! Better put the cuffs on me."

"It wouldn't be the first time," he teased, "but no, you heard what Mason said. I need to get you out of town because people know where you work and live. You're officially in my custody, and I have to make sure you're in court Monday morning. Grab your coat and purse."

"This whole thing is insane," she muttered, shutting down her laptop. She put it away in her Vera Bradley computer bag, but he crossed to the desk and put a hand on the zipper.

"Do you have any of Burrows' accounts on your laptop?"

"Of course. I can retrieve his records from his central accounting program."

Once again, he was being torn between doing his job and getting the information they needed to help The Association. "I'm sorry, Jilly. I can't allow you to access his information since he's the one who made the accusations against you."

"I figured that much, but it's my personal laptop."

"Sorry. I'm going to have to impound the device. I'll store it in a safe place until we report to police headquarters Monday morning. The two accountants at your CPA firm who worked on his business records are also banned."

"If I know Burrows, he's already had his techs change the passwords. He's going to need a shady accounting firm to go in and adjust the records to reflect the money I embezzled."

"He's probably had that done without your knowledge. His lawyers are going to have to produce the figures for the court."

"That won't be good enough. I'm going to demand an independent accounting firm review those accounts." A cunning gleam filled her hazel eyes. "That horny deviant thinks he's dealing with a stupid woman. Well, I'm one step ahead of him."

"Stop!" Ryder shot his hand up like he was stopping traffic. "Horny? He made a play for you?"

Watson sensed a threat and barked an alert.

Jillianne gave the dog an affectionate pat on the head. "Both of you back down. It didn't take but a few minutes in his company for me to recognize he's a dirty old man. He charges his hooker fees and Viagra to his business entertainment account."

"That's another reason my fist is going to meet with his ugly face." Ryder grabbed the case that contained her computer and opened the door. "Let's get going. We need to pick up my truck, and then we have a forty-minute drive to my grandfather's cabin. The media and bloodhounds won't be able to get to you there."

"How did you get here? Don't tell me you drove your motorcycle. It's November."

Ryder shrugged his shoulders. "When we left the house this morning, Watson hopped into the sidecar, plus the weather cooperated."

"I need to let my housekeeper and brother know what's happening and get some clothes."

"We don't have time to stop at your house. You can call Winifred and Neil on the way. After that, you won't be able to get a signal. I'll loan you some of my clothes."

They were headed down the stairs when she abruptly stopped. Watson had already reached the bottom and stared up at them as if to say, *Let's get going. You're wasting time.*

"I'm wearing nine-hundred-dollar wool blended trousers and an Adalyn silk blouse." She lifted her leg to show him her

Burberry block-heeled boots. "These babies were not meant to be worn on a motorcycle. Where am I supposed to sit?"

"Behind me, where you usually sit. I've got your helmet and leather jacket in the storage pouch on Watson's sidecar. What more do you need?" he asked with a laugh. "You're wearing pearls."

"Funny, Sherlock. What about my car?"

"I'm going to have it towed to the impound yard."

"My white Lexus? Are you crazy? That car is registered to me personally, not my business!"

"I know that, but there's a method to my madness. It's going to get back to Burrows that you were arrested and your car impounded. He'll enjoy the small thrill thinking his plan is working, ruining you and destroying your reputation."

A watery film covered her eyes and her chin quivered slightly, announcing she was slipping into phase five: giving up.

Ryder cupped her chin to keep his eyes steady on hers. "Jilly, love, he's playing a game, and we need him to think he's winning, but we'll be laughing behind his back, all of us, The Association and the Fabulous Four and the rest of your friends. I've never lied to you. Do you believe I'm a man of my word?"

Jillianne focused her gaze on him and nodded.

"I swear this will turn out okay and that bastard will be holding hands with the devil."

Chapter 2

Jillianne reluctantly followed her handsome jailer and his four-legged sidekick. Watson hopped up into the sidecar and patiently waited for Ryder to fasten the safety harness and adjust the strap on his doggie goggles.

He'd parked next to her Lexus, and she gazed longingly at the comfort she was forgoing. A brisk November wind snapped at her cheeks and penetrated her thin cashmere jacket. She shivered and swaddled her arms around her waist.

A scattering of dead leaves scratched against the surface of the parking lot, and her eyes were drawn to the barren tree limbs. Two weeks ago, the mighty limbs bore leaves of red, gold and rust. It was the perfect reflection of her day that had started out beautifully and turned ugly. Her arms tightened around her waist, and she didn't know how much longer she could hold it together.

Before getting on the motorcycle, she put the black biker's helmet on, crushing the perfectly styled layers Missi, her expert stylist, had just refreshed. As soon as she zipped up the black leather jacket, she felt blessedly warmer. *If the teetotalers from the country club could see me now.* Ryder had given her the custom-made jacket and matching leather pants two years ago for Christmas. She'd surprised him with two Bluetooth-equipped helmets that synchronized with the Bluetooth and GPS system on his bike.

It wasn't that she didn't enjoy riding a motorcycle. She loved the free-spirit experience and clinging to her love, but at the appropriate place and time. She had a reputation to uphold and maintain. *Jillianne, right now your reputation isn't worth a plug nickel.*

"Your turn," Ryder invited before glancing own at her feet. "At least you're wearing boots."

He grinned at his own joke, but his smile didn't reach his eyes, and she sensed his heart wasn't in the trying-to-be-funny remark that was meant to cheer her up. The phrase *opposites attract* fit them perfectly. She took life too seriously. He did, too, because of his job, but Ryder had the unique ability to make her laugh, more so at herself, and pull out the side that only her best friends enjoyed. With them, she didn't have to be any of the three P's that had been drilled into her head since she was a child: perfect, prim, proper.

"Funny, Sherlock. Where's my laptop?"

"Secured in the sidecar with your four-legged bodyguard."

Watson woofed in confirmation, and she cupped his strong jaw. "I can always depend on you to take care of me. The next time you see Cornelius Burrows, you have my permission to bite him on the ass."

Ryder lifted the face-protecting visor on his helmet. "That's after I've beaten the living shit out of him."

Jillianne was surprised at his vicious statement. Her cop was generally cool, calm and collected, and it took a lot to set him off. "I appreciate that you want to be my knight in shining armor, but I'd never expect you to jeopardize your career and a job that you love. It's also not your style. You have the unique skills of a negotiator."

"Let's just say this is a unique situation and leave it at that. We better get going. The sun is almost down, and there aren't any streetlights where we're heading once we leave my house."

Jillianne made herself comfortable behind him and adjusted the padding on the helmet that protected her chin. "Could you take the back streets?" His chuckle came through the speakers in the helmet.

"Why? Don't want anyone to know you're a sexy biker babe who wears black lace bikinis under her leather trousers?" he teased. "No one can see your face."

"Right, and no one will recognize Watson riding in the sidecar of a motorcycle wearing WWII flying goggles and helmet. Please? I'll make you breakfast in bed."

"You couldn't find your way around a kitchen with a compass."

"You don't have to be such a smartass. Please, don't make me beg."

"Jilly, whining isn't very becoming. Hold on tight, love."

The helmet muffled the sound of the powerful engine when he drove out of the parking lot, and she sighed with relief when they pulled out onto the almost empty Main Street in front of the theater. In another hour, theatergoers would be arriving to attend the sold-out performance of *A Christmas Carol.*

Ryder was true to his word and made his way down quiet side streets of well-maintained older homes with a Victorian influence. A squirrel cut in front of the bike, and Watson barked up a storm. Her cell vibrated in her pocket. Normally, she'd accept the call because she'd connected her phone to her helmet, but she really didn't want to talk to anyone right now. A dog barking, cell phone ringing, ignoring a call—all were normal, everyday things, but life as she'd known it when she'd gotten up this morning had changed forever. Memories that she'd buried from long ago threatened to come back to life, but she slammed the door in her mind to keep them at bay.

Concentrate on the present, she told herself. What had she done to Burrows that he would turn on her and want to destroy everything she'd worked hard to achieve?

"You're awfully quiet back there, Jilly."

His smooth, comforting voice came through the speakers in the helmet. "Just thinking about Burrows and why he wants to destroy me."

"Like I said before, he won't get away with it. We should be at my dad's house in a couple of minutes."

"It still boggles my mind that you're fifty years old and still live in the same house you grew up in."

"You know when I ended my tour in the Marines, my mom took sick and my dad couldn't handle things alone. He was like a lost soul when she passed away, so I never moved out."

"That was twenty years ago."

"We give each other space and don't interfere with each other's lives. Hell, my father has more of a sex life than I do."

"I'll take that as a personal dig because I'm the only one you have sex with, but our lives are determined by our jobs." Jillianne tensed, waiting for him to say, *You don't have one right now*. But all was silent.

"I hope your dad doesn't think I'm guilty and will want to help convict another member of the family." She hadn't meant to sound so sarcastic, but that, too, was something she had to worry about. She was no longer a teenager who had to live through an embarrassing scandal, but was now an adult who'd been thrust into another scandal not of her making.

"You're not being fair, and he's the last person to think you're guilty. If he ever heard you say that, he'd be very upset. He had a job to do, just like me. He felt sorry for you as a teenager and regretted the embarrassment reflected on your family. He was a cop and will want to help clear your name."

"Isn't it funny how history is repeating itself?"

"Jillianne, now you're being maudlin. Unless you decide to start wearing a funny red nose, nothing is comical about the current situation."

"Sorry. I'm not thinking clearly."

Five minutes later, Watson barked, announcing their arrival to the entire neighborhood made up of Cape Cod homes with grayish blue weathered siding. Here, too, the trees were bare, and the flower gardens that dominated the front of the Wayne residence were already sleeping. Dexter's hobby was woodworking, and spotlights shone on two life-size Thanksgiving turkeys that he'd staked on either side of the front walk. One held a sign that read, *Happy Thanksgiving*. The other read, *Eat Ham*.

Sensor lights on the corner of the house came on when Ryder pulled down the driveway that led to a three-car garage. He pushed a button on the handlebars, and one of the three doors opened up. Additional lights came on when he pulled in and shut down the motorcycle beside a black Ford F-350 with an extended cab and cap.

While she removed her own helmet, he took care of Watson. The moment the dog was free, he jumped out of the seat and headed for the doggie flap built into the back door of the house.

Jillianne twisted her hands together. "Maybe I should wait out here."

Ryder stored their helmets in the pouches built into the rear storage section of the sidecar and retrieved her laptop and cupped it under his arm. "I've never known you to be a coward. Plus, you're being ridiculous." He took her hand in a firm grip. "We have a forty-minute ride from here, and you'll want to hit the powder room. You can also make your phone calls."

She nodded and squeezed his hand that still had hers in a firm hold. "You seem to be the one thinking clearly."

Ryder opened the back door that led directly into the small country kitchen, and she hesitated before stepping inside. His father wasn't alone. Dexter and Polly, his girlfriend, were in a full-body clench, sharing a serious lip-lock. Both were in their early seventies and had let their full heads of hair turn a natural white. He was a good eight inches taller, but their height difference didn't hinder showing their affection.

Ryder purposely slammed the back door, making the short frilly curtain fly out. "You two should get a room."

They jumped apart, and a blush covered Polly's cheeks that she'd coated with a pale pink blush. The kiss had eaten away at her deep pink lipstick. Jillianne folded in her lips to hold back a smile. The rest of the lipstick was on Dexter Wayne's mouth.

He must have been making something in his woodworking shop, because he was still wearing his work apron over his trousers and green T-shirt. Polly was on the curvy side, and her head came to the top of his shoulders. She followed the popular trend to wear colorful leggings with a print tunic.

"Oh, sweetie, this is so terrible!" Polly rushed over to Jillianne and threw her arms around her shoulders. "I was so upset when I got that damn paperwork this morning, and I couldn't wait till I got out of there. Dexter picked me up."

Jillianne stepped back before her eyes shifted to Ryder's father. She'd been so silly thinking he might believe she'd done something wrong. His eyes were filled with sympathy and understanding. His lips tightened in a small smile, and he opened his arms. It was the invitation she was hoping for, and she let his long arms pull her in for a comforting embrace.

"We're going to make this right," he whispered in her ear.

She lifted her forehead from his shoulder. Fierce pride had her swallowing back the tears that had begun to gather as soon as Ryder told her she was under arrest. "Thanks, Pop Wayne. We're going to need the help from the Almighty to prove I'm innocent."

Polly ran a soothing hand up and down Jillianne's back. "Come on, sweetie. You have to eat. I made a pot of chicken soup, and the biscuits just came out of the oven."

Jillianne offered a tense smile to the caring couple. Eating was the last thing she wanted to do. She looked around the kitchen that had been built in the sixties and had been gently cared for. Watson was slurping water from a silver water bowl. "Where did Ryder go?"

"He went upstairs to get out of his uniform before you left for Pop's house. He also mentioned he wanted to put your laptop away," Dexter offered.

"I've got to call my brother, housekeeper and my lawyers before we leave, because the cell reception out there is spotty to none."

"I'm sure you'd like some privacy. Go in the den," Polly suggested. "You know the way."

The wood-paneled room shouted *men only*. A flat-screen television was mounted on the wall above the fireplace mantel. Two recliners were strategically placed to get the best view. Occupying the table between the two chairs were Ryder's handcrafted pipes in the mahogany and walnut pipe stand she'd given him for his birthday a few years ago.

They'd added a three-seater couch against the outside wall to accommodate guests. A magazine rack was overflowing with dog-eared copies of magazines on wildlife and woodcrafts. The four-legged member of the family hadn't been left out. An oversize dog bed occupied the slate floor in front of the hearth. Ryder must have recently smoked one of his pipes, because she caught the pleasant scent of cherrywood.

She walked over to the side-by-side glass curios that displayed a variety of trophies and framed awards from Ryder's growing-up years. The award he won in the fourth grade always brought a smile to her face. First place in Pie-Eating Contest. She was stalling. The words *I've been arrested for embezzlement* stuck in her throat.

She retrieved her phone from the pocket of her trousers, turned it on, and the incoming texts sounded like one continuous ring. Thirty in less than an hour. She sat on the edge of the recliner to review the messages. The Fabulous Four were outraged and were there if she needed anything. Calling her lawyers wouldn't be necessary. Kaitlyn Griffin had let her parents know what was happening with Jillianne. Sean and Nancy Harrigan were in Florida but would be home Sunday morning. She wasn't to speak to anyone, and they'd be at her home Sunday night at six. If she needed anything, she was to call. Kaitlyn was available to Jillianne if she had any problems.

Before calling her brother, she sent a group text to her friends letting them they would be going to his grandfather's cabin. It hurt to read the messages she received from irate customers demanding to know whether the allegations were true. So much for thinking they'd believe in her integrity and ignore the false accusation.

Now Neil. What would she say to the man who'd become her stepbrother when her socialite mother had given up on the idea that love didn't exist and found a man who made her genuinely happy? No way was she contacting her mother and stepfather, who were currently on a cruise down the Rhine river as part of a three-month tour of Europe celebrating their ten-year wedding anniversary.

Neil was her family, even if there weren't any blood ties. As the lighting and sound manager for the theater, she saw him when she worked at her office in the theater and spoke to him a few times a week. She looked upon his daughter, Paige, as her niece.

He was number two on her speed dial. Ryder was number one. Neil answered on the first ring.

"What the hell is going on?" he demanded before she could open her mouth. "Are you okay? I tried to call you, but it went straight to message."

"I turned my phone off. Ryder is taking good care of me, and we're going to his grandfather's house in the Pinelands. How did you find out so quickly?"

"Liam Thompson's wife and her niece were waiting to have their hair done at Beauty Works and didn't care who heard them say you were arrested for embezzling money from Cornelius Burrows Real Estate. Missi heard their conversation, and your favorite beautician went ballistic. She asked them to leave and politely announced that if anyone helped spread that vicious rumor, they were no longer welcome at her salon. She called her mother, Diane, who works for Mollie, and the word spread like wildfire. Your office manager called me when he couldn't get a hold of you."

"Jeez, and I was only arrested a little over an hour ago."

"There's more. Matilda Hennypenny is the head usher for the theater guild this evening and already set up a phone chain to debunk the rumor. Your friends have your back. What I can't understand is how Mrs. Thompson found out before you were arrested. Someone is deliberately spreading rumors to discredit you."

"It has to be that snake Burrows."

A wave of misery was sucking her down in its undertow, and right now she didn't know how to save herself. "Promise me you won't contact our parents. They've been looking forward to this trip for years. Plus, this is all a big misunderstanding. Please tell me you don't believe I'm guilty."

"Jillianne, I don't know of another person who is as honest as you are. I, too, have your back. Paige is doing the show tonight, and I came over to be with Winnie. Your housekeeper hasn't stopped crying. You know what happens when she gets upset. She starts cooking and baking. I convinced her to take two Advil and lay down. Oh, and there's a news van from the local cable station parked outside your house. I hardly got out of my car and was practically jumped. I hesitate calling the police, because it will only draw a crowd."

"Trent Media is at my house? That's Mason's father's company." Jillianne paused when a strong arm came around her waist and Ryder settled a soft, healing kiss on her forehead.

"Let me make a couple phone calls," Ryder said softly in her other ear and headed for the kitchen.

"Seems like you and the others have things well in hand," Jillianne said to Neil. "You and Paige have to work the lights and sound for the shows this weekend, but I prefer Winnie not be alone. I'm afraid she might go out there and beat the reporters with one of her cast-iron frying pans. She's close friends with Elsie Trent and Fred. Give the ladies a call and tell them I'll spot each one a thousand dollars to play at the casinos if they take Winnie into AC for the weekend. I've got a suite at the Golden Nugget that I use for clients."

"I'll do one better. I'll call Manny Symonds and give him a heads-up. He'll keep an eye on them so they don't get into trouble."

"You are the best brother. Thank you. I'm meeting Sean and Nancy Harrigan Sunday night, and I'm to be in court Monday morning." Jillianne turned, making sure she was alone and lowering her voice. "Neil, I know this is all a big mistake, but I'm worried, not just for myself, but you, Paige, our parents, my employees. I'm embarrassing Ryder and his dad."

"If I were in your shoes, I would've collapsed a long time ago. You're one of the strongest women I know. Your niece thinks her aunt walks on water. You have a man who loves you, as well as the best support team a person can wish for. We're going to beat this."

"Thanks for being my brother."

Jillianne put her phone away and wondered what happened to Ryder. She shrugged and decided she'd better use the powder room before they left.

Ryder closed the door to the powder room just off the kitchen and turned the lock. "Mason, tell me you didn't contact the local office of Trent Media to send a team to Jillianne's house. They're camped out like a bunch of vultures on a dead carcass."

"Back down, Sherlock. I didn't call them, but I know who did. Remember when Gianna Knight was here doing a story on the Bessandra Troy Museum in August? Her team showed up yesterday to finish the job, which includes a photoshoot of the interior. They'll be here for the next month. Gianna has arranged to do her nightly newscast from the museum to up the hype. Guess who will be conducting personal tours?"

"The media's favorite lovebirds, Everett and Laura Troy." Ryder shook his head. "If this wasn't so important, Laura would kick that reporter's ass right out of town."

"Needless to say, she's back to stick a few needles into our already precarious investigation. My father wanted to send someone else, but she insisted on finishing a job she started."

"I don't like the sound of that. She's got her own agenda and came back here for a reason, and it wasn't to finish the story on the museum. Do you think she knows we're on to her?"

"I don't think so. How's Jillianne?"

"Being Jillianne, stifling most of her emotions, but she's close to crashing. That's why I need to get her away from people. She doesn't want to show them Ms. Prim, Proper, Perfect can suffer like a normal human being. I hate that this is happening to Jillianne. We all got a bad feeling when Burrows hired her to manage his financial division. She's in the thick of this, and I don't know how much longer I can hold back from telling her what's been going on."

"I felt the same way when the demons went after Mollie. Jillianne is going to hit rock bottom, and it will be up to you to bring her back. Keep your lady safe. If I hear anything, I'll let you know. We'll set up a meeting for next week."

"We'll be leaving for my grandfather's place in a little while and will be back Sunday afternoon. Mason, thanks for keeping your ear to the ground."

Ryder opened the door, coming face-to-face with Jillianne, and took a step back. *How long has she been standing there?*

"You went into the bathroom to call Mason? What is this? High school?"

"We're pressed for time, and I'm perfectly capable of doing two things at once." He swept his hand in invitation. "It's all yours."

When he walked into the kitchen, he saw that Polly had set the small round table in front of the picture window that overlooked the backyard. She spent more time here than in her small apartment, and a seasonal tablecloth of fall leaves and pumpkins covered the table.

"We weren't going to take the time to eat," he announced and held out a hand when Jillianne joined him, Polly and his father in the kitchen.

"Dexter and I were talking about the trial. Jillianne, I hate to say this, but your problems have only just started," Polly informed them.

"You can eat, and we can talk at the same time," Dexter suggested.

Chapter 3

"Are you two trying to scare me?"

"That's the last thing we want to do," Dexter said. "Sit down, Jillianne, and we'll talk.

She looked to Ryder for confirmation. He nodded and pulled out a chair for her at the table before he took the seat next to her.

His dad had retired from his position as a detective captain on the Beacon Pointe Police Department, but he'd hardly stepped back from doing police work. Overseeing the school crossing-guard program for the town and working as an officer of the court kept him busy.

Ryder had no idea what his father needed to discuss, but decided it was pretty important if he wanted them to delay their trip. He wondered how much longer Jillianne was going to hold it together. When she reached for his hand under the table, he gave her a reassuring squeeze.

Normally, he enjoyed Polly's cooking. The delicious aroma coming from the bowl of hearty chicken soup in front of him confirmed she'd made another winner, but his appetite wasn't cooperating.

His father selected a warm biscuit from the basket in the center of the table and used a knife to slice it open, all the while looking at Jillianne. "You know Polly is the court clerk and handles the court calendar and works directly with the judges. She knew what was coming down, but her hands were tied."

"You don't have to make excuses for me, Dex, honey. The warrant has been served, and I'm on my own time, having dinner with dear friends in their kitchen. What's happening to Jillianne stinks."

Polly hesitated before continuing, and Dexter patted the back of her hand. "Tell them, sweetheart. What you say won't leave this room."

"Jillianne hasn't been formally arraigned, and things are stacked up against her. This is just my personal opinion, but I'm not sure she's going to get a fair hearing. The judge sitting on the bench is Victor Burrows, Cornelius' Jr.'s nephew."

"There's more than one judge," Ryder interrupted.

"I received a timely message from Judge Meadows's assistant this morning. He's made arrangements to have a medical procedure on Monday morning that he's been putting off for quite a while and will be unavailable for the rest of the week."

"Damn. Cornelius is lining up his ducks, all in his favor." Ryder wanted to say more, but couldn't.

"Damn is right! What the hell is going on?" Outrage filled Jillianne's voice. "I'm not saying this judge won't be fair, but I feel like I've been tried and convicted and I haven't put a foot into the courtroom."

Polly turned in her seat and stared pointedly at Jillianne. "Pay close attention to what I'm about to say. I once read a book with a similar scenario, and the defendant's lawyers requested a different judge because of a conflict of interest."

Ryder relaxed a little when the light of understanding shone in Jillianne's eyes.

"I read that Judy Kentrus suspense book, too. When I talk to my lawyers, I'm going to request a different judge claiming conflict of interest. What time do you get in the office on Monday morning?"

"I'm there by seven. Judge Burrows can bluster all he wants, but you have a valid claim. Technically, he should recuse himself."

"I can honestly say I haven't read the book, so where did they get a different judge?" Ryder asked, going along with Polly's idea.

"See, the municipal court clerk was a personal acquaintance of the county clerk, and she contacted her friend to get a list of approved judges that could step in when a town required temporary replacement. There was this great judge who didn't take any shit, pardon my French."

"Polly, what you've just told us about Judge Burrows is against the confidentiality demanded by your position. Please don't put your job in jeopardy," Ryder warned.

"As far as I'm concerned, we're discussing a great book. I'm hoping to reschedule the hearing for nine a.m. Tuesday."

"See how smart my Polly is?" Dexter complimented with a big grin.

"On a personal note," Polly added, "I've got a beef with Burrows Real Estate. I sell real estate on the side. His agents have been brokering a lot of short sales. These homes are in run-down neighborhoods all over the county and are sold in a matter of days. Plus, they're cash deals. A friend of mine said they're bulldozing the buildings."

Money laundering for the cartel. The words jumped into Ryder's head. He really needed to have that meeting with The Association.

Polly insisted they finish their dinner. Before they left, Ryder needed to speak to his father, alone. He placed his orange napkin on the table and stood up.

"Polly, that was delicious. Before we leave, I need to have a heart-to-heart with my dad."

"Give me your keys, and I'll take Watson out to the truck," Jillianne suggested. The dog, which had made himself comfortable next to Jillianne's chair, jumped up and barked in agreement, before running out the doggie door.

"Take the blue and black quilted jacket off the hook by the back door," Ryder advised before she walked out the door.

Ryder followed his father into the den. "Dad, I can't explain everything right now, but Burrows is dirty. I need you and Polly to be careful."

"I will and always am." Dexter sat on the edge of his favorite chair and rested his elbows on his knees. He drew in a deep breath and stared up at his son. "I've never told you this, but maybe if I'd believed you, this situation wouldn't have gotten so out of hand."

"What are you talking about?"

"The murder."

Ryder plopped his butt on the edge of the neighboring recliner, shocked that his father had knowledge about their investigation.

"I wasn't working that night you claimed to have witnessed a murder. Rather than act like a cop and believe my son, I acted the enraged parent when we got called into police headquarters. A cop's son, my son, getting stinking drunk, embarrassing your mother and me. You know the drill. I regret to this day I didn't believe you."

"You know who was murdered?"

"Years later, I put two and two together. When Margie Holcombe called to report her missing brother, Charlie McCarthy, you know, Mack, and I were the detectives assigned to question everyone about Marshall's disappearance."

"Did you question Cornelius Burrows personally?"

"Him and his son, the asshole realtor Polly is having a problem with. I remember them swearing they had no knowledge of Marshall's whereabouts. At the time, I was disturbed by their coldhearted, business-as-usual attitude. Can you confirm this mess with Jillianne goes back to Burrows and the cannery?"

Ryder nodded. "There's a great deal to this investigation that will take too much time to explain. In short, they're responsible for multiple murders and life-changing conspiracies that have affected The Association and the Fabulous Four. We're missing a lot of specifics and proof Burrows ordered the hit on Holcombe. We've recently brought Mack into our investigation as a consultant because he had pertinent information on another murder they committed. Do you still have your notes?"

"I've kept all my notebooks in order by date of the investigation."

"Great!" Ryder forced himself to contain his enthusiasm in getting more information about the incident. "Try to locate the one that includes your interview with Burrows."

"I think it would be a good idea if I met my former partner for coffee. We can hash out old times and pick each other's brains."

"If you two masterminds come up with something, let me know." Ryder stood up and moved away from the chair. "Dad, I've got to get going. Please don't discuss this with Polly. I know she can be trusted, but the fewer people who know about this the better. Burrows has been a step ahead of us every step of the way, so he's got a network of informants."

"I'll keep my eyes and ears open. Burrows and former mayor Liam Thompson frequent town hall, and I'll keep an ear out."

Ryder went to head back to the kitchen but paused when his father put a firm hand on his shoulder. "I haven't said this often enough, but I'm very proud of you as a cop and the man you've become. I'm sorry I didn't believe you."

Ryder drew his father in for a heartfelt clinch, closed his eyes and enjoyed this rare moment. "I've had the best teacher and role model. I love you, Dad."

When they returned to the kitchen, Polly was loading the bowls into the dishwasher. "Take the thermal bag on the table. I put in some milk, eggs and bread. We were there last weekend, so you'll find plenty of staples and coffee."

"Thanks, Polly. You're the best."

Ryder paused at the door to slip his arms into the sleeves of his red and black fleece-lined jacket. "If anyone calls looking for Jillianne or me, you don't know where we are. We'll be back Sunday afternoon." He offered Polly and his father a tense smile. "We need to make this right. Thanks for all your help."

Polly kissed Ryder on the cheek. "Go to your lady, and I'll do my magic from my end."

"You should think about putting a ring on this one's finger before she gets away," Ryder said to his father.

"I plan to, but you should take your own advice."

Ryder headed for the open garage door, but he paused to appreciate the scene in the front seat of his truck. Watson was sitting in the driver's seat with his head turned toward Jillianne as if they were having a conversation. He, too, was holding a conversation, the one he'd had with his father. If only he'd consulted with his dad about the murder years ago…

He opened the driver's door. "How many times have we had this conversation?" he said to Watson. "You're not old enough to drive. The best thing I can do is give you a backseat driver's license. Vamoose to the backseat."

The dog didn't have to be told twice, and Ryder stepped back to get out of the way of the whipping tail that swung in his direction when the dog stood up. He wasn't prepared for the fart of foul-smelling air from the dog's butt.

"Damn dog! No more stew for you!"

"Why do you think I've got the heater running with my window open? You need to teach him some manners."

"I need to teach him a lot of things, including manners." He put the small thermal bag on the floor behind the passenger seat. "You okay?"

Dumb question, of course she isn't okay.

"Just peachy. While you were in the house, I called my office manager to give him a heads-up. Brad knows it will be business as usual, and he'll field all complaints. I told him if anyone wants to close their account, we'll be happy to do so. If those clients are so shortsighted believing I'm guilty, I don't want or need their business. I know we're going to your grandfather's house, but are you sure it's okay if you take a wanted felon out of your jurisdiction?"

"Oh, you're a hardened criminal, all right. The most we can get arrested for is not wearing our seat belts. Relax for the next half hour or so."

Traffic was light. He appreciated this time of year because the tourists who frequented the seaside community had all gone home. After a short drive on the Garden State Parkway, he exited the interstate and took the back roads that wound through the Pinelands. With very few streetlights, he had to be watchful of wildlife crossing the road.

Jilly was unusually quiet. He mentally prepared for the crash he knew was coming. The dark, winding roads reflected the many twists and turns their lives had taken over the past thirty-plus years. One of the statements his father made—*you should take your own advice*—played in his head.

Jillianne had always professed she'd never marry a cop, plain and simple. Her staunch reasoning was he could walk out the door in the morning, and that might be the last time she would see him alive. In his mind, it went a lot deeper. Jillianne couldn't handle changes. Everything in her life was in precise order, like the numbers she worked with—plus, minus, perfect balance.

He'd never pressed the idea of marriage because of the problems The Association had been dealing with, but things had changed over the past ten months. Everett, Jackson and Mason had married the loves of their lives. This case was escalating, and the last thing he'd contemplate was getting married. Keeping her safe and out of jail was the top priority in his life.

He turned onto the dirt road leading to the ranch-style house, and the lights from the truck bounced off the dense woodlands on either side of the road. He momentarily glanced away. The side of her head was against the window, and her eyes were closed. At first, he thought she'd fallen asleep, but the lights on the dash reflected her fingers, tightened in a nail-biting grip. They were so well in tune, she didn't have to speak. He knew what was going through her mind.

Life as she knew it would never be the same. The nails digging into her palms began to hurt, and she relaxed her fingers, but tension still gripped her body. This was nighttime, and she'd go to bed and wake up tomorrow morning, and all of this would have been a bad dream, no, a horrible nightmare.

All these years, making sure she never made a mistake, especially in her business, shot to hell. She was under arrest! Arrested! If she'd done something wrong, it might help to understand why Burrows was accusing her of embezzlement. She hadn't sought him out. Her firm had a full plate of clients who had been with her for twenty years because of her accuracy. He'd personally wined and dined her, pleading dissatisfaction with his accounting division at the time.

Their meeting months ago popped into her mind. He'd asked her to meet him at the Plumb Beach Restaurant for cocktails to discuss business. He'd turned on the charm and confessed he'd requested the meet because he was interested in pursuing a "friendlier" relationship. He could do a lot for her business and recommend her to his clients. He was twenty plus years older, but she'd let him down lightly, stating she didn't date clients. Her rejection didn't sit well, and he came right out and sneered, "The cop must keep you well satisfied."

At the time, she'd wanted to throw her peach Bellini in his face and call him to task for his rudeness, but she'd been taught to always be a lady. She'd explained about Ryder and their permanent understanding. The devil inside her awakened, and she'd added, "Oh, yes, he keeps me well satisfied."

The truck tire hit a rut in the dirt road and jolted her head against the window. "Jeez, are you trying to scramble my brains?"

"Sorry, it rained hard the past couple of days, and the runoff creates ruts in the dirt road. The house is just up ahead. I'll pull up close to the open porch. The exterior sensor lights will come on, but stay in the truck until I turn on the lights inside the house."

No one had to tell Watson they were close to their destination. He barked three times and eagerly ran out when Ryder opened the back door. The first thing he did was scout out the nearest tree.

Jillianne decided not to wait for Ryder to open the door the way he usually did and stepped out. A jarring shock gripped her body when her foot sank into a deep puddle of cold water.

"My new boots!" she cried.

It was the wrong thing so say. The alarm in her voice drew Watson in her direction, and his two front paws slid into the same hole, splashing muddy water onto her clothes. She didn't need a mirror to know spatters of mud coated her cheeks and hair. "Ugh, Watson!"

"Jilly, are you okay?" Ryder asked, hurrying off of the porch. The gleam in his eyes was a sure sign he was trying not to laugh. "How many times have I told you not to play in the mud?" he teased.

"No, I'm not okay. You parked next to a watering hole, and I'm standing in cold water. The hems of my slacks are swimming in mud, and my boots are ruined! I've also got mud on my face and in my hair! You two are a menace to society!"

"Watering holes are a lot bigger," he explained with a small chuckle. "As for being a menace to society, I'll take your word for it since I don't hobnob with the rich and famous. I prefer country-western music, drink beer from a can and eat ribs with my hands."

"You know I didn't mean it that way!" The chill was beginning to seep into her body.

It had always been a sore contention between them. She'd been raised by the snobby rich, but she never looked down on Ryder because he came from a hardworking, loving family. She hadn't known what family was all about until she met him and the Fabulous Four in high school. They'd introduced her to a world where kids weren't expected to be perfect and it was okay to make a mistake. It was okay to have fun, okay to take a few risks, okay to laugh at yourself, okay to love someone with every breath you took. Ryder was her best friend, her protector, salvation and the only man she'd ever loved.

He'd also been her temptation, the teenager dressed in black leather, riding on a motorcycle. Her mother's housekeeper had kept her secrets. Winifred knew about the nights she'd snuck out of the house to meet him.

No, she wasn't a Sandra Dee—maybe a little—but now she was all grown up. Life had sucker-punched her in a way only the Fabulous For knew about. She'd persevered through heartbreak, scandal, betrayal, but this current situation… The cold, soggy wetness of her boots drew her back to man and dog.

"Watson, you owe the lady an apology."

Watson jumped up and put two muddy paws on the shoulders of her jacket, and he slobbered her face with a wet kiss. The dog's heavy weight almost made her lose her balance.

"Damn you, Ryder! You did that on purpose!"

Before she realized what she was doing, she bent down and grabbed a handful of mud and threw it at his laughing face. To her disappointment, he ducked and the mud caught only the side of his cheek. Watson thought it was time to play and jumped in and out of the puddle, splashing dirty water on both of them.

"My clothes! What am I going to wear?"

Ryder wiped the mud off of his face with the sleeve of his jacket. "I've got extra clothes here, or if you prefer, you can wear a towel."

"In your dreams!"

"I have them quite frequently about you, but I'm the one removing it."

"I can never get in the last word! Let's get inside. It's freezing out here."

Before stepping into the house, she removed her boots at the front door and carried them into the dated living room of the house she'd visited with Ryder and his dad over the years. The good-size room had comforting warmth, with a seasoned couch and a couple of well-used padded armchairs. A woodstove occupied an outer wall, and photos that Dexter had taken of the area in all seasons hung on the wood-paneled walls. Throw rugs covered the scratched but clean hardwood floors. The room was also blessedly warm.

She removed her soiled jacket and watched Ryder wipe the mud from the dog's paws. He was also quietly lecturing Watson on his bad manners. Like the four-legged rascal would understand. Her two loves shared a very special quality that she very much appreciated. They made her laugh, especially at herself. Normally, this type of situation would draw her out of her dignified, regimented life, but right now it wasn't working.

"I really need a shower and something to wear."

"Go ahead. I'll find something for you to sleep in. Your body wash and shampoo are in a box under the sink. Want a cup of tea? I think Dad still has some of your favorite, Dream by the Fire."

"When I come out." Instead of heading toward the bathroom down the hall, she hesitated, staring down at the floor and twisting her hands together. Asking for favors wasn't in her makeup, but this was the man she loved. He knew her better than anyone. He'd understand. "Please don't leave me alone tonight."

Her simple request cut right through him, but he understood. Standing before him was a young child, not a beautiful, mature woman. Little Miss Perfect didn't go running to Mommy or Daddy if she had a problem. She was to stand on her own two feet and deal with things on her own. Only a chosen few knew she was petrified of thunderstorms and spiders and hated snakes.

He erased the small space between them, cupped her chin to raise her head, needing her to see and hear the truth. "You're never alone, because you have me, and you didn't need to ask. I'll always be by your side. You're my lady, my love, Jilly." He brushed her lips with the lightest of kisses, sensitive to the slight trembling in her body. He wanted to give her more, but this wasn't the time, not yet. The mad, the fight in her had burned out.

She only nodded. When she turned and headed for the bathroom, his hate for Cornelius Burrows increased tenfold.

He walked past the bathroom door and paused just to make sure she'd gotten into the shower, then headed for one of the two bedrooms. The smaller room was sparsely furnished, with a queen-size bed, an old mahogany dresser and a pea green armchair from the sixties era. It had been a standard joke when growing up. If anyone had a piece of furniture they no longer needed and still had some life in it, the donation was brought to Grandpa's vacation house.

He retrieved a black t-shirt with a picture of, *The Association*, a singing group popular in the late sixties. They'd attended a reunion concert in Atlantic City a number of years ago. The Fabulous Four had thought it was great the singing group had the same name. Jillianne had purchased souvenir shirts for all of them, but she bought an extra shirt and mailed it to Everett so he wouldn't feel left out.

He found a pair of gray sweats she could wear and red and black argyle socks. Normally she wouldn't be caught dead wearing such a mish mosh of clothes, but beggars couldn't be choosers. She'd also look like his Jilly, not Jillianne Rose, the very rich socialite.

He suddenly remembered the thermal bag in the back of his truck and hurried to the back door. Of course, Watson wouldn't like it if he went outside without him. "You might as well hit a tree while I'm out here."

He'd just retrieved the thermal bag when his phone signaled a text message. Reception was spotty, but he could generally get a weak signal away from the house. It was from his captain. *Your dad and Polly are fine. They went out for ice cream, and someone broke into your house. Came in through back door. Your bedroom trashed. As per your dad, Jillianne's laptop is gone. I advised they stay at Polly's house for the rest of the weekend. Your father reluctantly agreed. Kaitlyn Griffin filing report.*

Chapter 4

Frustration had him bending over and picking up a good-size rock. With all his might, he shot it into the woods. Vital information to support their case had been in their hands, and now it was gone! That laptop had to contain explosive data if they'd had the balls to break into a cop's house. Discussing the contents on her laptop was totally off the table.

The reply to his captain wasn't pleasant, and he said he'd be in touch when they returned home late Sunday afternoon. At least his father and Polly were safe, but he didn't like that his father had been drawn further into the mess. He walked back to the porch and put his pinkies to the sides of his mouth and whistled. Watson came running and breathed out a puff of cold air, a sure sign winter was on its way.

"Come on, let's check on your girlfriend," he said as soon as they stepped into the living room. He tossed his quilted jacket over the chair closest to the door.

He frowned with concern at the sound of running water when he got to the bathroom door. The water heater couldn't supply hot water this long. "Jilly," he called but didn't get any answer. He opened the door to be greeted by a shroud of steam. The white, opaque shower curtain was still closed, and he quickly shoved it aside. His Jilly was huddled in the far corner of the tub with her face buried in her knees. The water was barely warm, and she was visibly shivering.

She'd finally crashed.

Pain clutched at his heart, but he forced himself to shift into cop mode and treat her like a wounded victim. "Okay, love. I'm here," he soothingly assured and turned off the water. He kicked off his boots and tossed the pink bath towel over his shoulder. "Let's get you out of here." He took hold of her chilled wet shoulders to help her stand up and leaned her against the tiled wall. "Don't move. I'm going to step out, and then I'll carry you into the bedroom."

She didn't even nod in response, but stared straight ahead. He draped the towel around her wet body before sweeping her up into his arms. Her sopping-wet head found a home on his shoulder, and his arms tightened when she shivered. The hot tears falling on his neck broke his heart. Jilly rarely cried. He'd once asked her why. Personal emotions were just that, personal, and she was to be a lady at all times.

Watson hadn't left his side and led them into the bedroom they used when they escaped for a weekend in the woods. He set her on the side of the bed and carefully wiped the water from her body like a parent would do for their child. He didn't do a thorough job drying her hair, but got most of the drips. She didn't protest when he finger-combed the wild strands off her face.

For once, there was nothing sexual in the way he touched every soft, sweeping line of her body. He forced his mind to ignore the sight of her upturned breasts, which puckered from the cold water, and the refreshing peachy scent of her skin.

As soon as he was done, he reached for the T-shirt at the bottom of the bed and drew it over her wet head. She'd remained silent through his ministrations, and the tears continued to run down her cheeks.

"Come on, Jilly love, get in under the covers." He quickly drew back the bedspread and top sheet and draped them over her.

He went to move away from the side of the bed, but a hand filled with tension gripped his wrist. "Don't leave me," she moaned.

"That's the last thing I'd ever do." Watson was already eyeing the space at the bottom of the bed. "Sorry, pal, this bed is too small for you and us. Stay close and sleep on the throw rug next to the bed."

Watson went into protective mode and sat close to the bed so he could rest his snout right next to Jillianne. "Watch over our girl," Ryder told him. "I'll be right back."

Ryder made sure the front door was locked, upped the thermostat two degrees and turned out the lights before returning to the bedroom. Jillianne had turned on her side and was running a soothing hand over Watson's head. The dog's eyes were closed in ecstasy.

Normally, Ryder slept naked, but he left his shorts on, not that it would be much of a barrier between them. He turned off the bedside lamp, but didn't bother to lower the shades on the two bedroom windows. Moonlight showered the room in a soft glow. He slid under the covers and, as if they were a longtime married couple, spooned their bodies together. They shared a pillow, and he brushed her wet hair off his face. His traitorous yearning was already reacting to the warm, soft body in his arms, but he took deep breaths, trying to beat back temptation.

Lying still, listening to her even breaths, he wasn't ready to settle down, reviewing the events that brought them here and what he had to do to clear her name. It wasn't going to be easy, and he'd need some very special help.

By the time he was done, Burrows was going to pay, big-time.

He'd been lost in thought, but was drawn back when a warm hand lifted his away from her waist and guided it under her shirt, urging him to cup her breast. He easily captured the fullness and kept a gentle, possessive hold. A deep sigh sent the message that she was back. His lips found their way to the tender flesh beneath her ear and lingered for extended heartbeats. He knew this, too, was what she needed and wanted.

In response, she whispered, "I love you."

The arm he had around her tightened a little more.

A cold wet nose on his neck and doggie breath woke him at six. Ryder reluctantly rolled away from the warm body wrapped around him. During the night, his love had turned over and, as was her habit, was cupping him. His hand crawled under her shirt to hold a very nice breast. She was still relaxed in slumber. Normally, he'd react to her possessive invitation, but he wasn't about to take advantage of her present emotional state. He'd wait for her to let him know when she was ready to make love.

"You've got rotten timing," he complained to the dog in a soft whisper and carefully removed her hand. He didn't bother reaching for his trousers because he had every intention coming back to bed to resume his enjoyable position.

"Hurry up, because I'm coming back to my comfortable bed."

The sun had risen enough for him to watch out the large front window in the living room to keep an eye on his wayward dog. Watson did his business, but the mischievous dog frolicked and tormented a squirrel on purpose, knowing Ryder watched and waited.

These few moments gave him pause to think about how he'd handle Jillianne when she was challenged with facing the new day. She'd suffered a dramatic, life-changing shock. Jillianne was strong, self-confident, regimented, but normalcy for her was gone. She was entitled to wallow in a little woe-is-me my-world-has-come-to-an-end suffering. He couldn't wait too long for her to heal, because they were going to need her help. His heart urged him to be sympathetic to her situation, but he knew, logically thinking, that that would be the wrong path to take. He needed to point her in the direction to fight and take her life back. It was going to hurt him as much as his love.

When the squirrel ran up a tree, Watson started barking. Enough was enough. Ryder opened the door and whistled, and Watson ran into the house and went right over to his bowl of water beside the counter in the kitchen. "You did that on purpose. You better hold this next round of pee for a couple of hours." In reply, the dog looked at him as if to say, *That's what you think.*

Jillianne was still in the middle of the bed when he crawled under the covers, but she immediately turned over and rolled into him.

"Hmm, you're cold. What time is it?"

Ryder gathered her close and urged her head to his shoulder. "A little after six. Go back to sleep for another couple hours."

"Okay, don't have a reason to get up."

And so it begins, he said to himself before he fell back to asleep.

The digital clock on the bedside table read ten a.m. Jillianne brushed wild strands of hair off her face. The bed beside her was empty. She hadn't slept like that in—she had to stop and think—her last weekend away with Ryder. There was never any question about their sleeping arrangements. It was understood their time together was special, precious, so they always took advantage of every moment, and that included sharing a bed.

When they were on vacation or on one of their escape weekends, it was obvious from the way they acted toward each other that they were lovers. Holding hands, quick, silly kisses, loving moments on a dance floor, sharing food and drinks. They'd been asked a number of times how long they'd been married. Neither had ever denied their marital state. She'd always reply, *Forever.*

Over the years they'd played the cat and mouse game and he'd pop the question, "Will you marry me," and she'd always reply "nope." He'd be surprised to learn she'd kept track of the number of times she refused his proposal—ninety-nine times. They hadn't played that game in a very long time. Had she protested too much, too adamantly, that she'd never marry him as long as he was a cop? It no longer mattered. She was now a criminal, and who'd want to tie himself to a woman with a tainted reputation. *You'll be lucky if he doesn't dump you,* her conscience warned. Your mother had faced a similar scenario…

"Stop!" Jillianne clutched the sides of her head when the nightmare remembrance generated a pounding in her skull. She flipped the covers off her body, and a piece of paper flew up in the air. She picked it up off the floor.

Morning, uptown girl. Drag your sweet body out of bed. Sweats and socks on dresser. Best I can come up with. Washing your sexy undies, what there is of them. Coffee made.

Her lips drew up in a small smile. Ryder teased her that Billy Joel had her in mind when he wrote the song *Uptown Girl*. Yes, her white-bread world was restrictive and regimented, but life as she knew it had changed forever when he walked into the guidance counselor's office and said he'd been assigned to show her around the high school. He'd introduced her to Laura, Tamie and Mollie, and her life had taken another turn, for the better. They'd all shown her a different side of life, but Ryder most of all.

A loving smile would fill his handsome face when her parents' driver dropped her off a block away from school. Her mother and father had reluctantly agreed to let her attend a public high school, but had drawn the line at letting her take a school bus. They'd thought she'd been going into school a half hour early to do extra work, but Ryder had become her reason to get up in the morning.

Her happiness had come to a screeching halt two weeks after she graduated from high school. In the past twenty-four years, she'd fought, crawled back and achieved success, only to have everything she'd worked hard to achieve wiped out by four words, 'you are under arrest.'

She went into the bathroom, and the face staring back at her in the square mirror over the sink was another eye-opener. Her hair was scattered like she'd been in a windstorm, dark circles cupped her sleep-heavy eyes, and red blotches from crying spotted her cheeks. A spark of outrage flared in her body.

This wasn't the face of a woman who ran a million-dollar business and courted rich clients.

The outrage immediately fizzled out. She wasn't that woman anymore.

Ryder had set out the spare toothbrush and toiletries she kept at the house. Face washed, teeth and hair brushed, she felt a little better and returned to the bedroom to get the clothes he'd left for her. It wouldn't be the first time she'd dressed without underwear. Along with Ryder, the Fabulous Four had introduced her to a sense of freedom in quite a number of ways.

She picked up the gray sweatshirt with the much-too-long sleeves and breathed in the earthy, outdoor scent that clung to the material. Ryder. The matching pants had stretch bands at the ankles, so she wouldn't have to worry about tripping. She finished rolling up the sleeves and looked into the mirror on the back of the closet door. "You look like a waif in someone else's hand-me-downs."

Out of habit, she reached for her phone that she set on the nightstand every night before she went to bed, but it wasn't there. Ryder locked it in the truck so she would be harassed. Tears escaped her eyes, and she used the sleeve of the sweatshirt to wipe her face. She wasn't that woman anymore.

She headed for the small kitchen that was off the living room. On the dark blue and white tiled counter that separated the dining area from the living room was the coffee pot, a mug and another note. *Outside chopping wood. Wrapped in foil is a piece of toasted "white bread." Add your own jelly. PS. Compass not required. Turn around and walk straight ahead to refrigerator. Jelly in door.*

"What a smartass." The kitchen had never been a part of her life. Winifred had seen to their meals and prepared anything she wanted to eat. Half the time, she'd have food delivered, since she always worked late.

A can of Maxwell House coffee was on the counter by the drip coffee maker. The coffee she normally drank came from freshly ground beans, a blend her housekeeper special-ordered. "Stop being such a prude. He went to the trouble to make the coffee because he knows you cannot function without your first cup of the day."

She poured a cup, sipped and decided it was good. She ignored the toast. That had been another dig, because he knew she never ate white bread. Rather than sit on one of the stools next to the counter that separated the kitchen and living room, she carried her cup of black coffee to the large picture window that overlooked the front of the house. The sight that greeted her caused the pace of her heartbeat to increase to a full sprint and made her mouth water.

Man and *beast*. Both terms fit Ryder. He'd removed his shirt, and his faded jeans rode low on his hips and clung to his cute ass. The morning sun enhanced the sweat-sheen gleam to his skin. He'd tied a red bandanna around his forehead to catch the perspiration. In all the years she'd known him, he'd always worn his russet-brown hair military short.

The muscles in his arms expanded, and his back muscles tightened every time he thrust his arms in the air before cleaving the piece of wood he'd balanced on a flat rock. Based on the stack of wood, he'd been at it a long time.

He kept himself in shape, claiming he needed to be able to move fast at a moment's notice. All he'd ever wanted to be was a cop.

To the right of his spine, just above his right hip, was a long, narrow scar he'd gotten trying to arrest a man with a knife. She'd been out of town at the time, and he'd been in serious condition. He'd ordered their friends not to let her know how badly he'd been hurt. She'd been royally pissed when she returned and went to see him at home. He'd jokingly said, "Aren't you glad you're not married to a cop?" His comment had hurt more than she cared to admit.

The thermometer on the wall beside the front door read forty-five degrees. She selected a green and white quilted jacket and then remembered her mud-covered boots were still wet. On the rack below the jackets was an assortment of well-used rubber boots. Along with the furniture, everyone donated footwear, jackets and foul-weather gear.

The jacket was too large and the black boots were floppy, but beggars couldn't be choosers. Watson was the first to spot her and barked in greeting when she walked out the door. She bent to one knee and wrapped an arm around his neck. "Here's my boy." She laughed when Watson jerked out of her hold and kissed her on the cheek.

Ryder set the ax to the side and picked up his aluminum cup filled with ice water and drank heartily. He should be cold without his shirt, but he'd worked up a lot of body heat the past hour.

"Morning. Day's a-wasting. Ready to go to work?" He realized too late what he'd said and silently called himself every kind of fool.

"I don't have a job, remember?" She swept a hand, indicating the pile of wood. "Are you planning to hibernate here for the winter?"

"Rules are if you use the woodstove, you have to replenish the wood. I always chop more because I don't want my dad splitting wood. How did you sleep?" He already knew. At one point, she'd rolled away so he wouldn't know she was crying, but he'd dragged her back and shushed her back to sleep.

Jillianne ran the tips of her fingers over the part of the bandanna that covered his forehead, before going up on tippy-toes to sweep his lips with a soft kiss. "You know, because you held me all night. Thank you. I can't believe the meltdown I had, and I'm sorry I behaved so badly."

"There's no need to apologize for being human. You're not that teenager who had to hide in the closet so her parents didn't know she was upset."

"That was before I was able to call you and pour my heart out." Jillianne slipped her arms around his waist and rested her cheek on his chest. "Ryder, you've grown inside me all these years, and I don't know if I could've made it without you in my life. The Fabulous Four helped me, too."

His love for her swelled, and he drew her closer. He kissed the top of her head. "Jilly, I feel the same way. And I believe I've mentioned a time or two that shit happens and we have to learn to deal." He didn't want to get deeper into their discussion, for now. He stepped back and bent over to pick up his ax.

"Make yourself useful. Pick up a piece of wood, balance it on the rock and move aside until I split it down the center."

She took a step back and acted like he'd asked her to chop down the entire tree. "Me? I've never done this before."

"I know. Every time I was outside splitting wood, you had to finish up some kind of work."

"They should have machines to do this kind of work."

"They do, but I'm also using it to relieve my frustration. Normally, when we sleep together, it's far from platonic. You kept holding my balls all night, and every time I moved my hand away from your lovely breast, you put it back."

"Sorry. You know I like holding you."

Ryder bent down and picked up an already split piece of wood and threw it into the woods. Watson thought it was time to play and went after it. "That's not the only thing that's causing my frustration. I want to beat the living shit out of Cornelius Burrows for doing this to the woman I love, but my boss warned me off because things are escalating and we have bigger things to worry about." Ryder realized too late what he'd said and hoped she wouldn't pick up on it. "So are you ready to help?" he quickly added.

"Me? Really? Split wood?"

"No. I'm splitting, you're assisting."

"But I'll mess up my nails."

Ryder walked over to the pile of uncut wood where he'd set his flannel shirt and picked up the extra set of work gloves he'd brought out just for her. "Put these on to cover your lily-white hands. Once we finish splitting, we'll load the wood into the wagon attached to the ride-on mower and stack the split pieces in the woodshed. I'll even let you drive."

"Deal."

Jillianne easily caught the rhythm of his swing, and they worked like a well-oiled team. Her hair kept falling in her face, and he reached in his back pocket and pulled out a yellow and black patterned handkerchief he'd purchased at a dollar store.

"Put this on. It's not a Louis Vuitton scarf, but it will serve the purpose." He'd purposely added the dig to see how she'd react to the snobby part of her life. She didn't, other than to shrug her shoulders.

"Thanks," she said and wrapped it around her head and tied it at the base of her neck before putting her gloves on.

They worked for another two hours and decided to stop when the sun disappeared behind gray clouds. With each swing of the ax, he'd hoped she'd open up and want to talk and spew, get rid of the inner torment he knew she was suppressing, but her depression overtook her need to want to fight back. It was time to push.

They sat on the thick cushions of the comfortable couch and drank cups of tomato soup and ate grilled cheese sandwiches. The fire he'd started in the woodstove was already spreading cozy warmth into the room. She hadn't removed the bandanna, and her cheeks had a healthy glow. The sadness in her eyes announced how she was feeling. If circumstances had been different, he'd have her stretched out on the couch and beautifully naked so he could sip at her, not tomato soup.

"Thank you for your help," he said. "There's enough wood for my father and Polly when they come on the weekends."

"I remember Gustave, my mother's distant relative, the one who owned the vineyard, saying the best way to appreciate hard work was by doing something physical with your body."

"You never talk about the six years you were away from Beacon Pointe. They were the longest of my life."

"I know. Mine, too. You know my mother wanted to shield me from the family scandal and shipped me off to France to live with a couple I never met. When I returned a year later, I wanted to attend college on the East Coast so I could be close to you."

"It wouldn't have mattered, because I was already in the Marines."

"I remember calling your house to speak to you. When your father said you were getting ready to be deployed to Iraq, I started to cry, because all I wanted to do was talk to you. He was so sweet and said he'd send me your address.

"Since my mother controlled the funds, and you were out of the country, I got my master's degree in accounting at USC. You know I kept in touch with the Fabulous Four and they welcomed me back to Beacon Pointe a week after I was twenty-five. My life was in limbo until you returned home."

"I understood why you had to leave, but it broke my heart. I wanted to escape, too, but I had to wait until my community service was over before I could enlist in the Marines."

"I remember the day you came home. The receptionist in my office said there was a Marine requesting to see me. I was on the phone with one of our new clients, and I hung up on him. I ran out of my office and couldn't get to you fast enough."

"You said in your letters that you'd always love me, and the kiss you gave me was positive proof you weren't lying."

"And the first thing you did was submit your application to the Beacon Pointe Police Department. I know it wasn't the FBI, like you wanted. It still bothers me that someone planted a handgun in your high school locker. I remember that day like it was yesterday. The principal and cops conducted their investigation right when classes were changing. I remember yelling at them that you'd never do such a thing, because you'd never disgrace your father."

Ryder chuckled lightly. "I remember Mason holding you by the shoulders. You were like a wild woman screaming I was being framed."

"I felt sorry for your father, because all he could do was stand there and watch his son be humiliated."

"I kept looking at my dad and shaking my head, denying it was mine. He understood and nodded in understanding. I was more worried about disappointing my parents than myself. My dad was furious that the chief refused to let him investigate the incident. I'd just turned eighteen and could've been locked up. Fortunately, he was able to call in a few favors, and I got community service for six months."

"It also bothered me that the chief of police opened your locker. The look on his face was like he was enjoying what he was doing. I know he's dead, but I'll bet he was dirty."

That's what I've thought for a long time. The chief refused to believe we witnessed a murder that fateful night. "It's funny you should say that. His cousin was the late Cornelius Burrows Sr. Both men are dead, so they've gotten away with whatever they were into."

"That family must have been born with a 'corrupt' gene. May they rot in Hell. It's a shame you never found out who planted that gun."

Evade the truth or give her a little background information? He took her hand and played with her fingers. "You remember Everett had drugs planted in his locker. Jackson and Mason lost their scholarships because someone doctored their grades, and the handgun was planted in my locker. We don't have any solid proof, but we've narrowed it down to Howard Blumberg, our old Intro to Psychology teacher. He just happens to be Cornelius Burrows' relative." Ryder hoped she didn't see a pattern to what he was revealing.

"Why would he do that to four eighteen-year-old boys? He should be castrated."

"As I say, it's only speculation."

Ryder lifted her ring finger that hadn't always been naked. "I've asked this question before, and you've always evaded answering. Let's try one more time. The night before you left town, we made love and you professed I was the love of your heart and no one would ever take my place in your life."

"It was and still is the truth. I loved you then and a million times more now."

"You wrote me a few letters, pouring out your love for me. Shortly after you turned twenty, they stopped. I found out in a letter from Laura that you got engaged to a rich guy socialite. I was upset, and that's putting it mildly, but when I gave it more thought, it made sense. Money and prestige have always been a top priority to you and have a lot to do with why you've refused my marriage proposals. I'm a cop with very little in the bank."

He relaxed against the back cushion and folded his arms over his chest. A spark of defiance flashed in her eyes. *So far, so good.*

Jillianne pulled her hand away and shoved up from the couch. "How *dare* you question my love for you? My mother introduced me to Marco because he came with money, power, and a society image she wanted, not me. He had the means to put her back on the pedestal she thought she needed to get on with her life, not mine. Yes, I accepted his proposal in a moment of weakness. He went to kiss me, and I felt sick with guilt because he wasn't you. It didn't go over too well when I refused to share a bed with him before we were married.

"We were engaged for a month, until I found him in bed with a man and a woman! They had the nerve to invite me to join them! Then the horny sicko informed me that he believed in an open marriage and affairs were perfectly acceptable. I took off the four-carat ring and told him to shove it up his ass. His father loved me because I had an unsoiled socialite reputation. He thought I could straighten out his wild son and clean up his image. I told the old coot I wasn't about to be played by some freewheeling socialite. I had a sense of pride, and no rich playboy was going to taint my standards and self-esteem.

"When I finished college, I gave my mother the option of staying in California or returning here with me. She came back and found a real love that didn't come with a big bank account. I picked up the reins of the poorly run business my father left. I poured my heart and soul into that firm and turned it into a million-dollar business. I'll be damned if someone is going to rain on my parade!"

The fire was back in her voice, and he added a little more to the flames. "All your work has been for nothing. Your clean-cut reputation is tarnished, and your business is shot to hell by another freewheeling socialite who has dumped a raging storm on your parade."

"Oh, shit, I forgot Burrows has ruined me." The fighting-edge mad in her voice dwindled, and she sat her butt on the edge of the cushion next to him and hung her head. "I've lost everything, my business and reputation."

He quickly changed tactics before the flame died. "I'll be your hero and fight for your honor, but I never thought you were one to give up. You're willing to let your business be destroyed, your name blackened, let people lose their jobs, let some snake ruin everything you've worked hard to achieve. I'm very disappointed in you, Jillianne Rose."

Ryder stood up and moved away from the couch. "What happened to the girl who defied her parents' strict rules and risked everything to be with me? Where's the girl who wanted to take on the police, declaring my innocence? Where's the woman who wouldn't let herself be used by some rich bastard? Where's the woman who took on the Alcoholic Beverage Control and the New Jersey State Police, declaring Mason's innocence when they wanted to charge him with selling illegal moonshine?"

"How dare you talk to me like that? He's destroyed everything I've worked hard to achieve."

"Oh, no, that's a cop-out. You're letting him get to the girl who hid in the closet because she was afraid."

He whistled, and Watson left the warmth of the rug in front of the woodstove to run over. "Let me know when you find the woman who is ready to fight and take her life back. I'm going out for a while."

"You're leaving me alone?"

"You're not alone. You can wallow in the company of cowardice, woe is me, bested, beaten and defeated. Pick one."

He grabbed his jacket and walked outside, debating whether he was doing the right thing. He waited on the porch until the dog did his business. "Come here, boy." It had to be the serious tone in his voice that urged Watson back to the porch.

"I need you to stay here and take care of our girl. She's sad, so keep her company." He opened the door and didn't bother to look at Jillianne. He couldn't. The devastated look on her face when he'd said he was leaving her alone had been gut-wrenching.

Gray clouds covered the sun, and he turned on his headlights so he could see down the dark road and hopefully avoid hitting the deepest potholes. He needed to make a couple of phone calls, one that included checking in with his dad.

He was so busy wool-gathering and thinking about Jillianne and the shit he'd dumped on her plate that he hit a pothole and his head slammed against the driver's side window, shaking his brain. He hoped she'd come to her senses.

Chapter 5

Jillianne was surprised to see the dog run into the room. Without prompting, he jumped up on the couch and stretched out beside her.

"He's a mean jerk!" she professed when Watson rested his head on her thigh. He barked in agreement before returning to his comfortable position next to her. "Who is he to talk to me like that? He thinks he understands, but it's not his business and reputation that's been destroyed.

"Look around this place, not even a television! On the other hand, that's good, so I don't have to watch my face being plastered all over the local cable channel like I'm a hardened criminal! At least if I had a cell phone, I could bitch and moan to my friends. Now what am I supposed to do?"

Watson jumped off the couch, walked over to the woodstove and barked. "You want me to add wood? I can do that, considering I helped split logs today." Jillianne remembered to put on the fireproof gloves that were setting next to the iron poker and opened the door. A blast of hot air hit her in the face. Sure enough, the fire was a bed of burning embers, and she added three pieces of wood.

She glanced at the time on the microwave on the counter, thinking it was much later than four thirty, considering how dark it was in the room. Someone had contributed a table lamp in the shape of a largemouth bass, and another duplicated a Gloucester fisherman in a yellow rain suit. She turned on the tacky table lamps and then remembered the gray clouds that had moved into the area early in the afternoon. She didn't feature being alone if a storm was moving in.

"Well, that killed all of ten minutes."

Watson ran into the kitchen and put two feet up on the counter, next to the jar shaped like a black cat. "Now you're telling me cookie time." She gave him two in the shape of fire hydrants. He'd no sooner finished chomping both treats when he ran to the front door and barked.

"You can go out. Do your business and no playing around. I don't feature going after you in the dark and it looks like we're going to get some rain."

She stood by the door and it was dark enough for the sensor lights to come on the moment he ran in front of the small open porch. "Sure, you can't pick a tree close to the house. You had to run down the path toward the pond. The wind shot a burst of cool damp air in her face and she quickly closed the door, but moved to look out the front window to keep an eye out for Watson.

The first boom of thunder made her jump, followed by a flash of lightning. "No, this can't be happening now!" Mother Nature ignored her plea and the heavens opened up and wind driven rain beat against the front window.

She shifted from foot to foot and wrapped her arms around her waist. Nights of hiding under the covers and shaking alone in her bed flashed through her head. "You will not be afraid. You will not be afraid. A volley of overhead thunder seemed to shake the house followed by almost instantaneous flashes of lightning. She prayed the power wouldn't go out. "Come on, dog, get back here!

A worried glance had her looking at the time on the microwave. He'd been gone twenty minutes. Her apprehension increased with every passing second. "Something isn't right." Without giving any thought to what she was about to do or face, she remembered the flashlights were in the cabinet next to the sink. She found an old police raincoat and black police-issue rain hat and slipped her sock covered feet into the boots she had on earlier.

"Jillianne, you can do this. Ryder and Watson are counting on you." Wind driven rain stole her breath and beat against her raincoat and wide-brimmed cap the moment she stepped off of the small open porch. The ground was already muddy, but she focused her eyes on the wide beam the flashlight put out when she left the lighted area around the house and started down the dark path toward the pond.

"Now I know what walking into hell must feel like," she muttered, trying not to look at the earie shadows bouncing off the naked trees and ground cover. Another boom of thunder caught her unawares and the too-big sloppy boots caused her to slip on the loose leaves under foot and she landed on her ass. In the distance she heard the crack of a tree limb and she automatically put her hands over the top of her head, not that it would do any good. The crashing boom said it landed closer to the road.

Despite the pounding of the rain, her ears picked up a whimper and then she saw him. Watson was lying in the path and her heart broke at the sight of his bloody paws. Her tears joined the water running down her face. She knelt down next to him and cradled his wet head in her lap. "Oh, my poor baby, what happened to you?" He licked her hand and wagged his tail letting her know he was glad to see her.

She focused the light to inspect his injuries. Blood was coming from a series of punctures in the bottom pads of his two front paws. Instinct had her taking off her raincoat and placing it over him. "Oh, baby, you're too heavy for me to carry you all the way back to the house.

"Damn, I can't even call for help." Then she remembered the ride-on-mower with the attached wagon. She stood up and patted him on the head when he tried to get up. "No, stay here and I'll be right back. I'm going to take good care of you." She kissed his wet head and he licked her cheek.

The storm continued with a vengeance. Without the raincoat, she was getting wetter by the minute, but she didn't allow herself to be distracted. The most important thing was getting Watson home safe and sound. She was relieved when the sensor activated lights came on and brightened the area that included the shed where the lawn tractor and wagon were stored. Luckily, Ryder had left the key in the starter and she sighed with relief when the four-wheeler started the first time.

The single front headlight made it easier to see down the dark path. Her soggy discomfort heightened, when the rubber tires hit rain-filled ruts and muddy water splashed up in her face. Her clothes and hair were plastered to her skin and the chill was already seeping into her bones, but she couldn't think about that now. The sight of the poor dog's paws made her feel sick to her stomach. She didn't have to be a police detective to know someone deliberately placed sharp objects in the path hoping to hurt the dog. "May their souls rot in hell," she muttered, but her words were muffled by another crash of thunder.

Just before she got to Watson, she took a short "u" shaped path and was able to come up beside him. She got down on her knees beside him and was heartened by his wagging tail. "See, my sweat boy, I told you I'd be back. Now we have to get you in the wagon." She opened the small back gate before slipping her arms under his soaking wet body.

"Damn, you're heavy," she groaned, sliding her arms out from under him when she set him down gently on the flat bed. She bent over to retrieve the rain coat so she could cover the dog and a pain shot up her spine. "Too many cookies. You're going on a diet." She wasn't surprised when he issued a small growl.

"Let's get you home and I'll bandage your paws."

A slew of curses filled the cab of his truck, some of them he made up on the spot. Rain beat against the front window and the wipers fought a losing battle to keep the windshield clear. "You're a first class bastard! Jillianne is alone and she's petrified in a thunder and lightning storm. You saw the storm clouds this afternoon. Like a jerk, you left her after issuing a guilt-laced tongue lashing.

People were smart enough to stay indoors so the main road had very little traffic. He sighed with relief when he saw the lane up ahead that led to his house. He'd picked up a pizza, antipasto and a meatball hero for their dinner and spoke to his dad. Everything was fine. The captain was personally conducting the investigation into the missing laptop. He wasn't about to name names, but it was brought to his attention that the Lieutenant hadn't followed procedure and the defendant's laptop hadn't been turned into the evidence clerk.

Mason gave him an update on what was being said about Jillianne. This evening, a rival cable channel aired a personal interview with Cornelius Burrows outside of his main offices and was questioned about his claim of embezzlement against Jillianne Bennett. He urged everyone who had their accounts with her to pull their business and follow up with an independent auditor."

This was why she couldn't back down. She'd have to work hard to get back what had been stolen, her unblemished reputation. He couldn't do that for her. The inner drive would have to come from her. It was inside her. That's what he'd been trying to do earlier. Wake up her will to fight back.

He made the right hand turn on the road that led directly to the house, but groaned at the sight of the red flashing lights up ahead. A fire rescue volunteer was parked on the shoulder and a row of orange caution cones blocked the road. It was then his headlights picked up the downed tree that was blocking the road. The curses started all over again.

He pulled up in back of the pick-up truck and got out, not caring about the torrential rain. One man was sitting in the cab, talking on his cell phone. Ryder knocked on the window and the guy rolled down his window.

"How long before you can get this tree out of here?" He had to shout over the raging winds.

"I'm waiting for help, can't move this sucker on my own. Trees are down all over the place and downed power lines are getting top priority. Name's Abner."

"My house is down the end of the road and I need to get home. I'll give you a hand. I've got a heavy chain in my equipment box. We can wrap it around the tree and I'll drag it with my truck."

While he and Abner attempted to get the chain around one of the larger limbs, all he could think about was Jillianne and how scared she must be.

Their first attempt to pull the tree off the road failed when a rotted limb snapped off. It took over an hour before they were finally able to get the tree to the side of the road. The rain continued to come down, but not as heavy as the beginning of the storm.

While the volunteer collected his cones, Ryder retrieved his chain, but paused when he saw where Abner had stopped and was shaking his head.

"What's wrong?"

"Been a volunteer for twenty years, but never seen anything like this in the middle of a storm," he said, pointing to the bottom of the trunk. "This tree isn't a product of the storm, it's been freshly cut. Who in their right mind would risk getting struck by lightning and cut down a tree? Lamebrain doesn't know you can't burn wet wood."

Ryder gave a hurried thank you to Abner and pulled out a twenty out of his pocket. "Buy yourself a cup of coffee." Cold and soaked to the skin, he gunned his engine to get home as fast as possible. Abner's comment jumped into his head. Had someone deliberately cut down the tree to delay him? A sigh of relief escaped when he spotted the house, but frowned when he saw all the outside lights were on. The lawn tractor and wagon was parked in front of the porch. "What the hell?"

"There, my sweetie, all nice and cozy. I'm sorry I said you needed to go on a diet. Have another cookie."

Jillianne sat back on her ankles and stared down at her patient as he munched on his third treat. The hardest part had been getting him into the house. She'd once read about people being able to bare a heavy weight and not know where they got the strength. She understood completely what they were talking about.

Watson's long body was stretched out on the soft blanket she'd spread on the couch. His fur was relatively dry, but still had a wet dog smell. He'd held perfectly still when she gently wiped the mud and blood off the bottom of his paws. She might've been a little over zealous in her bandaging technique, but Watson didn't seem to mind. Just for good measure, she'd found a mismatched pair of socks and slid them over the bandages. He didn't move when she covered his paws with another light blanket. They'd be taking him to the vet tomorrow morning.

She also felt a great deal better having taken a quick hot shower and commandeered another set of Ryder's sweats and thick wool socks. She'd even remembered to add wood to the fire. "You done good, Jilly," she complimented herself and sipped from the cup of tea she'd just made.

That's the sight that greeted Ryder when he rushed into the house. His Jilly was leaning against the couch next to his dog, safe and sound, with her hands cradling a cup of tea. She was wearing a different set of sweats and her hair was wet. She appeared relaxed, content, even though they still suffered occasional booms of thunder and flashes of lightning.

"You really shouldn't play in the rain," she teased.

"Are you okay?" She didn't even wince when a flash of lightning brightened the room.

She shrugged her shoulders before sipping more tea. "I'm fine, a lot better than you. You're dripping water on the floor."

"A tree came down and I helped a volunteer drag it off the road." His eyes shifted to Watson, wondering why the dog didn't get up off the couch to greet him. "Why is Watson swaddled up like a baby? Those aren't the clothes you were wearing when I left earlier. Why is the tractor and wagon in front of the house? What the hell's going on?"

"I've a lot to tell you, but first get out of your wet clothes and take a quick shower before you get a chill. I made a pot of coffee, but don't complain if it doesn't taste right."

"I will, but why are you sitting here so calm and we're in the midst of a thunder and lightning storm?"

"I'm not calm, it just looks that way." She stood up and gave him a quick kiss before putting her hands to his shoulders and pointing him in the direction of the bathroom. "I'm glad you're home safe and sound. Go. When you come back I'll answer your questions."

The clothes she was wearing were in a pile on the floor in the bathroom. He picked up the wet sweatshirt splattered with mud. The pants were in the same condition. What had she been up to while he was gone?

Seven minutes later he walked into the kitchen wearing flannel sleep pants and a sweat shirt and poured himself a cup of hot coffee. It was a little weak for his taste, but he wasn't about to complain. Jillianne had resumed her place on the floor beside Watson who was deep in slumber.

He sat down beside her, lifted his cup in a salute. "Great job on the coffee. The shower helped. I feel almost human." He set his almost empty cup on the floor. "Before you tell me what happened, I need this." He cupped her chin with his hands and lowered his mouth so he could steal a hushed, love-filled kiss. She moaned in acceptance and her head drifted back to the edge of the cushion. He needed more and was further seduced by the sweet taste of her lips and the soft pillow of her breasts pressed against his harder chest. Her hand moved to the back of his head and she relaxed further, urging him to deepen the kiss. They were lost in one another and Ryder didn't appreciate Watson waking up and licking their faces.

"I'm happy to see you too, but your timing sucks," Ryder said, wiping his cheek with the sleeve of his shirt. As an afterthought he wiped Jillianne's cheek, too.

Jillianne ran a soothing hand over the top of the Watson's head. "Go back to sleep."

"Now, I think I'm ready to hear what you have to tell me. I saw the dirty clothes on the floor in the bathroom. Are you really okay?"

"Yes and a heck of lot better now that you're here. It was touch and go for a while, but I made it."

"Now, tell me what happened." He was surprised when she stood up and started to pace.

"I am so angry right now I'm having a hard time keeping it together. Shortly after you left, Watson wanted to go out and when he didn't come back after twenty minutes, I knew something was wrong. I dressed in your old police raincoat and hat, grabbed your police flashlight and walked down the path toward the pond.

"In the thunder and lightning?"

"The weather was the least of my worries. I found Watson laying in the path close the pond." Jillianne moved to the couch and lifted the blanket away from his front legs.

"Why is he wearing mismatched argyle socks?"

"Sorry for the fashion booboo." Jillianne slowly revealed the heavy bandages around the dog's front legs.

"What the hell happened?"

The alarm in Ryder's voice instantly woke Watson from doggie slumber. He woofed and sat up on the soft cushion. Jillianne had put so much padding on his front paws his injury didn't appear to cause him discomfort.

"Some heartless son of a bitch put something sharp on the path and Watson stepped on it. In my mind it was deliberate."

"Someone deliberately wanted our dog to get hurt!"

"I just said that. I'm so angry I could punch something!" Jillianne continued to pace. "It isn't a secret that your family owns this piece of property that's in the heart of the area where the supposed New Jersey Devil was spawned."

"I can remember coming out here as teenagers and The Association would play capture the flag with the Fabulous Four. Mason purchased devil masks and staked them in the woods. The first time we played that trick, we could hear you girls screaming. Please don't tell me you saw the devil."

"No, but it was scary enough. Your grandfather believed the legend was real. When did he purchase the property?"

"He didn't purchase it. According to my grandfather, he used to play cards with Cornelius Burrows Sr. They were having their weekly game and Cornelius ran out of money. He jokingly bet the property and lost it to my grandfather."

"So it would be logical to think that his grandson knew about the property."

"Of course. It's been in the family since the mid-forties."

"And everyone knows Watson belongs to you."

"Just like everyone knows you belong to me," Ryder added.

"Unless you have a tracking device on your truck, it would be logical you'd bring me here to protect me from further humiliation, and of course we'd bring Watson with us for added security."

Realization of where their conversation was heading showed in his eyes. Anger in her body sharpened when she finished putting two and two together. "Don't say it! In other words, don't rain on my parade. He's behind this vicious move, and if it's the last thing I ever do, that lowlife is going to pay for hurting our dog! Someway, somehow, I'm going to make it my business to destroy that lower than a snake's corporation!"

Four words flashed through Ryder's head. *She's ready to fight*. He made himself comfortable beside Watson, and they both watched her pace. The dog's head moved back and forth, following her every move. Ryder might have taken the wrong approach to inciting her anger, but as he gave it more thought, he realized that all he had to do was make her unleash the protective, fight-for-the-underdog side she never acknowledged. She was magnificent!

He stood up and took her by the shoulders to make her stop pacing. "I owe you an apology. I said some pretty nasty things before I left. It was a piss-poor way to fire up your mad to make you want to fight back."

"What are you talking about?"

"Come here." He made himself comfortable on the couch and pulled her onto his lap. Watson didn't want to be left out and moved his head to her knees. "Think about what you just said. You want to go after him for hurting our dog. You didn't say you want to go after him because of what he did to you. You overcame your fear of thunderstorms and went out to save Watson. Like I mentioned earlier, when they were trying to arrest me, you didn't care about your own reputation, but screamed and challenged the authorities in my defense. You took on the establishment to protect Mason and saved him from going to jail." He brushed the hair away from her cheek and grinned. "You're a force to be reckoned with, Jillianne Rose. I think I'll get you a special shirt that reads Lady Underdog."

"Lady Underdog? I like that," she said with a laugh. "Leave it to you to point out a part of myself I never recognized. She'll have to be my alter ego."

"I'm very proud of you, Jilly. I know we're facing a lot of trouble, but we know you're innocent. It's not going to be easy, but we're going to make this right, I promise. If Burrows sees you backing down and hiding with your tail between your legs, you'll be giving him a win. Your office staff and their families will suffer if they lose their jobs. That alone should piss off Lady Underdog." He drew her head to his shoulder. "You also have a small army of friends who are willing to stand and fight right alongside you."

"While I was wallowing in self-pity, I forgot about them. Thanks for reminding me. I'm sorry for behaving so badly. I don't know how you put up with me."

"There was never any question. I love you, Jilly, and that will never change."

"I love you, too, Sherlock. You'll need all of your police skills to help get me out of this. No more hiding in the shadows. I'm ready to hold my head high and fight. Before we do that, we need to take Watson to the vet to get his paws checked out."

"My vet has an emergency number. I'll call him in the morning. Before we leave, I plan to check out the path to find whatever they planted."

Watson chose that moment to jump off the couch, and he didn't appear to be in much discomfort as he made his way to his empty food bowl and pushed it in their direction with his nose.

"Food! Our dinner is in the truck. I picked up a pizza, salad and a hero. Why don't you feed him while I get ours?"

Jillianne collected the used paper plates from dinner and put them in the garbage can under the sink. "Thank you for a delicious dinner. I didn't think I could eat, but I feel a lot better. You may think I'm crazy after spending all that time in the rain, but I need to take another shower and wash my hair."

"I understand, believe me. While you're doing that, I'll tamp down the fire in the woodstove and take Watson out."

The dog's head popped up at the mention of the word *out*, and he jumped off the couch without discomfort. "I know you're going to want to smell around and investigate, but no free running around for you tonight, my friend. You'll stay by my side. You can ride in the back of the wagon while I put the tractor away."

Ryder wanted to take a look around the perimeter of the house. More than ever, he was convinced the tree had been deliberately cut down to delay him from getting back to the house. What was more frightening: He'd left her alone at the mercy of the demons. *But you left Watson here to protect her,* his conscience jumped in. Not enough.

"His feet are going to be muddy, so I'll replace the bandages when he comes in the house."

"I'll take care of it, love. Enjoy the warm water. If you're not out in fifteen minutes, I'm coming in."

"I'm fine, Sherlock, really."

"I believe you. Go."

Despite the exterior lighting, Ryder grabbed a flashlight. After putting the mower back in the storage shed, he took a slow walk around the house, but he didn't find any footsteps in the soft ground, other than the ones he made. Watson wanted to veer off and head down the path to the pond, but the serious tone in Ryder's voice when he issued their established command *by my side* threw the dog into cop mode.

Confident the demons hadn't gotten close to the house, he went back inside. Before turning off the lights, he cleaned Watson's paws and replaced the bandages. On the way to the bedroom, concern had him pausing at the bathroom door, listening to the water running in the shower. His hand moved toward the doorknob, but Watson poked him in the thigh with his nose.

"What?" The look on Watson's face said, *You said you believed her, so don't start doubting her newfound courage.*

"You're right and too damn smart." He walked into the bedroom and smiled when the dog walked over to his newly made bed. Jillianne had piled three blankets on the floor so he would have something comfortable to sleep on. She would have made a great mother. That dream had ended a long time ago. Her hot flashes and mood swings during her hormonal changes had driven them both crazy.

He crawled under the covers, naked and turned on his side to check the time on the bedside clock. At fourteen minutes, the water shut off and the bathroom door opened.

His lungs filled with a sigh of relief, but his heart rate picked up at the sight of Lady Underdog walking into the bedroom wearing a small towel tucked between her breasts. It barely covered her hips. Her body smelled of fresh peaches. She'd towel-dried her hair, but left it wonderfully wild. An orchard of taste and beauty, he thought, and nodded toward the dresser. "Looking for your nightshirt? I sure hope not," he quickly added.

"I'm sure you're tired from cutting wood and moving the tree and stuff, but I've got an ache in my lower back, probably from carrying the dog. Any chance you can give me a good back rub?" She pouted, whipping off towel. To emphasize her discomfort, she thrust out her beautiful breasts and put a hand to her lower back. "I even come prepared with oil. I found a bag in the cabinet under the bathroom sink with a half-dozen bottles of massage oils. Polly left a note that said, 'Help yourself. We can't use them all.'"

"Thank you for putting that picture in my head, but what I'm seeing before me is pure perfection." No matter how many times they made love, he never got tired of indulging his senses on every gentle curve and sleek line of her gorgeous, unclothed body. He loved the heart-shaped birthmark on her right upper arm, because it was a symbol of the deep, everlasting love they shared.

"I'm sure I can manage that, and a whole lot more." He got out of bed, not caring that he was just as naked and already obviously aroused. "Stretch out on the bed, and I'll see what I can do."

She purposely wiggled her ass when she walked around to the other side of the bed and twisted her body in flirtatious poses before getting comfortable. "My cop has magic hands," she complimented before giving him an air kiss.

He read the label on the bottle. "Shea and honey, that's quite a combination." He poured a few drops into his hands before rubbing them together. "Now relax and enjoy." He straddled her legs and slowly glided his palms up her back, starting at the swell of her buttocks. When he got to her shoulders, he brushed the hair away from her neck and rotated the tips of his fingers down the length of her neck before traveling across her shoulder blades and down her arms, which she'd stretched out on either side of her head.

"Feel the heat yet?" he murmured, moving his palms down the outer edges of her ribs, framing her hips with his open hands.

"Hmmm, harder, more toward my lower back. Use more oil."

"Coming right up."

"From the feel of the stiffness between my legs, you already are," she teased and spread her legs a little more. "Make yourself at home."

He had no problem accepting her invitation and slid forward, but forced himself not to move. This part was for her.

"Get ready for more heat, baby," he warned and applied more oil to his hands. Once again, his palms traveled up her back, moving in a circular motion, adding the slightest bit more pressure. Her moan of satisfaction filled the room, and he made one more sweep of her back, ending with the pink skin of her cute butt. He gently treated the soft mounds with the light-scented oil before using a coaxing finger to coat the narrow cleft with this finger. "Any pains here?"

"Sherlock, you've got to be kidding," she squirmed as he continued to move his exploring finger from top to bottom. "The ache has traveled to another spot, and it requires your immediate attention. Lift up so I can roll over."

She flipped over, and he settled between her legs when her eyes dropped to his obvious erection. "Ah, poor baby, I'm not the only one with a stiff muscle," she teased and reached for the massage oil and poured some in the palm of her hand. "Hold still and I'll see if I can make you feel better."

"You little tease, I like it just the way I am, and there's only one way to make my pain go away." He inhaled quickly, and his personal discomfort increased when she took him between her oiled hands and massaged the hard length that tightened from her slow, easy petting.

"Nothing seems to be working," she baited and took his hand and brought it to the swollen tip of her breast. "I've got a new ache right here."

"Can't have a dissatisfied customer." This time, he tipped the bottle and let the fragrant oil slither in the valley between her breasts. The silky stream pooled at her navel. Rather than use his palms, he dipped his fingertips into the silky solution and coated her stomach before seeking out her breasts. He gently took the tips between his fingertips and rolled the stiffness.

"How's the discomfort?" he challenged, already knowing she was aching all over. He certainly was. A dreamy glow coated her eyes and reflected the glimmer of excitement in her body. She lifted her legs and entangled them around his hips, moving on her own to probe for his hardness that was reaching the breaking point.

Once again, he reached for the bottle of oil, poured some in his palms and ran his hands up and down her slender thighs that gripped him tighter with her building need. Up and down, back and forth, his fingertips explored the crease in her groin, but pulled back at the last minute, deliberately avoiding touching the throbbing center of her heat.

"Damn you, why didn't you touch me? My entire body is on fire," she moaned in frustration and took him in hand and squeezed. "You know exactly how to work me up. Time to put the fire out."

"'Bout damn time," he agreed. "It's going to be quick," he warned before lifting her hips. His plunging entry was silky smooth, and her inner muscles took possession. He felt her all over. His Jilly. His love. They were one.

Chapter 6

The following morning, they walked the path Jillianne had driven the night before. The air was crisp and clear, the sky a brilliant blue, Mother Nature's apology for the previous ugly night. His anger at what had been done to his four-legged pal bested Jillianne's. Burrows had pulled a triple play—endangering his love, his father and his dog—to send him a message.

The flip-flop sound from Jilly's too-big boots filled his ears. He held her hand so she wouldn't slip in the mud or on the wet leaves. "Watson wasn't happy when we told him he had to stay in the house."

"When I changed his bandages this morning, his paws looked better. As soon as you get a cell signal, call the vet. We're close to where I found him. In the daylight, it isn't so bad, but last night I felt like I was walking into hell."

"You were, considering the weather." The cop in him needed to ask this question so he could put a timeline together. It was going to raise her suspicion. "You said Watson had to go out shortly after I drove away, even though he did his business before I left."

"He went to the door and barked a couple of times. Are you thinking he heard someone?"

Oh yeah, he silently noted. "That dog can hear an acorn drop, so it's a good possibility." He focused his attention on the ground as soon as the tractor's tire marks stopped and tugged on her hand, indicating she should stop. Wet leaves with what appeared to be reddish-brown stains had been disturbed. His temper swelled as he pictured his dog out for run and being lured into a trap.

"Damn it all to hell!" Ryder bent down and carefully brushed away a few leaves to discover a strip of wall and fence spikes. A couple of the sharp points were discolored from Watson's blood. He picked it up and would add it to their growing pile of evidence against the bastards.

"What is that? It's lethal-looking."

"If you don't want critters crawling up your fence or on a wall, you install these. I've seen buildings with bird-control spikes to keep away pigeons."

Jillianne gasped. "That's cruel and inhumane."

"I agree, so you know who and what we're dealing with. Stay here, I want to check the path that follows the pond. If they left any more strips, I need to remove them so wild animals don't get hurt."

"Oh, no. I'm coming with you. Lady Underdog can handle it." Jillianne paused and squeezed his hand. "I love the name you gave me, and I know what you're trying to do. Teasing and making me laugh is very good therapy, and it's your way of trying to take my mind off the nightmare I'm facing. I appreciate it, but I promise I won't cower in his presence, hide in a closet or pull a hood over my head."

She lowered her eyes and stared down at the ground. "Last night, you said I disappointed you."

Ryder immediately cupped her chin and forced her to face him. "I shouldn't have said that, Jilly."

"No, you're right, because I disappointed myself, too. I also recognize that I can't fight the fight alone, and I'll need you more than ever. I'm sure I'll have wavering moments, tears of frustration, but I'll have you beside me and, of course, our friends." Jillianne removed his hand from her chin and kissed his palm. "Let's go look for clues and make sure no other animals get hurt."

The ground was muddier the closer they got to the lake. Sunlight bounced off the small ripples. "The first time my dad brought us here, we couldn't get over the tea-colored water. Then we found out the water is a product of the iron and tannin content from the abundance of fallen cedar leaves along the water's edge. We were able to catch some nice bass." He nodded toward the man-made path around the water's edge. "This is the only way from the main road."

They followed the trail that ended at the dirt road he'd traveled the night before, and he was relieved not to have found any more strips. He was just about to suggest they start back to the house when Jillianne spotted the downed tree.

He never should've brought her along, because Lady Underdog was too smart for her own good. It was too late to stop her when she dropped his hand and walked a few feet down the shoulder of the road and stopped at the freshly cut base.

"Is that the tree you had to remove last evening? Look at that pile of wood chips. Ryder, call me crazy, but someone deliberately cut down this tree."

"Abner, the volunteer fireman, brought it to my attention last night," he hurriedly noted, not wanting to give her too much time to dwell on the situation. It was only wishful thinking.

"I'll bet it was the same malicious human beings that put down that dangerous strip for Watson to get hurt. They knew you left the house and downed the tree in the terrible weather, hoping you wouldn't see it in the poor visibility. If Burrows was behind this, he was trying to hurt both of you because of me!"

Tears welled in her eyes and ran down her cheeks, but she quickly wiped them away with the sleeve of the quilted jacket she wore over his borrowed sweats. "I can take whatever happens to me, but I couldn't live with myself if something happened to you or Watson. You should walk away right now."

Inside, he felt like a shit and wanted to shout, *No, it's because of me that you are being tortured at the hands a heartless devil.* He drew her into his arms and linked their bodies together. "No one is walking away. Things are going to get a whole lot tougher, uglier. Neither of us knows what's going to happen, but I'll be with you every step of the way." He lifted her head from his chest, needing her to see the truth in his eyes. "Jilly love, what we have together will never end, but I want a promise from you, too. No matter what happens, you'll always have faith in me and know what I have to do is the right thing for us. Never stop loving me."

"When you use your no-nonsense tone of voice, I know this is a whole lot serious. I vow never to stop loving or believing in you."

He leaned into her when her arms wrapped around his neck, and he sealed their lips to share a kiss filled with love and promise.

They checked the path again on their way back to the house, just in case they missed something the first time. They were almost back to the house when Ryder spotted the piece of paper in a plastic bag, covered with a good-size rock. This was how the demons had left notes for The Association over the years. He didn't have the option of leaving it here, but prepared himself for the questions Jillianne would ask, questions that would require clever wording, right down to lying.

"Looks like Watson did hear someone," he said and tossed the rock into the woods.

The envelope was addressed to him. They had yet to find a fingerprint on any of the other notes they'd received, so he didn't expect they would on this one either. He opened the back flap and pulled out the piece of paper. He really wanted to read it in private, but that wasn't about to happen. Jillianne leaned over his shoulder.

We've destroyed every piece of evidence you've uncovered, including the laptop, and eliminated all witnesses. Your girlfriend should've kept her nose out of our business. Now she's paying the price. You can't win.

"Who are these people? What are they talking about?" Jillianne asked as she jerked back, wide-eyed. "Are they referring to my laptop?"

"I wanted to wait until tomorrow to tell you, because you've been through enough hell this weekend, but someone broke into my father's house and stole your laptop."

"Oh my God! Are he and Polly all right?"

"They're fine and weren't in the house at the time. The captain is investigating the incident. Let's get back to the house. Watson is probably pacing like an expectant father."

"What did they mean by your girlfriend sticking her nose into their business?" Jillianne asked when they were approaching the house.

Before he could offer up an explanation, Jillianne abruptly halted at the base of the porch steps. Her eyes widened in self-conclusion. "I'll bet it has to do with those questionable accounts I wanted to discuss with Burrows, the ones that he said I'd made a mistake about and weren't part of his business. Does he think I'm a stupid woman? Going after my man and hurting our dog has pissed me off big-time, but don't tell me how to do my job! Oh, I'm going to get that back-stabbing pervert if it's the last thing I do!"

Ryder decided he'd just unleashed a new female superhero. Cornelius Burrows had no idea what Lady Underdog was capable of doing. He needed to warn the Fabulous Four and The Association that a loose cannon would be in their midst. "He's totally underestimated Lady Underdog."

"Damn straight!" Jillianne declared and threw her arms around his neck. She kissed him with so much force he backed into the door and banded his arms around her. He poured everything into returning the kiss, letting her know he totally agreed with her declaration.

Watson was watching out the front window and started barking.

"Let's get our dog and take him to the vet," Ryder said, just before he opened the door to be greeted by a very happy dog and sloppy wet kisses.

On their way home, Ryder called the emergency number he had for the vet and found out the office would be open until two, so they could take Watson right over.

The vet's office was on the outskirts of Beacon Pointe, surrounded by a dense wooded area. Dr. Bones had been taking care of Watson since he was a pup. Ryder opened the back door of the truck, and the dog didn't move. "Don't start this nonsense. I get that you hate going to the vet, but you need to get checked out."

Watson stood up on the seat, turned around and gave Ryder a perfect view of his ass.

"You know he's got boarding services. Keep up that attitude, and you'll be spending a few days here."

"What's holding you guys up?" Jillianne said, walking around to their side of the truck.

"The wimp is scared. He'd rather run into a burning building than go to the vet."

"You're using the wrong technique, Sherlock. Step aside."

"Be my guest," he replied and moved out of the way.

"Come here, sweetheart," Jillianne coaxed, and the damned dog turned around and kissed her on the cheek. "Be a good boy for Mommy, and I'll have Winnie fix you a steak when we get home."

Ryder gritted his teeth when the dog gave him a look that said, *See, that's how it's done. Plus. I'm getting a steak.*

The walls of the reception office were decorated with framed collages of dogs and cats that the vet had taken care of over the years. Fortunately, the room was empty. From experience, Ryder knew that some people stared at German shepherds with unease.

The pretty woman behind the counter was new. The name Madison was embroidered on her smock, which was covered with imprints of dogs and cats.

"You must be Ryder Wayne. Dr. Parisi will be right with you."

"What happened to Dr. Bones? Watson is somewhat of a scaredy-cat."

"He semiretired two months ago and is a mobile vet for farm animals. His wife was his receptionist and retired also. Actually, Dr. Parisi is Dr. Bones's nephew. Don't worry, all the notes on our patients are in the computer. I looked up Watson's chart, and it says he needs extra TLC. I'm filling in for the regular vet tech today. You have a beautiful dog. What happened to his front paws?"

Ryder gave Jillianne a quick shake of his head before answering the receptionist. "He accidentally stepped on barbed wire. We need his pads to be checked out so he doesn't get an infection."

The door to the exam room opened, and the doctor stepped out. Ryder judged him to be in his early thirties, twenty years younger than Dr. Bones. His copper-brown hair was trimmed close to his head, and dark-framed glasses covered blue eyes that rivaled a summer's day. His T-shirt, which he'd paired with dark blue jeans, had puppies tugging on a rope and read, *Dogs just want to have fun*. Ryder was a little apprehensive, but the doctor's greeting to Watson was four-star.

"So you're a police officer. Thanks for your service. Let's take a look at those paws." Watson preened and followed the doctor like he was being invited to enjoy a steak.

With the doctor's strong build, he had no problem lifting the dog and carefully setting Watson on the stainless-steel surface of the exam table. "When did this happen?" His hands were large, but he gently removed the now soiled bandages.

"Last evening, in the middle of a thunderstorm. I've tried to keep the wounds clean and changed his bandages a number of times," Jillianne assured.

Dr. Parisi used the beam of a small LED flashlight to examine Watson's paws. "You did a good job, and I don't see any sign of infection." He turned off the light and stared directly at Ryder. "These punctures are bigger than barbed wire. More like wall and fence spikes."

Ryder's respect for the doctor went up. "You're correct, and I have every intention of finding out who put them on my property."

"Hurting helpless creatures is inhumane. I hope you find them. I'll clean his paws again and apply Vetericyn Plus, an antimicrobial hydrogel spray, before I bandage his paws. Remove the bandages tomorrow and apply the spray again and repeat the following day. If you see him in any discomfort, give me a call."

"I like him," Jillianne said when they got back into the truck.

"I'm just glad Watson is okay."

Ryder hesitated before leaving the secluded spot. Once they were back in cell phone range, a dozen texts would pop up on his phone. Reality and communication with the outside world could no longer be denied. He reached into his glove box and hesitated before passing Jillianne her phone.

The stare of apprehension on her face said it all when she accepted it. "I'm surprised you didn't ask me for this sooner," he said. "The old Jillianne couldn't be parted from immediate interaction with life around her. Before you turn it on, prepare yourself for the good, bad and the ugly."

She glanced down at the device cradled in her hand, before giving him a small smile. "The past couple of days weren't all pleasant, but I liked the part that it was just you, me and Watson. Now it's time to face what I briefly escaped from. Once I meet with Nancy and Sean and hear their take on the situation, I'll feel a little better." Jillianne's sigh filled the entire car.

"Let the battle begin."

Her house was located in an exclusive neighborhood of homes owned by doctors, lawyers and corporate executives, many of whom were her clients. No sooner had they pulled down the drive that bordered Jillianne's sprawling one-story home than the side door to the three-car garage opened and Winifred came running out. Her arms were spread in welcome, and tears ran down her age-wrinkled cheeks. She was wearing her customary flower-patterned housedress over her short, round body. Loving the new trend of sassy hair colors, she'd recently added blue tips to her short white hair. She kept Jillianne's home in top running order. Watson was the only dog she allowed to enter the spotless house.

Jillianne had barely gotten out of the truck when she was bombarded with a welcome-home embrace.

"My sweet girl! I've been so worried. Those aren't your clothes."

"I'm fine. Ryder took good care of me," Jillianne assured, pulling back from Winnie's loving arms. "My clothes got ruined, so Ryder let me borrow his."

"Watson! How are you, baby?" The housekeeper got down on her knees and threw her arms around the dog's neck. "Those bad people hurt you. I made dog cookies as a special treat." She lifted her hand to Ryder. "Help me up, handsome. These old bones don't always want to cooperate."

"Winnie, you can hold your own with the best of them," Ryder said and kissed her on the cheek. "Let's get inside. I thought I saw a truck from a cable channel heading in our direction."

"Not surprised. A reporter from KF Cable showed up here Friday asking to speak to Jillianne, but I told him she was unavailable to him and all representatives from the media. When he left, I gave him the finger.

"I had a wonderful weekend with Elsie and Fred in Atlantic City. They assured me the gossip train is knocking down all negative gossip toward Jillianne. I won a hundred dollars on the slots. Manny took us to dinner and a show with a few of his friends. Those men are beautiful and fun."

Jillianne put her arm around her dearest friend. It felt good to be home. The moment they stepped into the big, modern kitchen, they were greeted by a mouthwatering aroma.

Winnie moved to the stove and stirred whatever was in the large pot. Watson ran over to his water bowl first and then accepted a homemade cookie. Ryder helped himself to a cup of freshly brewed coffee and selected a freshly made pumpkin donut from a nearby plate.

On the surface, everything appeared to be totally normal, but it wasn't. The knots in Jillianne's stomach were already tightening. *You're not going to lose it.* She smiled when Ryder passed her a cup.

"Drink, take a shower, and then we'll sit in your den and make some notes before your lawyers get here. If you need me, just holler."

"I always need you," she assured and gave him a brief kiss, stepped back, but captured his mouth a second time, tasting the cinnamon spice on his lips. He settled a warm, comforting hand on the side of her neck.

"What's wrong, Jilly?"

"I warned you there would be wavering moments, and I'm having one now. Knowing you're here keeps me from wanting to pull the covers over my head."

A half hour later, she walked out of her marble-tiled bathroom and felt a great deal better after her shower. She'd recently changed the color décor in her bedroom to pretty shades of lavender, white and moss green. When she was growing up, her mother and father had decided on the color of her bedroom, which was usually white and had to be kept neat at all times. They never entered her walk-in closet to see pictures of Ryder, the Fabulous Four and posters of rock stars hidden behind her racks of clothes.

She walked to one of her two walk-in closets, contemplating what she should wear. Lying on the bed was Ryder's much-too-large-for-her sweats. He'd probably laugh if she told him wearing them had offered surrounding comfort. They were hers now, and she'd buy him new ones.

She settled for black leggings and a long tunic in black, white and purple. Her hair was almost dry and would fall into fashion-cut layers, and she'd go makeup-free.

When she walked into the kitchen, Ryder was sitting at the table talking on his cell phone. Winnie had set out two soup bowls on the fall-themed placemats on the country pine table. The gold-jarred candle in the center of the table had the scent of pumpkin spice. She loved that Winnie brought seasonal decorating into the house. It had been unheard of when she was growing up.

She took a seat next to Ryder and poured a cup of tea from her personal teapot, while she picked up some of his side of the conversation. "Bastards left another note. Hurt Jillianne, my dad and Watson. He's a dead man. See you Tuesday night."

"Sorry, first it was Everett and then Jackson checking up on us."

Winifred set a soup tureen next to a dish of roasted vegetables. "Help yourself to chicken and dumplings. While you were in the shower, Neil called to say he and Paige are working both shows at the Footlight Theater. You're to call if you need anything. I really appreciate that they house-sat this weekend. Paige let me know she handled calls from your friends and business colleagues. Most of them were to support you. Shortly after I got home this morning, we had a personal visit from the media, but Neil took care of Gianna Knight."

"Why is she back in town?" Jillianne asked.

"She's back to do a follow-up story on the opening of the museum and a photo shoot," Ryder replied.

"It's funny. She arrived without any cameraman and specifically wanted to talk to Neil. He didn't invite her into the house and spoke to her on the patio. Whatever was being said, he wasn't happy, and I recognized the anger on his face. I caught a couple of words—baby, conceited bitch, life. They spoke for about twenty minutes, and he stormed into the house and left her standing there.

"After he calmed down, I asked what she wanted. He said she wanted him to arrange a personal interview with his stepsister. He said he told the bitch to kiss his ass. He'd arrange an interview with the devil before her."

Ryder looked at Winnie and then Jillianne. "Neil is never hostile and is one of the most calm, easygoing guys I know. What am I missing here?"

"My brother is a very private person and hasn't told anyone that Gianna Knight is Paige's mother."

Jillianne wondered why the look on Ryder's face was that of a man ready to spit nails.

Chapter 7

Ryder had to take numerous mental deep breaths. Jillianne had just dropped a bomb he'd never seen coming. Now, more than ever, he needed that meeting with The Association. The onslaught of complications with this eye-opener was going to cause another scandal in her life. With all his heart, he wished he could avoid the inevitable, but all he could do was offer comfort.

He needed to talk to Mason and used the dog as an excuse. "Winifred, everything was delicious, but I want to take Watson for a walk before Jillianne's lawyers arrive."

"Do you want me to come with you?" Jillianne asked.

He kissed her on the corner of her brow. "No, I'll only be a few minutes. You can bring two cups of coffee to the den, and we can get started as soon as I get back."

Watson was already barking at the door. The very efficient housekeeper thrust a plastic bag at him. "Don't forget to pick up his business. The uppity snobs in this neighborhood would call the cops even if you are one."

"Don't worry. I always obey the poop laws."

Watson wasn't accustomed to walking with a leash and literally pulled Ryder down the driveway. "Damn, dog, slow down!" He managed to take out his cell phone and punch in Mason's number.

"I didn't expect to speak to you until Tuesday night," Mason said. "How is Jillianne?"

"Pretty good. Mentally gearing up to take on Burrows and his organization."

"My wife is off-the-wall angry. You know what Burrows tried to do to her, and she'd finally calmed down. But she's back to being royally pissed off because of what Burrows has done to Jillianne. I'm glad she never got that angry with me."

"How soon we forget, bridegroom, but that isn't the reason I called. Gianna Knight showed up at Jillianne's, hoping for a one-on-one interview, but Neil gave her the heave-ho. I hope you're sitting down, because I just found out Gianna Knight is Paige's mother."

There was dead silence on the other end of the phone.

"Mason, are you still with me?"

"I'm here," he replied in a flat tone. "In all the years I've known the bitch, she never indicated she has a child. I guess it was wishful thinking that our case couldn't get any more complicated."

"I felt the same way, knowing what this is going to do to Jillianne, Neil and especially Paige when the public finds out about that two-faced reporter," Ryder said. "I'm heartsick that Jillianne is being put through this horror, knowing it stems back to me, to The Association. I'm barely keeping it together…"

"You're preaching to the choir, friend. How do you think I felt when they were going after Mollie? Vent to all of us, because we've all been through hell together and separately."

Ryder paused when Watson peed on his third tree trunk. "When we meet on Tuesday night, I think Everett should give us a quick course on how to live with scandal. In the meantime, I'll try to find out more about Neil's relationship with your favorite girl reporter."

"Don't let my wife hear you say that. You eat a lot of your meals at the Book and Brew, and you could find something in your food that you might not like."

"The timeline, as it stands now, is that Jillianne is meeting with her lawyers tonight, and we'll push to get a different judge and move the initial hearing to Tuesday."

"What's wrong with using one of our hometown judges?"

"One is conveniently having a medical procedure tomorrow, and the other is Victor Burrows. The judge specifically requested to hear the case." Ryder tugged on the leash to let Watson know it was time to head back home.

"Damn, nothing like stacking the deck against her. Can't you ever call me with some happy news?"

"At this point, it will be a cold day in hell."

When he returned from walking Watson, he and Jillianne made notes about what occurred over the weekend with Watson being injured and their discussion with Pollyanna Friday night. Ryder had been bracing himself for this meeting with the lawyers. Hopefully, Jillianne could handle what they were about to discuss.

Winnie showed Nancy Jean and Sean Harrigan into the den at precisely six o'clock. The husband-and-wife team bore beautiful tans, but their normal happy smiles were absent. They sat together on the tan leather couch and set a laptop and a yellow pad on the coffee table in front of them.

Nancy rubbed her hands up and down the arms of her long-sleeved black sweater. "Thanks for turning on your gas fireplace. This weather change takes a bit of adjusting for the body. This morning it was eighty degrees in Florida, and when we got off the plane here, it was forty." She gave Winnie an appreciative nod. "Thanks for the hot apple cider."

"If I can get you something else, let me know. Take good care of my Jillianne Rose."

"We will, Winifred," Sean assured, raising his cup of coffee in thanks before the housekeeper left the room. He directed his first statement to Jillianne and Ryder sitting on the opposite loveseat. "Before we start, I have to say these accusations are the biggest load of bullshit that I've ever encountered in all my years as a lawyer and investment banker. Jillianne, you are without a doubt the most honest CPA I've ever had the pleasure of working with. If we weren't defending you, I'd put myself on the stand as a witness to attest to your integrity."

"Thank you, Sean, but we need to get me out of this mess with as much of my personal and business reputation intact as we can. I couldn't have a better defense team. Nancy is a great defense attorney, and you're a lawyer who ran your own investment banking firm, so you've got additional qualifications dealing with finances." Jillianne squeezed his hand. "Ryder has been wonderful, and I'll admit to having had a number of weak moments, but I'm ready to fight Burrows."

"What happened to Watson?" Nancy asked.

Jillianne leaned into Ryder. "You tell them. Just thinking about it makes my temper soar."

Ryder explained about the strips that had been set out to deliberately hurt Watson as well as the tree being cut down. He also told them about the theft of the laptop from his house.

He reached into his pocket and took out the plastic bag that contained the note. The lawyers were privy to what was going on with The Association and knew they couldn't ask too many questions in front of Jillianne. "Found this under a rock outside my grandfather's cabin. I'll be putting it into evidence when I go into work tomorrow morning. Jillianne scanned a copy into her desktop computer and emailed both you and me copies for your files."

"Sick, absolutely sick." Disgust filled Nancy's voice. "It may not have Burrows's name on the bottom, but it's obvious who the note came from. Unfortunately, it wouldn't be admissible in court. Personally, I'd like to castrate him for what he did to Watson. Technically, our favorite pooch is a police officer, and I'm going to request that the prosecutor files the charges as assault on a police officer."

Watson was sound asleep on the floor next to the couch, but barked and batted his tail on the hardwood floor in agreement with Nancy's statement. She leaned over and patted him on the head. "We'll get him, you'll see."

"I support your idea, my love, but everything he's done skirts the line. That's why we have to work a lot harder to prove his guilt," Sean said.

Nancy took over the discussion. "We've been working on your case and are ready to file official paperwork tomorrow morning requesting a different judge because of a conflict of interest."

"But you were on vacation," Jillianne noted.

"We're like cops and can't always escape from our responsibilities," Nancy said. "Pollyanna called me yesterday morning to explain what was happening with the judge situation. In her capacity as the municipal court clerk, she's been in contact with the county court clerk to request a different judge. She's pushing to move the trial to Tuesday morning at ten. We'll be at her office tomorrow morning to make it official."

"I'm so grateful for what you've already done on my behalf, but I'm supposed to be in court at nine tomorrow morning."

"Polly contacted Judge Burrows over the weekend, under the guise of looking out for his reputation, stressing she knew him as a man of principle. According to the gossip, the defense is claiming a conflict of interest and plans to take the case to the county level if he doesn't agree to recuse himself. She said His Honor lightly protested, but gave in."

Ryder reviewed the points that had to be discussed and set the yellow pad on the accent table next to the couch. "You covered all our notes."

Sean drank a little more coffee before directing his next question to Jillianne. "I have to ask, what precipitated these accusations from Burrows that made him initiate this claim against you?"

Jillianne shook her head. "I don't have a clue. I will say his financial records were a mess, and I don't understand how he's been able to keep his business running, as far as the federal government is concerned. He has plenty of money, but a great deal of it hadn't been applied to the correct accounts."

"So you basically saved him from experiencing problems if he was subject to a federal audit," Sean confirmed, typing on his laptop. "My other question is, if his accounts were such a mess, how does he expect to prove that you stole a hundred thousand dollars? I'm going to file a motion to see proof of this theft before your case goes to trial."

"I found other accounts from over thirty years ago just sitting there that were eventually funneled into his present corporation. The influx of cash was questionable, so I called him. He went on the defensive and said I'd made a big mistake, because they weren't part of his business. When I stressed they were tied to his present finances, he reluctantly agreed to meet with me this week to go over my findings. On a personal note, he offered to refer his friends to my accounting firm if I took our relationship to a personal level."

"Sick pervert bastard," Ryder muttered with a dark scowl.

"That's sexual harassment. Add that to our countercharges," Nancy told her husband.

"That will be hard to prove since it will be Jillianne's word against his," Ryder noted.

Nancy brought up the subject of bail and said they'd take care of it from their end.

"Technically, I'm under arrest and in Ryder's custody until my hearing. Since we've objected to a judge being related to Burrows, they could also accuse us of having a conflict of interest because Ryder and I are in a relationship."

"Jillianne, my lovely wife is damn smart and one of the shrewdest defense attorneys around. If they want to get technical, you've been in the custody of two police officers. These people mean business, so don't give them a chance to bring other charges against you. Remain in Ryder's custody until bail has been arranged."

"She'll be going to work with me tomorrow and spend the day at police headquarters."

"Oh, jolly. What do you expect me to do?"

"Keep Watson company," Ryder added with a chuckle.

It was after ten p.m. when they finished. Nancy and Sean would contact Jillianne once the official paperwork had been filed. She'd see them at nine a.m. on Tuesday so they could talk further about their defense strategy before they went into court.

Before going to bed for the night, Ryder called his dad to bring him up to date. Dexter planned to spend the night at Polly's and would see Ryder at police headquarters because he had a crossing-guard meeting. He reported that Mollie's brother had repaired the damage to the frame molding at the house and replaced the back door with one without windows.

Jillianne was already in bed when Ryder came back from taking Watson for his nightly walk. She'd left one light on next to the bed, and he sat next to her. Strawberry-blond hair fanned her pale lavender pillowcase, and he ran his fingers through the soft locks. The covers barely covered her lovely breasts.

"You've been extremely quiet since Sean and Nancy left. I was very proud of the way you handled yourself. It's going to be okay. Talk to me."

"I hate that you know me so well. It freaked me out when Nancy said they'd handle my bail. That made it all too real what I'm facing. Don't get me wrong. I know it's real and all-consuming. I have every confidence in their ability to prove I'm innocent."

He smoothed the length of her eyebrow with the tip of his finger and swallowed back the words he wanted to say. *I'm worried because Burrows is a clever, sneaky bastard who's been making our lives hell for thirty years.*

"I share your sentiment." He took a deep breath and drew in the scent of honeysuckle that clung to her skin from her shower. “You know Winnie isn’t happy when I share your bed, because your ring finger is bare.”

“She’s been blustering moral codes at us since we were teenagers, but she loves you. She can’t object, because I’m officially in your custody and can’t be out of your sight.” His body was already responding when she opened the buttons on his red and black flannel shirt. Her warm hand slid up and slowly explored his chest before she pinched his nipple.

“There is that.” He tugged off his shirt and threw it on the fancy upholstered chair in the corner next to her girlie dressing table. “Do I need my handcuffs?”

“Not necessary tonight, but Lady Underdog does plan to do some investigating as soon as you ditch those clothes.”

“Oh, she does?” He laughed, standing up and shedding his jeans and shorts. She was in a mood and was ready to play. So was he.

“I’m just warning you. Your prisoner is randy and will probably overtake her guard.” Jillianne flipped back the covers and presented herself to him in all her naked glory. In her hand was their favorite bottle of massage oil.

“Get on your back, Sherlock, and spread ’em. I’ll be the one frisking you tonight.”

“I’ve never heard of frisking a naked prisoner,” he teased in return. His throbbing need for her built with every step he took to the other side of the bed. He’d no sooner made himself comfortable when she opened the bottle and dribbled the contents directly onto his body, starting at his chest and pooling it in his navel. He forced himself not to shudder from the driving need for his love building in his body.

“And how do you plan to spread this stuff around?” His answer was in the form of a silly grin before she stretched out on top of him. Her already hardened nipples poked him in the chest when her arms came up and she laced their fingers together.

“I’m about to give you my version of a full-body massage. We can enjoy the heat together. Then I plan to ride you, hard." Her mouth lowered to his, and she planted a kiss that was meant to stir up his already raging need for her.

His last conscious thought was they needed to order a case of that oil.

The following morning, Jillianne sat on the couch in Ryder's office and looked around, deciding it could stand some redecorating. The plain brown desk, dated visitor chairs and small meeting table were ancient, right down to his desktop computer. It was eleven o'clock, and this was the first time she'd sat down to relax.

Her alarm had gone off at five thirty. After a quick shower, she hesitated to put on the clothes she'd set out the night before. A coffee-beige dress suit, heather-blue silk blouse and Christian Louboutin patent-leather pumps. Meet-and-greet, wine-and-dine client's clothes. She put everything back in her closet and chose her True Religion navy jeans and a cropped cashmere sweater to wear with her black fitted leather boots.

Ryder grinned and gave her a thumbs-up. Before they drove to his house to get his uniform, she changed Watson's bandages.

At seven, they'd walked into police headquarters, and you would have thought Everett Troy had arrived to sign autographs, but the star was Watson. Word had gotten back to headquarters about the malicious way the dog had been injured. Ryder had left Jillianne alone, and she became the dog's personal social diva. People kept coming in to see the injured hero, and like a ham, he lapped up every loving sentiment. The round meeting table in the corner of the office was filled with plastic containers of homemade dog cookies.

She'd been anxious to hear from her lawyers, and they'd walked into Ryder's office at nine thirty, wearing big smiles. Their paperwork had been filed and accepted. Pollyanna had worked her magic, and a new judge would handle the case at ten tomorrow morning.

She'd recalled what Ryder said over the weekend about showing Burrows she wasn't cowed by his accusations and reached out to her office manager. The report she'd gotten wasn't all good, but many of their clients had called in support of her personally and her company. Others had expressed their fear and were pulling their accounts. An investigator from the prosecutor's office had shown up with legal paperwork requesting all their files pertinent to their case. It was exactly what she'd expected. The office staff were worried she'd be closing the firm, but she assured her manager that no one would be losing their jobs.

She walked over to the window that faced the front of police headquarters. The sun was shining on the naked trees, and the sky was clear and blue. She decided she could use some fresh air, so could Watson.

She collected his leash from the bottom drawer of the desk and approached the star stretched out on his LL Bean bed. "You need to visit a tree. Since you're a cop, I won't be out of police custody," she teased, attaching the hook to the ring on his harness. She scribbled a note to Ryder saying she was going to take the dog for a walk and would be right back.

She waved to the officer sitting at the front window in the reception area and walked out the front door. "Slow down, Watson," she ordered as they made their way down the steps to follow the concrete path to the sidewalk. The building was surrounded by hometown business offices and a few Victorian homes that had been turned into law offices and professional buildings. She closed her eyes and lifted her face to the sun to absorb the warmth. Her jacket had a light fleece lining, but she hadn't bothered to put on a pair of gloves.

Watson was selective of the tree he wanted to use and then decided to play cat and mouse with a squirrel. He barked his head off, and it took all her strength to keep the strong dog under control. "That's not good for your paws!" she scolded, reeling in the retractable extend-a-leash. "If you don't stop, you won't get any more cookies!"

The threat of being denied his favorite treats worked, and she headed back to police headquarters. Her carefree walk was interrupted when a news van pulled up in front of the building. Jillianne groaned when Gianna Knight got out. Her black hair was free-flowing, and from the smartness of her jacket and trousers, she'd come prepared to conduct an interview. Her cameraman came around from the other side of the truck.

Watson's doggie sense told him this wasn't a friend, and he started to growl. Jillianne bent to one knee and wrapped her arm around his neck. "Yes, she's annoying, but whatever you do, don't bite her. She's mean enough to press charges."

The reporter was all smiles. "Sorry I missed you yesterday. Neil said you were away for the weekend. Must be nice having friends in the police department, especially the one you're sleeping with, that give a criminal free reign."

"You've forgotten that I'm innocent until proven guilty, plus the courts are closed on the weekend." Jillianne dipped her head toward Watson. "I'm in official police custody."

"A dog? Give me a break," she sneered.

"Fair warning. Watch what you say around him." Watson had been sitting down at parade rest, but stood up and moved a step in the reporter's direction, offering the slightest growl.

"You appear to very confident, but confidence won't save your business and reputation. I was getting my hair done earlier this morning and I overhead three women discussing how you helped yourself to their husbands' accounts and they fired your firm a few months ago. One of them said you came onto her husband."

Temper, temper, Jillianne. She's only trying to egg you on. "My guess is they were paid to start malicious gossip to discredit my reputation. I do recall one sick pervert who came on to me. He buys Viagra by the case."

"By any chance, are you referring to Cornelius Burrows?"

"Why am I not surprised. Did the oversexed degenerate come onto you too?"

"No comment. How about a one-on-one? I just finished interviewing him, so this is your chance to speak up."

"You're a big-time reporter. Why are you so interested in a case in this small town?"

"News is news, but you're the endowment curator and director of funds for the Footlight Theater, and Everett Troy's museum is connected to the theater, and he is on the board of directors. You're also his accountant. It's all connected. People will talk."

Jillianne couldn't believe how this manipulative bitch had come up with such ridiculousness. "Are you out of your mind? My problems have nothing to do with Everett Troy. Inciting an ugly rumor could cast a dark shadow on Everett's dream."

"Squash the rumors now and talk to me."

"Gianna, my brother was right. You're a first-class bitch."

"That's why I'm so good at what I do," she replied with a catty smile. "So are we doing a one-on-one?"

"First, I have a question for you. How could you be so cold and heartless and walk away from your newborn baby?"

"Your brother got what he wanted, and it's really none of your business. My turn. Why did you embezzle funds from Cornelius Burrows?"

Stupid, stupid, you walked right into the slam-dunk question. But she was saved by three referees.

"If it isn't the bitch in sheep's clothing," Mollie Trent declared, approaching the women.

"Aren't you supposed to be at the museum taking pictures?" Laura Troy asked.

Tamie Elise Vance wasn't to be outdone and asked, "She's too busy taking over the gossip column."

Watson wagged his tail in greeting and moved to stand beside the Fabulous Four to get his next round of loving sympathy.

Jillianne enjoyed an inner sigh of relief. She hadn't heard them approach from behind and snubbed the reporter. "What are you three doing here?"

"Apparently saving your ass," Mollie said and moved to stand in front of Gianna. "You want a story? Here it is. The person making accusations against my best friend is a rotten, dishonest scoundrel who tried to put me out of business. Jillianne Bennett is the most honest businesswoman I've ever known. On top of that, someone out for revenge tried to hurt her dog. Watson is a decorated police officer. Make sure your cameraman takes a picture of the bandages on the dog's paws."

Laura took her turn at the microphone. "She single-handedly brought in hundreds of thousands of dollars to keep the Footlight Theater, a nonprofit organization, from going under. She's also too modest to admit it, but she started a charitable organization to help premature babies and those born with birth defects."

"She didn't want anyone to know she personally paid for all of the renovations to accommodate the children's programs at the Footlight Theater," Tamie added.

Laura surprised Jillianne when the angry blonde took a step closer to the reporter. "We heard what you inferred, and if you print one word disparaging my husband's name and the Bessandra Troy Museum, I'll personally sue your ass for everything you own and then some."

"Since you technically work for my husband," Mollie noted, "that should give you a great human-interest story, rather than one that will slander a person's reputation."

"You really think you've won now that you have his ring on your finger?" Gianna asked.

Jillianne wasn't the only one to hear the sarcasm in Gianna's voice.

"I'm also carrying his child," Mollie boldly announced.

The reporter's eyes widened before dropping to Mollie's still very flat stomach, which was visible because she hadn't bothered to zip up her fleece-lined jacket.

"Seems your skills for sniffing out a story are getting weak," Mollie added with a sneer.

Gianna nodded to her cameraman, indicating the so-called interview was over, but she turned back to Jillianne and spoke for her ears alone.

"This round belongs to you. I'm not going anywhere, because we're far from done. You think they're your friends, but they've been keeping secrets from you, along with your lover and his friends, since they were teenagers. You're just another in their long line of casualties."

Inside, Jillianne was shaken by what the reporter said, but didn't have time to entertain more problems in her life. She offered up a smile to her best friends. "So, what did I do to deserve the pleasure of the Fabulous Four coming to see me?"

"We're here to have lunch with you," Tamie said.

"Technically, I can't leave."

Mollie held up two cloth bags. "We brought lunch to you. We'll take over Ryder's office."

All four women stopped in their tracks when Gianna Knight called out, "Word of advice, ladies. You can't win!"

Ryder walked out of his captain's office and headed downstairs to finish the endless pile of paperwork on his desk. The closed-door meeting had been to fill him in on what happened over the weekend and to make tentative plans for Jillianne's hearing tomorrow morning. Paul Clark had taken possession of the note and would put it in a safe place. He was convinced there was a snitch on the force, but couldn't move on his suspicion because it involved The Association's case.

He stopped at the dispatcher's station and studied the electronic board that listed the locations of their squad cars. Everything appeared normal, and he checked the time on his watch. Mollie had called him that morning to ask if the Fabulous Four could meet in his office at lunchtime. They wanted to cheer Jillianne up and give her their support. He agreed and said he'd have a little surprise for all of them.

He paused in the open doorway. As expected, there was a party going on. Watson was by his feed bowl, finishing off a hamburger, and the ladies sat at the round table in the corner of his office. They all seemed to be talking at once. Friends, no, more than friends, sisters who supported one another since they were in high school. They shared secrets even their husbands didn't know and might never know. Husbands—that title, too, sounded strange. In the past ten months, three of The Association had taken the plunge with their ladies. Before he and Jillianne entertained getting married, he had to make some changes in his life.

"Nothing like walking into your office to find four beautiful women," he complimented and slipped his arm around Jillianne's shoulder.

"Damn, you're handsome in that uniform."

"Don't let your husband hear you say that, Mollie Trent."

"He knows I love him, and there's nothing wrong with a woman appreciating a handsome public servant."

"Jillianne, do we tell him what just happened, or do you want to?" Tamie Elise asked.

"Somebody better tell me, because Jilly hasn't been out of this building."

"I went for a walk, but I left a note on your desk."

His temper shot up, along with his voice. "I've been in a meeting and didn't see it. After what happened this weekend, you went outside alone? Why the hell do you think I brought you to work with me?"

Jillianne shoved up from her. "Step back, Sherlock. I needed some fresh air, and I had Watson with me! Gianna Knight showed up and asked for a one-on-one. Don't worry, it never happened. Let's just say our meeting didn't end on a pleasant note."

"What else happened this weekend other than Watson getting hurt?" Mollie tossed out.

"I got another love note!" Ryder realized too late what he'd revealed.

It was like turning off a switch, snuffing out their demand to know what happened.

Mollie softly muttered, "Oh, shit."

Laura mumbled, "Oh, no."

Tamie finished off with, "Not another one."

He needed a quick distraction and thought about his surprise. First, he apologized. He slipped his arm around her waist and drew Jilly's chin up with his knuckle. He wasn't the least bit intimidated by her dark scowl. "I didn't mean to yell at you, but I need and want you to be safe." Then he pressed his lips to hers in a soothing kiss of apology before addressing the Fabulous Four. "I have a little surprise." Ryder opened the door to a small storage closet where he kept Watson's food and took out four gift bags stuffed with white tissue paper. One was red, and the other three were yellow.

"What's this?" Jillianne asked.

"Ladies, we have a new superhero in our midst. Jilly will go first, and then the rest of you can open your bags."

He stood back and watched her remove the black knit shirt that displayed a picture of a slender woman in a white bodysuit that called attention to her generous breasts. A white Venetian mask hid her identity, and a sparkling tiara was nestled in her strawberry-blond hair. Her right arm was thrusting a glittery gold sword, and small gold dog bones were scattered at her white, calf-hugging boots. The words *Lady Underdog* were clearly spelled out below the sexy character.

"Oh, Sherlock! I love it! Jillianne threw her arms around his neck and squeezed tightly before turning to her smiling friends, who were opening their gift bags.

"Team Underdog! We love it," Laura laughed, already putting the shirt on over her long-sleeved knit top.

While the ladies adored their shirts and the rest of their lunch, he sat at his desk and enjoyed the ham and cheese on rye that Mollie had made for him. He glanced away from the ladies when his cell indicated an incoming text message. He frowned at the sender and darted a glance at the table. Laura was nowhere in sight. He read the message.

I'm in the ladies' room. Gianna Knight was big trouble. Will tell you more at the meeting tomorrow night. We saved Jillianne from being roasted by the bitch. Before she left with her cameraman, she called out, "Word of advice, ladies. You can't win." Apparently, she knows about everything.

His silent sentiment echoed Mollie's favorite expression. *Oh, shit!*

Chapter 8

Tuesday morning, Jillianne sat at the defense table in the courtroom located on the second floor of police headquarters. The room was also used to hold special town-hall meetings, and the pew-like seats were generally filled. She'd seen Dexter before entering the room and said he'd limit entrance to only those who had anything to do with the case.

Wanting to appear the confident businesswoman, she wore a two-piece black suit with a white silk blouse and simple pearls with matching earrings. Her hair had cooperated and had fallen into place, cupping her chin and the back of her neck. Before she'd left the house, Winifred had approved and said she looked formidable and confident.

Only one person knew what she was hiding. Ryder had walked out of the bathroom wearing a towel. He burst out laughing when he saw she was covering her Lady Underdog shirt with her blouse. Her cheeks had turned pink from being caught, but he thought it was great. "Superman covered his superpower shirt with regular clothes," he teased. Then she'd glanced at the time on the bedside clock and figured they had an extra twenty minutes to spare. Lady Underdog used her superpowers after his towel was history.

Nancy Jean and Sean were in the back of the courtroom, talking to Ryder and his father. Ryder wore his full dress uniform and looked so handsome. She loved him so much and was grateful for his strength that was supporting her through this terrible ordeal.

He surprised her and brought Watson into court, knowing the dog had a calming effect on her nerves. Like his master, he, too, looked handsome, in a neon dog vest with the word *Police* boldly visible. He was currently lying next to her feet.

Dexter Wayne looked smart in a blue dress shirt and tie with his black trousers, the standard court officer uniform. Standing side by side, she appreciated how much Ryder took after his dad. Before coming into court, she'd stopped in the ladies' room, and Pollyanna had rushed in. She hadn't wanted anyone to see them communicating, but said she needed to wish Jillianne good luck.

Inside, Jillianne was a nervous wreck, but she could get through this. Thoughts of what Gianna Knight had said played with her already troubled mind. Yesterday, when Ryder had blurted the statement about the newest note, her friends had immediately clammed up. That was so unusual, because they were like a dog with a bone—persistent and not letting go until they got answers. She needed to get through this before she could contemplate getting answers on her own.

She turned in her hard wooden chair when Sean and Nancy Jean took their seats next to her.

They, too, presented a united front, dressed in formal business suits of dark gray. Sean had added a wine-colored tie to his lighter gray shirt.

"Everything okay?" Jillianne asked.

"Fine. I think you'll like the judge. She's fair and, according to Polly, doesn't take any bullshit," Nancy said and ran her hand over the dog's head. "I'm glad Ryder put the police vest on Watson. His presence is pertinent to your case."

"I was under the impression he brought Watson because his presence is a calming influence on me."

Sean opened a legal-size portfolio and removed clipped sheets of notes. "Watson is here for that, too. Like we discussed, you won't have to take the stand."

Shortly before ten, she turned around at the sound of the soft voices of spectators coming into the court. She was relieved to see familiar faces, but pursed her lips when she recognized some of the people she'd worked with at Burrows's corporate offices. Gianna Knight accompanied them.

"Like a bad penny, the press showed up," she whispered to Sean.

"They're treating this like a trial, not a preliminary hearing. Don't worry, Nancy and I are prepared. She'll be taking lead chair. I'm here for backup."

"You two make quite a team."

"We think so, too."

The knots in her stomach tightened when Cornelius Burrows and his legal representative entered the court and sat at the opposite table. The snarky fool had the audacity to give her a cocky grin and wink at her. His custom navy suit shouted money and prestige, and it wasn't her imagination that his white hair appeared to be a glaring white. His skin was a dark tan, indicating he'd just returned from vacation in a warm climate.

Their attention was drawn to the front of the court when Dexter Wayne announced, "All rise for the Honorable Margaret Taylor."

Talk about formidable. Jillianne took her age to be mid-fifties. The judge's white hair was drawn back in a tight bun at the back of her neck, and a string of pearls graced the front of her black robe. Gold-rimmed half glasses were balanced on her nose. The last name, Taylor, sounded familiar. It could be just a coincidence, since it was a common name.

"Good morning. I've been asked to oversee these proceedings. Judge Burrows recused himself due to a conflict of interest since Cornelius Burrows is a relative. Who will be prosecuting?"

"I will, Your Honor. Liam Thompson , former mayor of Beacon Pointe."

"I'm sure you were a wonderful mayor, but the court clerk provided the name of the prosecutor overseeing this case, and it's not Thompson."

"He came down with laryngitis this morning, and I'm familiar with the case."

"Who will be representing the defendant?"

"We will. Nancy Jean Harrigan and Sean Harrigan, my partner."

"How does your client plead?"

"Not guilty, Your Honor," Nancy Jean supplied.

The butterflies in Jillianne's stomach went crazy when she picked up the troubled glance Sean gave his wife. He scribbled a note and slid it in front of her. *Pulled a fast one already.*

"Be seated. I was told this was a bail hearing, but the court clerk advised me there are a number of objections on the part of the prosecutor due to improprieties in the way the defendant was remanded into custody."

"Before we begin, Your Honor, I need to clarify something with Lieutenant Wayne, the arresting officer and my witness."

"You have two minutes, Ms. Harrigan."

"What's going on?" Jillianne whispered to Sean when Nancy walked to the back of the room to speak to Ryder.

"Nothing for you to worry about. It's under control."

Jillianne didn't believe him.

Ryder's gut churned, and the trial had barely started. His mind was filled with the picture of his hands around Burrows's throat. Once again, the demons had pulled a fast one and they were forced to remain silent. He glanced at Everett, Jackson and Mason, and all three of his friends shared the same look of loathing. Their wives, too, shared worried glances.

He wasn't surprised when Nancy asked to speak to him in private.

"Ryder, what do you want me to do? Thompson is a major player in the case you're building against Burrows's corporation. I can approach the judge and claim another conflict of interest, but Thompson will be standing right next to me. Trying to explain our objection will give away your lawsuit."

"I hear you, and right now our hands are tied. We really thought we'd covered our bases on this one, but once again they've tricked us. It sickens me that Jillianne is being put through this and we can't reveal what's really going on and defend her."

"I understand, because you love her and you have to wear the blindfold of justice, but defending her will be my job."

"I know you'll do your best, Nancy Jean. I've got a good feeling about this judge."

"Thank you, Your Honor," Nancy said, sitting down next to Jillianne.

The judge addressed Liam Thompson. "Let's begin with your objections to the defendant's arrest."

He stood up and authoritatively thrust out his chest. "A warrant was served on Friday, and the defendant has yet to spend a night in jail. She went away for the weekend with Lieutenant Wayne, her longtime boyfriend. He also took possession of her laptop that contained vital information about Mr. Burrows's corporation. It wasn't turned in to evidence, and she had access to the device, allowing her the opportunity to amend confidential files."

"And you know this how?"

"My nephew is a sergeant on the Beacon Pointe Police Department."

"You have a reliable source, someone who tells you what's really going on within the department," the judge confirmed.

"Yes. I trust him completely."

"Is he here in court today to confirm the information he provided?"

"Well, no. I didn't think it was necessary. He's a respected police officer."

"Since I don't know you or your nephew, it's hearsay. Sit down, Counselor."

"But I'm not finished."

"You are for now."

She addressed Nancy Jean. "Counselor, since your witness is in court, I'd like him to take the witness stand."

Snake in the grass were the words that filled Ryder's head when he approached the bench and his father held out the Bible to swear him in.

"Wayne and Wayne. Any relation?" the judge asked.

"Father and son, Your Honor," Dexter supplied.

"Nothing like keeping it in the family, in more ways than one. Gotta love living in small towns," the judge added and drew a number of laughs.

Ryder liked this judge, especially when Liam Thompson stood up to start asking questions and was shot down.

"Sit down, Counselor. I'll be questioning the witness. I'm sure you're a man of integrity, but I can't take the chance you might be prejudiced against the witness since you've spoken to your informant, excuse me, your nephew. I'd call that a conflict of interest."

Yes, Ryder silently cheered.

"Lieutenant Wayne, I don't need the blah-blah particulars on how long you've been a police officer. You served the initial warrant to arrest Ms. Bennett."

"Yes, Your Honor."

"The clerk informed me the court closes at four o'clock, and there is no presiding judge on the weekends. The prosecutor claims Ms. Bennett is your girlfriend and you took her away for a romantic weekend."

"We went to my grandfather's cabin in the woods, but we remained in the county."

"I wouldn't call that romantic."

"It wasn't. She even split wood."

"I'd call that hard labor. At any time, did the defendant leave your sight?"

Ryder took a deep breath, zeroed in on the worried look on Jillianne's face and told the truth. "Yes, Your Honor."

Liam Thompson jumped up. "See, Your Honor? He should be charged with dereliction of duty! She's got lots of money and could've taken off for parts unknown."

The judge banged her gavel. "Sit down, Mr. Thompson. She obviously didn't escape, because she's in court."

"Your Honor, I can explain. Ms. Bennett was never out of police custody." Ryder dipped his head toward his dog. "I went out to get us something to eat, and Watson was guarding her."

"Lieutenant Wayne, you want the court to believe Ms. Bennett was under police guard twenty-four seven?"

"Correct."

"Your Honor, I object." Liam Thompson pointed an insulting finger at Ryder. "He's sleeping with her and is painting a cozy picture to cover his badge."

"Have you ever tried to run away from a police-trained German shepherd, Mr. Thompson?" Ryder countered.

"He's got you there, Counselor. Why are there bandages on his front paws?"

"Someone deliberately put spike strips on the path that he takes when he goes out to do his business."

"That's inhumane! If you ever find this person and I'm sitting on this bench, they will feel my wrath. Moving on. Tell me about the defendant's laptop."

"I filled out the necessary forms listing it as evidence, and Captain Clark advised I keep it because the office of the property clerk was closed. I brought it home, and the house I share with my father was broken into over the weekend. An official police report was filed."

The judge addressed Dexter. "You weren't hurt?"

"No, Your Honor. I was out for the evening with my girlfriend. As soon as I noticed the back door had been jimmied open, I called the police."

"It's an unfortunate set of circumstances. Did Ms. Bennett have access to the laptop from the time you took it in as evidence?"

Ryder shook his head. "Absolutely not. Watson was guarding it from the time I removed it from her office until I brought it to my home."

"You're Honor, I object. This is getting out of hand. Lieutenant Ryder expects us to believe this super dog is capable of guarding the defendant and evidence critical to this case."

"Mr. Thompson makes a good case, Lieutenant."

"If Watson could talk, he'd confirm my testimony. What Mr. Thompson failed to mention is that Ms. Bennett was notified by her staff that the passwords to access Mr. Burrows's accounts were changed, so she couldn't have altered information if she'd had access to the laptop, which she didn't. She's also a woman of integrity."

"Thank you, Lieutenant. Is there anything else you can add before you're dismissed?"

A thousand things, his mind shouted, but he shook his head.

"Let's get on with this, shall we? The charges against Ms. Bennett are embezzlement of one hundred thousand dollars from Burrows Real Estate Organization. An addendum to the charges was filed this morning by two members of the board for the Footlight Theater Organization that Ms. Bennett embezzled seventy-five thousand dollars, money that was slated for the renovation of the theater."

Nancy jumped up. "Objection, Your Honor. We weren't notified of these additional charges against Ms. Bennett."

"That's a lie!" Jillianne shoved away from her seat at the table before Sean could stop her. Watson was startled by her abrupt move and jumped up, too. "Every cent Everett Troy donated is accounted for, and I have every damn receipt to prove it!"

"Jillianne, sit down," Nancy urged and directed her attention to the judge. "Sorry, Your Honor. These unfounded additional charges are very upsetting to my client."

"Mr. Thompson, I may be a visiting judge, but I'm not stupid. I don't like surprises and expect all charges in this case to be fully disclosed to the defendant's lawyers."

Ryder was livid and leaned forward to get Everett's attention. "You need to get up there and clear this up now."

Laura pulled a pad out of her purse and wrote a quick note. "Take this to Nancy Jean."

Ryder silently approached the lawyer and gave her the note. She gave him a grateful nod.

"Your Honor, I believe we can clear up this unfounded accusation right now. Mr. Troy is present in court, and he'll be glad to answer any questions you might have."

"Everett Troy, the actor, the movie star, is in court?"

"Yes, and he's willing to testify."

"This is a highly unusual set of circumstances, so as they say on *The Price Is Right*, come on down."

Jillianne had never been so grateful to see Everett walk past her, especially when he gave her a reassuring smile. She agreed with the judge, whom she really liked. This had turned into a fiasco. She was aware that Burrows and Thompson were very good friends. She'd been in their combined company at the country club and at board meetings many times. Why the hostility? To accuse her of stealing from the theater, which had been in her life since she was a teenager, was unthinkable.

She watched Everett put his hand on the bible before sitting down in the witness chair.

"Mr. Troy, it is indeed an honor to meet you, but not under these circumstances. Tell me about this donation."

"It's a pleasure to meet you, too, Judge Taylor," he returned, giving the woman his signature grin that melted women's hearts. "Last year, I donated a substantial sum to the theater, which needed a great deal of renovation. Ms. Bennett set up a special account to draw the funds and sent me copies of the bids and subsequent payment when the work was completed. Every penny was accounted for. Actually, there was two thousand dollars left over, and I donated it to the charitable foundation she maintains for premature infants and newborns with birth defects. And before you ask, I received a letter thanking me for my donation.

"Judge, if I might add, I was recently elected president of the board for the Footlight Theater, and we have no plans to replace Ms. Bennett as the endowment curator and director of funds. She's a woman with impeccable honesty. Those members initiated these charges without the knowledge of the rest of the board."

"Thank you, Mr. Troy, for clearing up this additional charge of embezzlement."

Jillianne breathed a sigh of relief and wished this was over. She turned her head and settled her eyes on Ryder, sending a silent message that she needed a hug. He understood and blew her a kiss.

"Mr. Thompson, I question the validity of these charges as it seems they were conveniently initiated by you and Mr. Burrows at the last minute. Unless you can provide validated proof, I'm satisfied with Mr. Troy's testimony, and those additional charges will be dropped."

The judge reached for the carafe on her bench and poured a glass of water. She expelled a deep sigh after taking a long drink. "I've reviewed the affidavits filed on behalf of Mr. Burrows, and as of right now, it's his word against the defendant's."

Liam Thompson didn't waste any time and stood up and swept a hand toward his client. "Mr. Burrows has been in business for over thirty years. He took over the company from his father. He's a member of the Board of Education and supports the teams at our youth center that, through his generosity, was recently expanded. He's a member of the

Rotary and Better Business Bureaus here and in Atlantic City, where he maintains his home office. This is a man of principle and honesty. He hired Ms. Bennett, thinking he was getting a trustworthy, aboveboard firm. The past month, his on-staff accountants brought to his attention discrepancies in some of the accounts, and he hired a firm to look into her background."

Liam Thompson turned and stared directly at her. "Actually, she's following in her father's footsteps. Little did my client know that he'd hired the daughter of a thief."

Chapter 9

I will not cry, I will not cry.

She'd never felt so humiliated, and it took everything in her not to get up and run out of the courtroom. All these years, she'd fought to overcome the stigma her father had put on their family's name.

Nancy Jean ran a soothing hand up and down Jillianne's back. "What a bastard," she whispered. "They're so done."

This time, it was Sean who stood up. "Objection, Your Honor. My client's father has nothing to do with this case."

"Sustained. Mr. Thompson, unless it's pertinent to our present case, keep your derogatory comments to yourself. Counselor," she said to Nancy Jean, "does your client need a few moments to compose herself before I render my decision?"

Jillianne shook her head. It would take more than a few moments for the sick feeling in her stomach and heart to go away. *Lady Underdog, you can do it.*

"I'm a judge, not an accountant, so the financial figures I reviewed are Greek to me. Mr. Burrows claims Ms. Bennett stole from him, and the defendant professes she's innocent. Both appear to be people with impeccable honesty. There is only one way to settle this. I'm ordering an audit by an independent accounting firm."

"You ignorant ass! Stop this!" Cornelius's demand of his lawyer filled the room.

"She's the judge," Liam argued right back.

"I object!" Cornelius Burrows shoved up from his chair and thrust a finger at Jillianne. "She stole my money."

The judge banged her gavel three times. "He's correct. I am the judge, and you're out of order! Counselor, control your client. This is my courtroom, and I have the first and last say about what happens in here! Now I'll continue. Mr. Burrows, you will give the court-appointed auditing firm complete access to all your records. If you don't cooperate to the fullest, I'll charge you with contempt of court, have you arrested and shut down your entire operation."

"You can't do that!" Burrows charged back.

"Don't try me! I'd shut my mouth before you're charged with contempt of court and taken out of here in handcuffs."

"So that means she'll be getting away scot-free?" Liam Thompson appeared quite flustered when he questioned the judge.

"Absolutely not. Ms. Bennett, you'll be free on bail of twenty-five thousand dollars and surrender your passport to the court. You'll make yourself available to the auditors if they have any questions."

Jillianne only nodded.

"Judge, my client has a business to run and needs to conduct the affairs at the Footlight Theater," Nancy said.

"She can go back to work at both places, as long as she doesn't come in contact with any of Mr. Burrows's accounts."

"Thank you, Your Honor," Nancy said.

The judge banged her gavel. "Court dismissed."

Her feeling of relief slowly died when Cornelius Burrows paused next to her chair.

"Congratulations, Jillianne. Round one belongs to you, but we're far from done. Your father paid the price for his dishonesty, and so will you. I'm not the bad guy here. The people you call your friends could've saved you from this humiliation, but they tossed you in front of a firing squad. Ask about the secrets they've been keeping from you for thirty-four years."

"Don't you have someplace else to be?" Ryder sarcastically challenged as he approached. When he slipped his arm around her waist, she leaned into him to absorb his strength.

"I'm not done with you either," Burrows sneered directly in Ryder's face.

"What a piece of garbage," Ryder whispered in her ear before she gave Sean and Nancy a grateful smile.

"Thank you both, so much," Jillianne said. "I never thought they'd bring up the subject of my father. It's a part of my past I've worked very hard to put behind me."

"Those two misfits will be getting letters from the theater board notifying them they're no longer board members after falsely accusing you of embezzlement," Everett said, standing next Ryder.

Gianna Knight approached them, wearing a catty smile, and Jillianne patted Watson on his head when he gave off a protective growl.

The reporter paled and took a step back. "You had your hands slapped."

"I think the judge was fair in her decision. Guess you're disappointed I wasn't put in handcuffs and carted off to jail."

"That is still a possibility. See you around." She paused in front of Everett. "Like a hero in the movies, you rode in on your white horse and saved the day. I'll be mentioning it tonight in my broadcast. Hometown justice as seen through the eyes of Everett Troy. I'll see you tomorrow morning at the museum."

"I don't know how you can stand working with her," Jillianne said. "Thanks for stepping up to the plate and saving this damsel in distress."

"I only told the truth. Jillianne, we need you back at the helm of the theater."

Laura moved around her husband and gave Jillianne a special embrace shared by deeply felt friends. "Once that auditor checks out those records, you should sue that weasel for making false allegations. I hate to bring this up now, but we need to have a meeting about the children's toy drive and show. Manny's chairing and I'm co-chairing, but you control the funds."

"I agree, this is something very important. As soon as I clear things up at work, I'll set up a time and date for the meeting."

They were just about to leave when Dexter Wayne came over and kissed her on the cheek. "I'm so glad things worked out the way they did. Polly sends her love."

Jillianne thanked all her friends for coming and walked back to Ryder's office. She gave Watson two cookies, and he settled in his bed.

Ryder purposely closed his office door, sat on the edge of his desk and held out his arms. "Lady Underdog, one hug coming up."

That's when the tears of relief escaped. She buried her face in his shoulder and wrapped her arms around him like a vine. He was warm, strong, loving. In the past week, they'd gotten closer than ever before. Each morning, she'd open her eyes and he was already awake, watching her greet the new day. Then he'd give her a silky kiss that set the mood for the hours ahead. How was she going to face each sunrise without him?

"Are you okay?"

She pulled back and forced a smile. "I am, because of you."

"Are you comfortable with the judge's decision?"

"Absolutely. Basically, I'm a free woman. Any plans this evening?"

"I've a meeting, but tomorrow night is open. Actually, I'm on days for the next two weeks."

She fingered the marksman medal on his jacket. "Will you be sleeping at home tonight?"

He nodded. "I'm sorry to disappoint you, love, but I don't want to leave my dad alone. If you need me, I'll come right over. I'll miss spooning with you and the way you wiggle your sweet cheeks against me until I'm rock hard. What a turn-on, Lady Underdog. Just thinking about it makes me want to do this."

The power that was in his arms poured into his kiss, and once again, she clung to him. Not for his reassurance, but in love. She stepped in closer, and his arms tightened. She stroked his bottom lip with her tongue, and he opened his mouth to give entrance to her exploring touch. There'd never been a question about the love they shared, but it had deepened and grown these past couple of weeks. Thank God he was hers.

She reluctantly lowered her arms. "I believe that kiss was very inappropriate for an office in police headquarters."

"That's why you need to get out of here, because I can think of a lot more inappropriate things I want to do to you. What are you going to do this afternoon?"

"I need to make sure I still have a company, but I'll need my car."

"It's parked out back." Ryder pulled open the top drawer of his desk to retrieve her keys. "Drive safe."

She slid the key ring around her pointer finger. "Thanks. Now I'm going to get out of here and test my newfound freedom." She walked over and bent to kiss Watson on the top of his head. "You be a good boy. Watch out for your master because we both love him. You won't have to put up with those bandages after today."

Her heart was heavy when she walked toward the door, but paused with her hand on the doorknob when Ryder called her name. "Jilly, remember what I said. No matter what happens, or how things may seem, I love you, Lady Underdog."

"I love you, too, Sherlock."

She found her car in the back parking area used by employees and visitors and decided a visit to the car wash was needed. The drained feeling in her entire body had her leaning her head back against the headrest.

She was free on bail, but it was a whole lot more.

She was personally free. The personal drive to succeed was gone.

For years, she'd been working to clean up the dark shadow of dishonesty her father had left behind when he was charged with embezzling a hundred and seventy-five thousand dollars from his own firm to cover gambling debts. The disgrace and embarrassment had sent her and her mother running to California to stay with her grandparents. They'd barely gotten settled when her mother shipped her off to France to stay with distant relatives she'd never met.

Despite being separated from those she loved, she'd been happy thinking of the future, but one day that happiness was shattered, compounded by the message she'd received from her mother that her father had taken his own life in prison.

Not engaging in her personal rat race the past few days, she'd felt a change in herself as a person and how she thought her life should be lived. The old Jillianne would have been rushing to her office to reach out to prospective clients. Thanks to her maternal grandparents, she had plenty of money, but she'd become an obsessive workaholic.

Was it all worth it? This horrible experience was a wakeup call.

She'd also loved being with Ryder and the dog all the time. Simple, relaxing and very loving. She was being sappy, but she missed them already. Changes in her life were needed.

She called Winnie to let her know about the judge's decision and that she'd be home later this afternoon for dinner. Ryder wouldn't be with her. She followed up with a call to her office manager to let him know the outcome of the trial. He was relieved and couldn't wait for her to return to work. She'd be in the office by eight tomorrow morning. There'd be a staff meeting at ten, and everyone was expected to be there.

She opened her purse and took out a slice of Juicy Fruit gum, her favorite. Chewing gum hadn't been allowed when she was growing up. She chewed and pondered Burrows's statement about her friends keeping secrets for thirty-four years and Ryder's comment that, no matter what happens, he'd always love her. Thirty-four years? The guys would've been sixteen years old when it began. Something was definitely going on behind her back, and she knew where to get some answers on the past and present.

She pulled out of the parking lot and headed for the public library.

At eight o'clock, Ryder knocked briefly on the back door of the Book and Brew and walked down the hall that led to the parlor. Mollie was setting out coffee and cookies on the table under the window, and Mason lined up bottles of water. Both wore jeans and white cable-knit sweaters.

"You two are so damn domesticated," he teased and helped himself to a bottle of cold water.

"You should try it, Sherlock. I didn't know I could be this happy. Clare calls me Daddy, and every night I read her stories by Mark Twain." He lovingly patted Mollie's flat stomach. "In seven months, we'll be giving her a brother or a sister."

"He's a wonderful father," Mollie added, giving her new husband a loving smile.

Ryder had barely made himself comfortable on one of the two couches when Laura and Everett arrived, holding hands. They sat so close on the couch there was hardly a space between them, and they continued to hold hands. Tamie and Jackson were just as bad. He put his arm around her shoulders to draw her close.

Happiness and love radiated from these three couples. He'd loved Jillianne forever, and the closeness they'd enjoyed this past week was proof they could make a life together, but there were so many things they had to overcome. Despite being surrounded by his best friends, he felt alone for the very first time and set apart because she wasn't here.

He looked at Everett. "Where's your bodyguard? Hudson has become your shadow."

Mollie replied with a smile that danced in her eyes. "I can answer that. Matilda stopped in at the Book and Brew to get a pumpkin latte to go and told me Hudson is accompanying her to the girls' Thanksgiving show at their school."

"Don't get your hopes up, Moll," Mason warned.

"I'd better start before another one bites the dust," Ryder teased. "First, I want to thank you for being there today for Jillianne. It's been rough, but she's going to get through this. Everyone in this room surmised something was fishy when Burrows asked her to take over his accounting division. It makes me sick that we couldn't spare her."

"How do you think we feel?" Laura sniffed, and Everett used his handkerchief to dab at the tear escaping her eye. "To see her sit there today in court, being humiliated! And it's all trumped-up lies! I wanted to punch Burrows."

"You never came right out and said it, but Taylor and Taylor…" Jackson remarked, raising a brow.

"I'm not going there," Ryder replied, giving everyone a meaningful stare. "We can't testify to something we don't know."

Mason accepted a cup of coffee from Mollie and kissed her on the corner of her brow. "Who are they going to hire to audit Burrows's accounts?"

"I received a ray of sunshine in the form of a text earlier from Pollyanna, our favorite court clerk. Before leaving, the judge provided a list of five firms that would be acceptable to do the audit. One was starred." Ryder's voice trailed off, and he studied the row of books on the nearby shelf to let his friends draw their own conclusion in his statement.

Tamie Elise fisted her hand and punched the air. "Yes!"

"When you think about it, we've been doing as much manipulating as Burrows, but at least ours is honest," Ryder continued. "Polly sells real estate on the side, and I found out a little more about Burrows's dirty dealings. He's scarfing up short-sale properties and turning them around within days."

"He has to be laundering money for the Magellan Cartel," Everett decided. "Too bad you can't tell Polly what we're doing."

"I also found out my dad interviewed the employees at the cannery when Marshall went missing. He apologized for not believing me, us, and is eager to help. I filled him in on many of the particulars, and he'll work with his old partner, Charlie McCarthy, aka Mack, if we need an extra set of eyes."

"Do you have any leads on who stole the laptop?" Tamie asked.

Ryder shook his head. "None. It irked me when Thompson brought up the laptop in court. Either he was playing dumb, or he doesn't know Burrows had it stolen from my house. The right hand doesn't know what the left hand is doing."

"Personally, I think there's trouble in paradise. Burrows wasn't very happy with his counsel in court today. I came in on the tail end of what Burrows said to Jillianne after the trial, and he's trying to stir up more trouble." Mason looked at his wife. "Has Jillianne approached any of you girls and asked about secrets you've been keeping?"

"No, and I, too, didn't like what he said. The old coot is trying to make us look like the bad guys," Mollie said.

Ryder was the first one to notice that Tamie leaned forward on the couch, and her fingers were laced together in a tight fist. "Burrows is right." The somber tone in her voice drew everyone's attention. "We are the bad guys, because we let him do that to Jillianne, our sister. He's an expert manipulator, and he's been manipulating—first, the guys' lives and now ours—for a very long time."

She looked at Ryder. "The psychologist in me says you feel like the odd man out, and my heart is breaking for you. We've been where you are and know the problems you're facing, but you need to make up your mind, very soon, to tell her what's happening. I also understand that you're scared for her, but Burrows has already done a great deal of damage to her life. Again, we stood back and let her go through this. We're terrible people." Tamie buried her head on her husband's shoulder, and Jackson drew her close.

Ryder was about to agree with her when his phone signaled an incoming text message from Hudson. He read it out loud. "'Just heard from Preston. He's been officially assigned to audit. Contacting Burrows's office tomorrow. He knows Jillianne isn't allowed to work on accounts, but he could get the job done faster if she could, in a roundabout way, point him in the direction of the accounts we need from the cannery. Get back to me ASAP.'"

"That's the best news, but Jillianne will be suffering additional embarrassment once I tell her what's going on. It will be like pouring salt into an open wound."

"What are you talking about? Ryder, that poor girl can't take any more shit," Mollie said. "Her reputation suffered another bruise when that lowlife Thompson brought up her father, so what's left?"

"It's about her stepbrother, Neil. I found out Gianna Knight is Paige's mother." Numerous gasps filled the room.

"That two-faced, double-tongued liar gave birth to that beautiful person?" Laura gripped Everett's hand. "Once Gianna is arrested for her part in the dirty dealings of the Magellan Cartel, the fallout for Paige will be devastating."

"So where do we go from here?" Jackson asked.

"Keep our eyes and ears open, watch each other's backs. I'll have a talk with Jillianne about the murder that took place thirty-four years ago. I had to move my canister to my house, since they started renovating the old cannery.

"Invite her to dinner," Laura suggested. "Ply her with wine and pumpkin pie, her favorite."

"Speaking of pumpkin pie, Mollie, Laura and I were talking about Thanksgiving. Jackson and I will host a traditional feast. Our new den is big enough to set up long tables. The fireplace is already decorated with cornstalks, pumpkins and lights."

"I mentioned it to Elsie and Fred, and they were thrilled," Mollie said. "Elsie will bring books from the library on Thanksgiving to entertain the kids."

"I spoke to Manny, and he'll be there with Robyn and invite a couple of his friends," Laura added. "Luckily, Noreen has off, and if all goes well, Ben will be home."

"Belvedere and Valerie are on board, especially since they don't have any immediate family. I just might try my hand at deep-frying a turkey," Jackson said with a big grin.

"Better notify the fire department ahead of time," Mason teased.

"I'm working the day shift until three," Ryder said.

"Party pooper. Ryder, you're not getting out of it that easily. We'll eat dinner at three thirty," Mollie said. "We'll let Jillianne and Winifred know. Of course, Neil and Paige are invited. All we'll need is a head count and who's making what."

"Sounds like a plan," Ryder said, just before his cell phone rang. He wondered why Captain Clark was calling. Something told him to put the call on speaker.

"Hi, Captain, tell me something good."

"I need to come straight out with this. What have you been doing the past hour, and is Watson with you?"

"I'm at a meeting with The Association at the Book and Brew, and I left the dog at home to keep an eye on my dad. You're on speaker, so everyone can confirm my whereabouts."

"He's been here since eight o'clock," Mason called out.

"Why?" Ryder asked.

"Liam Thompson Sr.'s body was just found in the parking lot across the street from the theater. The officers on scene determined he was mauled by a dog before someone slammed him on the side of a head with a police-issue billy club."

"You're accusing me and Watson of murder?" The idea was incredulous.

"Of course not, but I have to follow procedure and had to ask. You of all people should know that."

"Who are the cops on scene?"

"Officers Griffin and Deakins, the new patrolman. Sergeant Thompson arrived, but I ordered him off scene because he was very upset. He was going to notify his aunt of her husband's murder."

"Deakins has a newly minted degree in crime scene investigation," Ryder said. "Do they know what Thompson was doing in that area?"

"Sergeant Thompson just called me with the answer to that question. According to Liam's wife, you called and asked to meet him in the parking lot at nine o'clock. She said you needed to talk to him about the trial."

"That's a load of bullshit. I've got a room full of witnesses. For the record, I don't carry and have never used a billy club."

"The one found at the crime scene was an old-fashioned piece made of wood. It had the initial W carved on the bottom. Ryder, I'm asking this question as a friend. When they broke into your house, could they have stolen your father's billy club?"

"Jeez, I don't like where you're going with this. As a friend, this is another load of bullshit. My father's old billy club has a W engraved on the bottom. He wanted to give it to me when I became a rookie cop. I'm sure the murderer used gloves, and if there are any prints on the club, they'll belong to my father."

"This is all circumstantial, and someone has gone to a great deal of trouble to try to set you up, but again, I need to follow procedure. We need to ask your father about his whereabouts this evening and about his club."

Fury surged anew in Ryder's body. "You're not going to drag him down to headquarters like some common criminal!"

"Lieutenant, now you're out of line. He's a decorated police officer, and I would never subject him to such humiliation. We're waiting for the coroner, and then the two officers will go over to your house. Just make sure Watson is there."

"I want to be present when they question my dad. You know Watson would never do something like. He's trained to stop a criminal, not maul someone to death."

"You and I know that, but clutched in Thompson's hand was the same type of bandage you wrapped around Watson's paws. They took it into evidence, along with the club."

"Damn, they thought of everything. Are you quarantining him?" Ryder almost choked on his own question.

"Not at this time, but as his handler, the dog is not to be out of your sight until he is cleared."

"Before I come into headquarters, I'll go see Dr. Parisi, his veterinarian. There has to be a way to prove Watson's innocence. See you in the morning."

Ryder immediately called his dad's cell, and it went right to voice mail. He checked the time. Ten o'clock. His dad was already in bed because he had to be up early to report to his crossing-guard location.

"This entire scenario is a load of crap," Tamie said in disgust. "That sweet dog wouldn't hurt a fly! He smells the flowers and eats homemade cookies!"

Laura chimed in, "And to infer your father is a murderer!"

"Along with Everett, Watson was the hero in that courtroom today, and apparently, Thompson screwed up and was no longer useful to Burrows," Mason determined.

"They took your comment, 'Did you ever try to run away from a police-trained German shepherd, Mr. Thompson?' seriously," Everett reminded everyone.

"That's not all. Before Burrows left the courtroom this morning, the bastard stared directly at me and said, 'I'm not done with you either.' He wasn't satisfied going after my Jilly, now he's gone after my father and the dog. Everett, watch your back."

"Hudson's been with me every day at the museum, especially now that Gianna Knight is around, but I'll be extra careful."

"So what do you want us to do now?" Mollie asked. "Team Underdog is ready to help."

"Go home and pray for my woman, my father and my dog."

Chapter 10

Ryder gripped the steering wheel of his truck so hard he could feel the blood pressure building up in his fingers. He was driving over the speed limit on the residential streets. The first cop that pulled him over for speeding would get his head chewed off. A few blocks later, he almost ran a red light and jammed on his brakes. "Goddammit, slow down. You can't prove Jillianne's, your father's or dog's innocence if you're dead."

He'd always considered himself even-tempered and maintained a cool head, a requirement of being a police officer, but right now he'd exhausted every ounce of the principles he'd come to live by. During their investigation into Burrows's and the cartel's dirty dealings, they'd been outmaneuvered and beaten back. Now it felt like they were running on ice. One step forward, and twenty back.

He really needed to talk to Jillianne, needed to hear the sound of her voice, but changed his mind. She'd been through enough hell for one day.

As expected, the house was dark when he pulled down the drive and parked in front of the garage. The moment Ryder got out of the truck, Watson barged through the doggie door to meet him. His first thought was to order the dog to open his mouth so he could examine his teeth and gums, but he'd wait for the vet to do it in the morning. If the case ever went to court, he could be charged with evidence tampering.

"I wish you could tell me you and Pop stayed home all night."

Watson replied with two barks and barreled through the doggie flap before Ryder could unlock the door.

The light was on over the stove, and he hung his jacket on the coatrack next to the door. He hated what had to be done, but as a retired cop, his father would understand. Ryder walked down the hall and knocked softy before opening his father's bedroom door. He was greeted by light snoring. He approached the bed and put a hand to his father's shoulder. "Dad, I need to talk to you."

A startled snort was followed by, "What? What's the matter, boy? Did I oversleep?"

"No, but there's been an incident, and we need to talk."

At the sound of the word *incident*, his father's slow wakefulness came to full alert, a residual effect from being a cop. He tossed off the blankets and groaned when he swung his legs over the side of the bed and reached for his glasses sitting on the bedside table.

"What happened?"

"Come into the kitchen, and I'll make some decaf.

"Give me a minute to go to the bathroom."

When his dad walked into the kitchen, Ryder smiled at the sight of his father's flannel pajamas. "It takes a real man to wear pajamas with dancing polar bears and red hearts."

"I like them. Polly gave me these for my birthday because my old furnace doesn't heat up my body like it used to." Dexter picked up the cup of coffee Ryder had set on the counter and brought it over to the table and sat down. "What happened at"— he paused to look at the time on the microwave—"eleven at night?"

"Liam Thompson was murdered this evening, around nine o'clock in the parking lot across from the Footlight Theater."

"Jeez, we just saw him in court this morning!"

"It gets complicated. A wooden billy club with the initial W was found at the scene. Officers Griffin and Deakins are on their way over to question you. You'll need to put on some trousers."

"That club sounds like mine, but I had nothing to do with Thompson's death. Polly and I played poker, our kind, and she left at nine thirty because she has to be in work early tomorrow morning. The damn dog was driving us crazy. He kept running in and out of the doggie door, barking his head off. Something was out there. I checked outside a couple of times, but didn't see anything. He lost the bandage on one of his paws, so I took off the other one."

Once again, Ryder didn't like where this was heading. In his haste to get home, he hadn't noticed that the bandages were gone from Watson's paws. "What did you do with it?"

"It's in the garbage can over there in a little plastic bag."

Ryder reluctantly retrieved the bag that contained the other bandage. Technically, it was evidence that could implicate his four-legged best friend in a murder.

"What's so important about the bandage?"

"Thompson was mauled by a vicious dog, and a piece of bandage was found in his hand."

His father's cheeks turned red, an obvious sign his blood pressure was on the rise. "Those guttersnipes are trying to make it look like Watson attacked Thompson! I'll bet that's who the dog heard outside!"

"Dad, calm down, I don't need you having a heart attack. Can you determine how long he was outside?"

Dexter suddenly found interest in the basket of fruit sitting in the middle of the table. "To tell you the truth, son, Polly and I got a little frisky and retreated to my bedroom for a while, say, forty-five minutes."

"I really didn't need to know that, but that leaves Watson's whereabouts up in the air."

Watson barked, drawing their attention to the back door. "They're here. Get some clothes on. Answer their questions as best you can. I'm here as your son, not a cop."

Ryder opened the door. It always amazed him how much Kaitlyn Griffin looked like her mother, right down to her golden-blond hair and lovely face. She was a cop, through and through, and was currently going for her degree in criminal justice, majoring in forensic science.

Officer Deakins was a recent hire, but a seasoned cop, having put in ten years on the Jersey City Police Department. He had a sturdy build and brown eyes that took in everything going on around him. With a degree in crime scene investigation, he was on the fast track to becoming a detective.

"Can I get either of you something to drink? My dad will join us in a minute. He's getting dressed." Kaitlyn avoided looking at him. He understood she was very uncomfortable with what they had to do.

"Sorry to keep you waiting," Dexter said, hurrying into the room.

Out of respect, Kaitlyn introduced her partner. "Detective Wayne, this is Officer Graham Deakins."

"Nice to meet you, sir," Deakins said. "Kaitlyn explained who you are on our way here. I've never had to question a retired, decorated detective, but I'm sure you know we have to follow procedure."

"It's a first time for me, too, but do your job and don't let my son, your lieutenant, intimidate you."

"I explained what happened and why you have to question him," Ryder informed his officers.

Ryder pretended he had duct tape over his mouth when the officers asked his father if he was home all evening with the dog. His father gave a cleaned-up version of his guest being here until nine thirty and noted the disturbance that had the dog running in and out of the house. Dexter purposely added that there were raccoons and opossums in the neighborhood.

Officer Deakins mentioned the piece of bandage found in the victim's hand and brought up the subject of Watson's bandages. That was when things got sticky.

Ryder had been raised with a strong sense of honesty and principles. It broke his heart, but he succumbed to doing the right thing. He reached into his pocket and pulled out the plastic bag, but was reluctant to pass it to the officers right away.

"I'm aware of the bandage found with the victim, and this will probably implicate Watson in the murder. We could have both pieces tested for DNA, and it will likely prove they came from my dog. There's no way to prove his innocence, other than I know he'd never maliciously harm a person." Watson chose that moment to put his feet on Ryder's knee and kiss him on the cheek. "I know, boy," he said and ran his hand down the dog's back in a loving gesture.

"Lieutenant, you know I just finished my CSI training and I'm constantly doing research. There is such a thing as dog-bite forensics. Bites are unique, like fingerprints. Sometimes it's obvious when looking at the bite marks on a victim's body. You can tell the difference in size of the bites. If Watson did the damage to the victim, there might be some trauma inside his mouth."

"Captain Clark is aware I'm taking Watson to the vet in the morning to get checked out." The word *vet* set the dog on alert. Watson ran into the other room, adding a bit of comic relief to the tense atmosphere. "My big, brave police dog is afraid of the vet."

Kaitlyn cleared her throat before looking at Ryder with respectful hesitation. "Lieutenant, we have one other question for Detective Wayne."

"Officer Griffin, I'd feel the same way if I had to question your mother about a murder. Proceed."

"Sir, an old-fashioned wooden billy club was found at the scene and was possibly used to murder Mr. Thompson. The letter W was engraved on it."

"Let me stop you now. It sounds like mine. I gave it to the lieutenant when he became a rookie cop."

"Dad, I haven't seen it since you gave it to me. I've never believed in using brute force."

"It's in a shoe box in the top of your closet."

"If you recall, my closet was tossed when they broke into the house. I stored Jillianne's laptop in my old gym bag from high school. Officer Griffin took the report."

"Hopefully, the box wasn't disturbed," his dad said and led them upstairs to Ryder's bedroom.

Ryder opened the door to the walk-in closet and turned on the light. "Since the break-in, I haven't had time to reorganize my possessions. Dad, point me in the right direction."

His father stepped around a pile of clothes and storage bins and headed for the corner and shifted a number of undisturbed boxes aside. "Here it is. I used the box your first pair of police shoes came in to store the billy club. He passed it to Ryder. "I don't want to look."

It felt much too light. Before lifting the lid, he already knew the box was empty.

The following morning, Ryder stared at his dog. "Don't pull this crap with me. You have to get out of the truck. Dr. Parisi is waiting for us." Ryder left the door open and paced a few feet away. "This is crazy. I'm the human here and the one in charge, but I'm trying to convince a dog to get out of the truck." His only option left was a decent bribe. "Steak for a week."

As anticipated, Watson jumped out of the truck and headed for the building. A different receptionist was at the desk. A lovely woman with blond hair wore a smock with pictures of a variety of animals and offered a friendly smile.

"You must be Lieutenant Wayne, and this has to be Watson. I'm Sydney, the doctor's vet tech."

"Sorry to drag you guys in at seven thirty in the morning, but I appreciate you meeting me. Technically, it's police business, but more important, it's about proving Watson's innocence."

"Dr. Parisi was glad you explained the severity of the situation to our emergency service. He's waiting in exam room one for Watson."

Sydney came around the side of the high desk and patted Watson on the head. "You wouldn't hurt anyone, you handsome boy."

There was something in her smile that made Ryder think he might have seen her before. "Your face and smile seem so familiar. Are you from around here?"

"No, I was raised on a farm in Idaho."

"Did your parents ever live around here? Maybe I know your folks."

"Their last name is Waters, and as far as I know, they've always lived in Idaho." She hesitated before adding, "I was adopted and have no idea where my biological parents lived."

When they walked into the office, Dr. Parisi was talking on his cell phone and flipping his fingers across the screen of his tablet. "I just got your information, and thanks for getting back to me so quickly. I'll take the molds in a little while," he said, ending the call.

"Morning. Nothing like starting my day off with an interesting challenge. Hi, Watson, sounds like you are in quite a pickle, but we're going to fix that."

"I really appreciate you seeing us so soon. There's no way Watson mauled the victim last evening," Ryder assured.

"That's what we're going to prove. I was just speaking to a buddy of mine from college. He's a forensic odontologist."

"I'm familiar with the term but have never used one."

"These specially trained dentists use their expertise to help identify remains and trace bite marks to a specific individual. He's highly sought after and works with the medical examiner and coroner in New York. In our case, he's going to compare the bite marks on the body to a mold we're going to take of Watson's teeth after I examine his gums."

Hope flared in Ryder's body. "How soon can he get here?"

"Lucky for you, he's on vacation and is driving to Florida to see his parents. We need a request giving him authorization to attend the autopsy on behalf of the police. Foster Scanlon's testimony will hold up in any court."

"I know the coroner, so there shouldn't be any problem getting permission on the autopsy. Tell the doctor to send the bill for his services directly to me, along with yours."

"Foster already told me your case is pro bono. His German shepherd is riding shotgun in his truck. I'll need the phone number and address of where he is to do the examination. It won't be until late this afternoon.

"Now, Watson, my friend, let's get you on the table so we can examine your teeth and gums. To make this official, Sydney is going to take pictures, so you're going to have to smile."

"I can do that," Ryder offered.

"You're here as his handler and loving owner. We're doing this by the book, so no one can accuse you of doctoring the pictures. Give us about a half hour."

"While you're doing that, I'll contact the coroner's office." Before leaving the room, he spoke directly to the dog that preened with an *I'm going to be a star* attitude. "Behave, or no cookies for a week."

Before contacting the coroner, he called Captain Clark to give him an update on what they were doing to prove Watson's innocence. He was much relieved. To keep things official, he'd call the coroner to ask him not to perform the autopsy until Dr. Scanlon, the forensic odontologist, was able to do his examination.

The captain informed Ryder that all hell was breaking loose at headquarters with reporters from the cable channels asking about the murder of the former mayor. The chief had assured them everything possible was being done, but someone asked about the billy club being owned by a former police detective on the force. He responded that all avenues were being investigated.

"Ah, horse hockey. Burrows is deliberately pointing fingers at my father. Tell me they didn't ask about Watson."

"Funny you should say that. Someone referenced your comment directed at Liam Thompson about running away from a German shepherd and specifically asked about Watson."

"That information has Gianna Knight's name all over it."

"For the next five days, you're working the evening shift. Babysit your father and the dog during the day, and Pollyanna can keep them company in the evening. You don't need reporters showing up at your house."

"What about his school crossing-guard job?"

"Dexter requested extra help because they're short-handed. He's assigned to the high school, and we require two guards. Get yourself a neon vest. Looks like you're back to directing traffic."

"What about the dog?"

"Jackson's the principal. He can keep Watson in his office."

"Captain, if this situation wasn't so life threatening, I'd burst out laughing at the calamity. How am I to prove Jillianne's innocence, along with my father's and dog's?"

"It's time to call in the troops, aka, The Association. Report in after your crossing-guard assignment."

Sydney was wiping a white substance from Watson's upper lip when Ryder returned to the exam room. "He whimpered like a baby when we had to poke at his gums, so Dr. Parisi gave him a small shot to calm him down. On the whole, he did very well."

The vet finished washing his hands at the sink and used paper towel to dry his hands. "If Watson mauled a person last night, you couldn't prove it by me. There's no sign of residual blood, skin tissue, nothing. The mold is setting and will be ready for Foster later this afternoon."

"That's something positive. The coroner is being notified as we speak not to perform the autopsy until Dr.

Scanlon examines the body. I'll need the doctor's contact information." The words had barely left his mouth when Sydney passed him a piece of paper with the information he needed.

The vet tech gave him a sheepish smile. "Just so you know, I had to bribe Watson with cookies when he saw the needle in Dr. Parisi's hand. You owe him four treats."

"No problem. When can I get the pictures?"

"You're not," Sydney informed him. "Hannah and Paul Clark bring their dog, Sparkles, here, and I reached out to her for the captain's direct email address so we can send the photos to him. We need to keep you out of the loop for now."

He set Watson on the floor and clipped the leash to his harness. "Thank you again. Doc, you need to take your"—he hesitated when Sydney wiggled her ring finger—"fiancée out to dinner. When's the big day?"

"That's the big question," the doc replied.

Late Tuesday afternoon, Jillianne parked her car in the library parking lot. This was her second trip here in two days. She wanted to speak to Elsie Trent, Mason's aunt, who ran the reference section, but she'd been off yesterday afternoon. Not wanting to miss her again, Jillianne had called the library this morning to make sure she'd be coming into work today. Elsie would be working until five.

It had felt good to get back to her normal work routine this morning, and she'd concentrated on what was going on in her office and not the outside world, which would surely be talking about her trial. To her delight, her employees and loyal customers had filled her office with balloons and flowers. The Fabulous Four had sent a bouquet of iced sugar cookies. Irene, the baker at the Book and Brew, had duplicated the figure of Lady Underdog. That had raised a lot of questions that she refrained from answering.

Facing her employees at the staff meeting had started out awkward, but she'd addressed them in the professional manner they'd become accustomed to and assured everyone that it was business as usual. The company had lost three percent of its accounts, but she was surprised to learn they'd gotten calls from prospective clients wanting to use her services because they had had bad experiences with Burrows Real Estate Organization.

A half-dozen times during the day, she'd wanted to call Ryder, but changed her mind. He was probably up to his ears deflecting questions about their relationship and the trial. She missed him like crazy, especially when she woke up this morning and didn't see his beautiful face and enjoy his loving, good-morning kiss. No Watson to rest his chin on her foot or lap. They'd made tentative plans to have dinner this evening, but he'd sent her a short text saying his shift had been changed and he'd be working nights the rest of the week.

At four o'clock, she'd shocked her office manager when she walked out of her office and announced she was done for the day. No one was to work beyond four thirty. They had families at home, so clients would just have to wait, unless there were unusual circumstances that had to be approved by her or him.

The Beacon Pointe Library, housed in a gray stone building, had been one of the first elementary schools in town. A row of bright green holly bushes bordered the walk leading to the main entrance.

She passed through one of the three glass doors and offered a friendly wave to the woman at the main checkout desk and headed for the reference room.

Elsie Trent was sitting at an antique lady's writing desk, filling out a file card. A small blue bow was buried in her curls, and pale peach blush accented her soft cheeks. Three strands of beads in various shades of blue graced the front of her long-sleeved shirtwaist. Jillianne knew for a fact that the sweet, soft-spoken, seventy-five-year-old had a very healthy bank account.

She'd been overseeing the reference room for over twenty-five years, and there was more information in her head than in the two-story room. The library had been updated with a modern computer system, but the screen on the nearby table was dark. A few of the chairs were occupied with people referencing hardcover books and working on laptops. The quiet was almost unnerving.

She was greeted by Elsie's beaming smile when she approached the desk. Elsie stood and opened her arms. "Oh, my dear, I was so happy to get your message."

Jillianne sighed with relief and returned Elsie's greeting hug. "Thank you for believing in me."

"Of course I do, my dear. Fred believes in you, too. She's disliked the Burrows family ever since she had to work for Burrows Sr. at the cannery all those years ago. What can we do to help?"

"How long ago was that?"

"About thirty-four years."

Same number. "Is there someplace we can go talk in private?"

"It's just five, so I'm done for the day. I'm meeting Fred for dinner at Scannelli's around seven. We love pizza. She's putting in extra time at the paper helping Mason. The office, no, the whole town is suffering the aftershocks of Liam Thompson's murder."

Shock gripped Jillian's entire body. "What are you talking about? When was he murdered? I've stayed away from all news media and the internet."

A couple of the people at the tables shushed them. "Let's go upstairs and sit at the tables behind the bookshelves. That's where the kids like to hide and neck, or don't they say that word anymore?"

Elsie held on to the shiny brass handrail of the steps that led to the upper level and led the way to the far rear corner. One of the tables was occupied. Kaitlyn and Paige, Jillianne's niece, were working on laptops. The girls were close friends and had graduated together. They were also attending the same college.

"Oh, Aunt Jillianne, this is so awful," Paige cried, getting up from her chair and giving Jillianne a hug. "Daddy has been dodging reporters, and Gianna Knight was waiting for me when I walked out of school. This whole thing sucks, because you didn't do anything wrong."

"I'm so sorry you're being subjected to all this embarrassment."

"There may not be any blood between us, but I consider you my aunt, and that makes us family. I'm more furious than embarrassed."

Jillianne had always felt the same way. "We certainly are. How did you handle Gianna Knight?"

"I told her to leave me alone and I'd prefer she never contact me again. Then she had the nerve to ask me if I knew she was my mother."

"Nothing like being direct. What did you say?"

"I was tempted to say kiss my ass, but my father taught me better manners. What I did do was toss my chin and tell her the only parent I've ever had is my wonderful father. I got in my car and drove away. She just stood there, dumbfounded. What are you doing here? You usually work until eight or nine o'clock."

"The past week has been a real eye-opener for me, so I've decided not to put in so much time at the office so I can enjoy my family and friends. I'm a member of the Historical Society and decided to do a little research on the town's history." She dipped her head toward Elsie. "I was told if I wanted to find out about a specific event, talk to Elsie Trent. But before that, I need to find out about Liam Thompson's murder."

Kaitlyn, dressed in jeans and a bulky hooded sweatshirt displaying a logo from the Beacon Pointe Police Department, waved her over. "Why don't you ladies join us at our table?"

"We need to keep our voices down. There's a part of this room that sends out an echo, and everyone below can hear what you're saying," Elsie reminded them.

"Liam Thompson was murdered in the parking lot across from the Footlight Theater last evening around nine o'clock," Kaitlyn explained.

Jillianne put a hand over her mouth to shield her gasp. "Across from my theater! Do they have any suspects?"

Kaitlyn's cop eyes shifted nervously to Elsie and then Paige before she explained the circumstances of Thompson's death.

"Watson! That's ridiculous! He wouldn't hurt a fly. Ryder must be going out of his mind worrying about his father and the dog. I can't believe he didn't call me."

"He probably thought you'd been through enough hell." Elsie patted Jillianne's hand. "Is there anything specific you wanted to ask me?"

She really wanted to call him, but would wait until his shift was over. "Something significant happened in Beacon Pointe thirty-four years ago, possibly involving Burrows Sr. You mentioned Frederica didn't like working for him at the cannery. I always thought the cannery belonged to the Holcombe family."

"I can answer that question," Elsie said with an easy smile. "They did, but the company got into financial difficulties and Cornelius Burrows Sr. bailed them out. The company enjoyed an economic boom for a number of years, and everything was great. He even brought his son on board. When Marshall Holcombe went missing, Burrows Sr. took over the company."

"I researched a paper on the cannery for economics in high school and how much the town depended on the one big company to survive," Kaitlyn added. "When the EPA shut them down for falsifying reports, the town suffered greatly. I interviewed a couple of my friends' grandfathers, and they swore Burrows stole their pension money."

"Was their claim ever investigated?" Jillianne asked.

"No, because there was some fancy clause in the contract that eliminated all the pensions if the company went under," Elsie answered.

"Does anyone know what happened to Marshall Holcombe?" Jillianne directed her question to Elsie, but was surprised when her niece spoke up first.

Paige ran her fingers through her long black hair that she'd unfortunately inherited from her mother. "He disappeared and was never heard from again."

"How did you find out?" Jillianne asked her niece.

"From Matilda Hennypenny. You know she's head of the theater guild, and I had to go over to her house to bring her information that had to go in a program for one of the shows. Faith, Hope and Charity were playing dress-up and were wearing pretty costume jewelry. Many of the pieces were designed with the letter M. Matilda said she found them and a lot of antique gold pieces from Marshall and Margie, her grandparents, the owners of the cannery, in boxes in the attic.

"She also found her grandmother's old journals. Margie had become quite senile and wrote that she believed Burrows had her brother murdered. He wanted to take over the company because he and his son had funny money in the fish."

Jillianne shook her head. "None of that makes sense. Burrows is a lying snake, but I can't believe he'd order someone killed."

"The scribbling in the last journal was very hard to decipher. She babbled about the Beacon Pointe Light and talking to Lazarus Anderson, the ghost, who turned out to be Mollie Trent's great-great-grandfather. She ranted that Blumberg should get his hands slapped with a ruler and expelled. Matilda was really confused by Margie's last line about how she felt sorry for four boys because no one believed them about something. I remember so much because I found it fascinating."

"Blumberg? I had him in high school, and he was a terrible teacher. Jackson just fired him," Kaitlyn noted. "I recently learned that Charlie Mack and Dexter Wayne were detective partners way back when. They must have questioned Margie about her brother's disappearance. Haven't you ever noticed Mollie's ring? It's a Holcombe heirloom."

All this information was swimming around in her head, but one comment stuck out. "What four boys?" Jillianne asked, but a sixth sense told her she already knew. "Did she say how long ago this happened?"

"The pages dated thirty-four years ago," Paige answered.

Jillianne looked at Elsie, who'd become much too quiet and was twisting the longest strand of her beads around her finger. She reached for the woman's aged hand and laced their fingers together. "Did Fred ever suggest to you that she thought Burrows Sr. had Marshall Holcombe murdered?"

Elsie lowered her eyes to her lap and nodded.

"Oh, shit!" Kaitlyn said it so loud her curse echoed throughout the room. "The past, Burrows, the four boys, who are now men. Now it's starting to make sense. My lieutenant kept saying things were happening and that he wished he could give me an explanation, but couldn't."

"What are you talking about? But keep your voice low." Jillianne moved her chair closer.

"Excuse me, ladies." Elsie stood up and smoothed the front of her dress. "I'm going to leave you to your thoughts because I don't want to be accused of feeding your ideas. Before I leave, I will say you're headed in the right direction."

She patted Jillianne on the shoulder and kissed her on the cheek. "He's loved you for a long time and has wanted to keep you safe. Give him a chance to explain."

"Do you need me to walk you to your car?" Kaitlyn offered.

"No, I'm good. You ladies be careful. Too much knowledge isn't always safe."

Jillianne furrowed her brow, wondering what Elsie meant. Ryder wanted to keep her safe and she should give him a chance to explain? About what?

Kaitlyn instinctively looked from side to side to make sure they couldn't be overheard before she drew Jillianne's attention. "You were there the night Maya and Dylan were left trussed up on the beach smelling like they'd taken a bath in booze. It was reported as a misadventure by two teenagers, but they were actually kidnapped by two men with Russian accents."

"Aunt Jillianne, Mollie almost lost the Book and Brew. It's rumored the phony health inspector worked for Burrows and he deliberately infested her building with vermin and roaches. He had a Russian name."

"Shortly after Everett returned to Beacon Pointe, Manny was beat up and was told to give his boss a message to mind his own business. They spoke with heavy Russian accents," Kaitlyn added.

Paige counted off with her fingers. "Manny is connected to Everett. Jackson is connected to Maya. Mollie is connected to Mason."

"And I'm connected to Ryder." Jillianne spoke up, as the puzzle pieces formed a picture in her mind.

"The lieutenant recently found out the two guys responsible worked for Burrows."

"Worked?" Jillianne questioned Kaitlyn.

"The Russian health inspector was found dead on the beach near the Beacon Pointe Light, and his partner was recently murdered in Atlantic City," Kaitlyn added.

Cold, hard reality slapped Jillianne in the face. "Burrows is seeking revenge on those four boys, who are now men, and the bad guys who worked for him are being eliminated. Now he's going after me." Her voice trailed off as this was making too much sense.

"Jillianne, you don't think…" Kaitlyn's voice trailed off.

"Yeah, I do."

"My God, Aunt Jillianne. Those poor guys have had to live with this all these years and are still being subjected to treachery from Burrows."

She stared at both of the women. "Not a word of what we've discussed to anyone. Like Elsie said, knowledge can be dangerous. Paige, if you feel the least bit uncomfortable at any time, call the police."

"Aunt Jillianne, now you're scaring me, but I'll take your warning to heart."

"I'm going to research old records in police headquarters from when McCarthy and Wayne were detectives," Kaitlyn said. "I'll let you know if I come up with anything about Marshall Holcombe's disappearance."

"You, too, be careful. The best way to get revenge on this egotistical dirt bag is through his wallet. He's going down, once and for all," Jillianne declared.

Chapter 11

Jillianne hadn't been prepared for the drastic change in the weather when she left the building and cautiously picked up the pace to her car when ice pellets hit her in the face, shocking her already numb system. Ice had banded the naked tree limbs and lightly blanketed the ground. "Next time, check the weather," she scolded herself and shivered, despite the comfort of her down-filled coat.

A layer of ice coated her windshield. She turned on the defrosters and would wait until she could see out the front window before heading home. These few minutes gave her pause to think about the overwhelming information she'd just learned.

Secrets, lies, untruths, betrayal, not only from the man she loved with all her heart, but from her very best friends. The other members of the Fabulous Four had to have learned what was going on from their husbands. From what little she'd concluded, Burrows was a ruthless charlatan who had been cheating people for many years. He'd been making The Association, and those they loved, pay for what those innocent boys had witnessed. Confirmation of what they'd seen was still up in the air.

Another reality-shattering thought came to mind. Her dearest friends and the man who loved her believed Burrows was dirty, but hadn't tried to stop her from accepting a job working with his financial division. Why? Would she have listened to them if they'd tried? Probably not, because she'd thought he was a well-respected businessman, and the account had added more prestige for her firm. In all fairness, she couldn't blame them for everything. Her selfish drive to succeed over and above what she'd already accomplished took a direct hit.

More bits and pieces jumped into her mind. When the boys were seniors in high school, each one had suffered a career disappointment. Jackson and Mason lost their scholarships to Ivy League schools. A gun was found in Ryder's locker, killing his chances to go into the FBI. Drugs were planted in Everett's locker, and he lost his acceptance into Juilliard. Blumberg, the psychology teacher, was a relative of Burrows and had had direct access to the eighteen-year-olds' lockers and records. The lowlife had sabotaged their dreams. Like Paige had said, the guys were slowly being made to pay for what they'd witnessed, and not just them, but everyone they loved. That now included her.

Ryder had suffered a personal hell when he had to arrest her, but he'd whisked her away so she wouldn't suffer additional humiliation. Burrows had retaliated by going after Watson and Dexter. Was there no stopping him?

Why didn't the guys strike back? *Stupid, Jillianne. They worry their families will suffer harm.* What had Margie Holcombe meant when she wrote about *fishy money*?

"Oh, shit! Oh, shit! Jillianne slammed her palm against the steering wheel. Fishy money. Those accounts she'd discovered were from thirty years ago. Burrows Jr. was following in his father's footsteps and laundering money. That was why his accounts were so irregular, and she'd cleaned them up so he could pass an audit. Laundering money for whom? Damn! She no longer had access to those accounts. And where did Gianna Knight come into this?

Despite what she'd learned, she couldn't find it in her heart to get angry with her friends. They'd seen her through hell and shared her own heartbreaking secret. Ryder was also going through hell. The best thing for her to do was act normal. She'd give him a day or so before she confronted him about what she'd learned. Elsie's advice came back. *He's loved you for a long time. Give him a chance to explain.* There were a lot of unanswered questions, but the pounding in her head said she'd done enough heavy thinking for tonight. It was time to go home and enjoy a glass of wine, no, make that two or three.

She pulled out of the parking lot, and her headlights reflected on the rain and ice-slick streets. She called Winnie to let her know she was on her way home but was taking her time because of the poor driving conditions. Dinner would be ready and Winnie had a nice bottle of rosé chilling. They were going to celebrate Jillianne's first day back to work.

The light at Madison Boulevard had just turned green, and she slowly entered the intersection. The force of the powerful truck plowing into the Lexus was the last thing she remembered.

Ryder had never been so happy to receive a phone call. Foster Scanlon had just called to say there was no way Watson mauled the victim. The jaw bite was wider, and the size of the teeth much larger. The punctures didn't even appear to have been made by an animal. He was emailing his conclusive report to Captain Clark.

Officer Deakins had inspected the billy club for prints, and the surface had been totally wiped clean. His father was officially off the suspect list, considering he was at home at the time of the murder and had Polly as an alibi. Dexter was thrilled and was taking Polly out for dinner. He wouldn't be home till tomorrow morning, after his school crossing-guard assignment.

Ryder leaned back in his armchair and rubbed his hands over his face, feeling emotionally spent. The stress had made him unusually tired. He glanced at the corner where Watson was snoring softly on his comfortable bed. "Catch some Z's for both of us." His body could use a good dose of his love. Jillianne would be the best cure in the world. He had two more hours until his shift ended. A night spooning in her bed would be the perfect medicine for both of them, after he made tender, sweet love to her.

In between worrying about his father and the dog, he'd given a great deal of thought to how and when he'd tell Jillianne about his past. His protective reasoning for not making a life with her, no longer mattered. Burrows had almost destroyed her. No more holding back. Before he made love to her again, he was going to tell her about that night all those years ago. Hopefully, she'd still love him after he'd deceived her all these years.

That left finding a way to convince her to marry him.

The radio in his office had come alive an hour ago when the rain and ice started. This was the first rain-ice incident of the season, and people didn't seem to remember how to drive in it. At the rate they were going, he'd have to go out and assist with the fender benders.

He was just about to get a cup of coffee when his cell phone rang. It was the dispatcher. "Lieutenant, we just got a call about an accident on Madison. Late-model white Lexus. Plates read JILLY. Vehicle flipped over on its side. Unit six is on their way. We've already called for an ambulance, rescue squad and a wrecker."

"On my way!" Oh, God, no. Jilly! His heart almost stopped, but he told himself she was alive. His tiredness disappeared, and adrenaline shot through his body like an out-of-control wildfire. "Watson, now, boy. Jilly needs us."

With his 360 lights and siren blaring, he cursed the bitch of the weather, anything he could think of and pressed the button on the microphone attached to his collar. "Unit six, give me a report."

"Car landed on driver's side, Lieutenant. Attempting to get the passenger door open."

"Any movement?" The words stuck in his throat. Waiting for the patrolman's answer felt like a lifetime.

"Can't tell. Fire rescue and ambulance just arrived."

"ETA one minute." *She's alive, she's alive.* He couldn't stop repeating the words. "What about the other vehicle?"

"Lieutenant, a witness said a truck plowed right into her and kept going. Big and heavy, like the kind that spreads road salt."

The intersection was a mass of red and blue flashing lights. Once again, Ryder's heart almost stopped at the sight of Jillianne's vehicle. He didn't bother to get his raincoat from the trunk of the car. His world was already frozen in time.

Watson jumped out of the car first and ran over to the scene of the accident. He barked at the first-aid volunteers, as if to say, *Stop standing around. Do something.*

Two officers had climbed up on the car and were using a crowbar to try to open the smashed passenger door. That wouldn't do. He needed to be the first one into the car to make sure she was still alive. He held up an arm to his officer to help him up onto the passenger side of the car.

"One of you set out the cones and direct traffic. Tell the rescue squad to get the jaws of life ready if I can't get this door open in a couple of minutes. Tell first aid to stand by with a backboard and gurney. As soon as I get Jillianne free of her seat belt, I'll need their help getting her out."

He summoned all the strength in his arms and body and applied it to the piece of cold steel in his bare hands. "Goddammit, you son of a bitch, give!" He expelled a momentary sigh of relief when the door finally cooperated. One of the men from the fire rescue squad joined him and helped pull back the mangled door.

He cautiously crawled into the car and set his feet in the passenger well. The strap from the seat belt supported Jillianne's head, and she was deathly still, just like his heart. Blood coated her face and hair. He put two fingers under her chin, and life returned to his body when he felt her pulse. There didn't appear to be other external injures that he could determine.

"She's alive," he shouted to the others. "Stand by."

"I'm here, baby. I'm here," he assured, not knowing if she could hear him. He managed to release the seat belt and braced her body as it fell into the broken window. He quickly slipped his hands under her arms and used all his strength to draw her to him. Her head flopped against his shoulder. "I've got you, Lady Underdog. It's going to hurt getting you out of here, but I'll try to be gentle."

"We're coming out," he hollered. One of his patrolmen and a member of the rescue squad offered their hands in aid. "I'm going to pass her up to you." More arms and hands reached out to get Jillianne onto the backboard and nearby gurney. Ryder poked his head out of the open doorway, and Watson yelped and spun around, doing a happy dance when they rushed her over to the waiting ambulance.

Cold water ran down Ryder's face, and he moved to the interior of the ambulance. His love appeared deathly pale, but she was breathing. He gripped her cold hand and watched the first-aid responder apply a bandage to the side of her head. His partner was on the phone to the hospital, giving them her vitals.

"Is she okay? It's a dumb question, but she's my…fiancée."

"She most likely has a concussion, but her pulse is strong. The hospital will check her for internal injuries. We need to go."

"I'll follow you to Beacon General." Ryder placed a light kiss on her lips. "I love you, Lady Underdog."

It wasn't his imagination that he felt her hand squeeze his in response.

Ryder checked the time on his watch. Nine o'clock in the morning. Had it been only forty-eight hours since he'd lived through the worst nightmare of his life? He hated hospitals, the antiseptic smells, the beeps coming from the heart monitor, the monotonous sound of the voice on the loudspeaker calling for doctors.

He hadn't been home in two days, and his father had brought him clean clothes. The Association and the Fabulous Four had invaded the emergency room an hour after they'd brought Jillianne to the hospital. The women had clung to their husbands and cried their hearts out, along with cursing Cornelius Burrows's soul to hell.

Luckily, Noreen, Laura and Everett's daughter, was the head nurse and approved the visitors as long as they didn't get in the way of the medical staff. He'd called Winnie and assured the housekeeper that Jillianne wasn't at death's door. Neil and Paige had arrived two hours later.

The scent of flowers, especially the ones that had accumulated in Jillianne's room, was annoying. It got to the point where he asked the nurses to distribute the posies to other patients. His temper shot through the ceiling when a note of get-well wishes was attached to a bouquet of flowers from Cornelius Burrows. He told the teenage candy striper to throw them in the garbage.

Mollie brought him food from the Book and Brew and hamburgers for the dog. Watson hadn't left Jillianne's side. The hospital staff objected to the dog's presence, but Ryder put on the dog's police vest and announced the patient was under guard due to the suspicious cause of the accident.

The captain assigned Kaitlyn Griffin and Graham Deakins to look into the accident. They'd found the county salt truck a couple miles down the road. They were waiting for results on the prints from the county.

He sat in the chair closest to her bed and settled his eyes on her beautiful face, which was a mass of purple and green bruises. She also had chest injuries from the seat belt, the device that saved her life, along with her down-filled coat. She'd suffered a concussion, but woke up in the emergency room two hours after the doctors had diagnosed her injuries. She'd been sleeping on and off, but the doctor assured him that was normal. If all went well, she could go home in a day or so.

The snaps on the thin hospital gown had come undone, exposing the heart-shaped birthmark high on her right arm. He stood up and kissed the warm spot that he loved before closing the snaps.

Sitting in this chair gave him too much time to think and face reality. As a cop, he'd been facing reality for twenty-plus years, but this was too close to his heart. He could've lost her, and his reasons for not making her a permanent part of his life now seemed ludicrous.

His eyes fell on the ring finger of her left hand. When he'd filled out the admitting paperwork, he'd listed himself as her fiancé. A half hour ago, he'd made it official, only she didn't know it yet. His father had gifted Ryder his mother's engagement ring. It wasn't flashy or large, but it came with many years of love.

Watson jerked up from the floor and moved toward the bed, announcing Jillianne was awake. He put his two front paws on the bed and rested his snout on her leg.

"Hey, my beautiful boy, taking care of me." Jillianne used her right hand to pat the dog on his head. Ryder walked around to the other side and sat next to her.

"And my other handsome love, watching over me." Jillianne used her right hand to press the button on the device to raise the head of the bed. "Are you ever going home?"

He leaned in close and stroked an airy kiss to her temple. "I will when you leave here, maybe tomorrow or the next day. How's the pain?"

"My boobs and ribs are sore. Every so often, I get a shooting pain in the back of my neck, but the meds help. I'm not happy they had to cut part of my hair away to put the stitches in the gash on the side of my head. On the whole, I feel lucky to be alive."

"You're going to have to take it easy for a couple of weeks. You suffered a concussion, also."

"Did they locate the driver of the truck that hit me?"

"Two of our best cops are on it, and you look beautiful," he added, brushing the hair away from her cheek, which displayed a blend of colorful bruises. *Here goes nothing*. "I love you, Jilly, more than life itself. When I saw your car, it felt like my heart had been ripped from my chest. Life returned to my body when your strong pulse beat against my fingertips."

"Seeing the man I love when I woke up convinced me I was still alive. I heard this faint voice when I was pinned in the car and knew you'd save me."

"I need you to put the accident and everything else that's been happening to you, us, out of your mind."

"That's almost impossible, but I'll try. Sherlock, I'm grateful to be alive so I can tell you again how much I love you. What's wrong?"

"Sitting in that chair, waiting, watching you sleep, gave me time to think. The cold, hard reality is I could've lost you. He picked up her left hand and kissed her knuckle above the ring. "I slipped this ring on your finger earlier, hoping you'll believe what I'm about to say. No more playing 'cat and mouse games'. Before you say no, I'm going to eliminate the one thing that has stopped you from saying yes. I'm going to put in my retirement papers."

Jillianne had *never* expected him to give up his dream. He was doing it, for her. Tears of happiness blurred the face of her love. He picked up the edge of the light sheet across her chest and carefully dabbed at the wetness on her bruised cheek.

"I didn't say that to make you cry."

"Nothing like knocking a girl off her feet. I wake up from a dream, and my handsome prince is right here in front of me, complete with a ring."

"It belonged to my mother. It's not big and flashy like a socialite would…"

She lifted her hand and pressed her fingertips to his mouth. The sunlight coming into the room bounced off the small diamond sitting on the plain gold band. "No, it's not a big, flashy, cold stone. It's quite beautiful and represents the deep love that your parents shared. I love it. Now it's our turn.

"I, too, have been thinking about us and decided, before this accident, to make necessary changes in my life. The most important one is the life I don't have with you."

"But you do have me."

"Not the life we deserve. The hell we've been through these past couple of weeks made me realize my reason for refusing your proposals has been selfish. No one has ever been willing to sacrifice their dream for me. I really appreciate your offer, but I'd never expect you to give up the job you love."

"So you won't marry me?"

"No, I didn't say that." It hurt when she shrugged. "You haven't asked."

"Jillianne Rose, Lady Underdog, will you please marry me?"

"I'd love to marry you. Now you're supposed to kiss me, but be gentle."

He leaned in, and his lips feathered hers ever so gently, before their mouths wedded in the softest of kisses. He braced his arms on either side of her to keep his weight off her body, but nothing kept him from deepening the kiss when her hand curled around his neck to urge him closer. She was alive, really alive. This was real. He was real. Her cop.

"I love you, Sherlock, so much."

"I love you, too, Jilly. When I filled out the admittance paperwork, I listed myself as your fiancé."

"Pretty sure of yourself."

"Are you sure you don't want me to retire?"

"Absolutely not."

She recalled the discussion in the library the other night. His ultimate dream had been stolen from him, and now he was willing to give up his love of being a police officer, for her. He was willing to sacrifice himself, for her. It wasn't just the present, but the ugliness in his past. To her, he wasn't a martyr, but a hero, and she loved him. She had to let him know she knew what he'd been hiding all these years. It would be a shock, but there might be a way to smooth the initial bombshell.

She drew in a small breath that didn't hurt too much. "Now it's my turn. I need you to put the accident and everything else that's been currently happening to you, us, out of your mind."

"Okay."

Skepticism filled his voice, but she continued. "I refuse to let you give up the job you love. Our friends are bringing pizza from Scannelli's for dinner, but I want you to have them pick up a couple bottles of champagne. Invite your dad and Polly, too."

"We can celebrate our engagement."

"I'd love that, but there's another reason."

"I can't think of a better reason."

Here goes. "We're going to drink to the demise, downfall, ruination—pick one—of Cornelius Burrows for ruining the lives of four teenagers three decades ago."

His eyes widened, and his voice hitched. "You know?"

Jillianne nodded and cupped his cheek. "Don't tell them. It will be an added surprise."

Chapter 12

Ryder now understood the meaning of someone being in a state of shock. "This is unbelievable. How did you find out? Who told you? Why aren't you furious with me for keeping this secret from you?"

"Those are a lot of questions. I'll give you brief answers, but I hope you and The Association will fill in the missing details. Question one, how did I find out? The other day, when I was confronted by Gianna Knight in front of police headquarters, she said my friends have been deceiving me for years. Cornelius Burrows said something similar the other day and threw in the mention of keeping secrets from me for thirty-four years."

"Those reprobates were trying to turn you against us."

Jillianne patted his hand. "I already figured that out myself. You're not the only one that's been thinking about making changes in their life. I returned to work the other day and realized that all these years I've been obsessive in needing to overcome the personal stigma I've been carrying since my father's embezzlement. Liam Thompson brought it to the forefront in court, and it opened my eyes. I've got money and prestige, but it's not what I want anymore. I'm going to work regular hours and am considering four days a week. My office manager can run things, and I'll give him a hefty raise."

"You? My Jilly?" he teased.

"I deserve that. My life has been rearranged, but that's okay." Her voice choked. "When my car started to flip, I can remember gasping, and the breath was sucked from my lungs, but my mind screamed, 'Ryder, I love you.' I need and want you in my life twenty-four seven. I'd marry you right now if it was possible. But I'm digressing. I left work at four the other day because I'd set up a meet with Elsie Trent to ask her if she knew something of importance that happened in Beacon Pointe thirty-four years ago."

"She told you?"

"Not exactly. Kaitlyn Griffin and Paige were working in the library. They were full of information. Kaitlyn said she did a paper in high school that focused on Beacon Pointe's economic dependency on the cannery and how the town was affected when the plant was shut down. Paige had occasion to speak to Matilda Hennypenny about the journals her grandmother wrote a couple of years before she passed away. I know Mollie's ring once belonged to Margie Holcombe."

"Damn! Margie has journals?"

"The old woman was suffering from dementia. No one believed her when she said her brother was murdered by Burrows, so she wrote it in one of her journals. She also wrote something about 'fishy money.' She mentioned feeling sorry for four boys because no one believed them."

"You figured out The Association are the four boys she mentioned in her journals?"

"That part came easy, but I used rational reasoning on everything else." Jillianne cupped his cheek. "I think I know, but tell me the truth. Did you witness someone killing Marshall Holcombe?"

"Yes. We were sixteen, drinking and smoking under the boardwalk. No one believed what we saw, not even my father, because we were drunk out of our minds. Paul Clark was a rookie and felt sorry for us. He drove us back to the beach afterward, but the body was gone. He knows what's going on and has been working with us."

"So you don't actually know who killed Marshall Holcombe?"

"No, but they worked for Burrows. A week after the murder, we received written notes in our school lockers that threatened us and our families if we ever spoke to anyone about what we saw."

"I remember what happened in your senior year, and now it makes more sense. Blumberg has to pay, too, for destroying your dreams." Jillianne pouted.

"He's on the list of bad guys. We've also been paying blackmail money all these years."

Her eyes opened wide in recognition. "One of the two accountants working on Burrows's jumbled files saw the money and brought it to my attention. A yearly donation from four unnamed sources. We didn't know where it was coming from. That was one of the things I was going to speak to Cornelius about. I figured out for myself what Margie meant by 'fishy money.'"

"You verified that he's laundering money for the Magellan Cartel?"

"That's who he's working with?"

"We think so, but have no proof. His real estate agents are gobbling up short-sale properties, and we haven't been able to trace them back to the cartel. Thirty-four years ago, they were dealing drugs and laundered money through the cannery."

"I personally saw that money, too. My gut feeling says Gianna Knight is involved, because of what she said to me."

"She's been working with the cartel, but again, we don't have any solid proof. She was responsible for Mason being thrown in prison."

"That bitch! I can't believe Mollie hasn't pulled every black hair out of that back-stabbing reporter's head for what she did to Mason."

"Jilly, there are a lot of holes and missing information in our investigation. Believe it or not, you, my love, are the key to solving our problem. We're hoping Judge Taylor's ruling will pan out when they conduct an independent audit on Burrows' accounts. Preston Reynolds, the forensic accountant is excellent and is well aware of what's been going on. Between the two of you, we should be able to nail Burrows and his entire organization."

"You've had someone working on it already?"

"Burrows isn't the only one who's been sneaky. We haven't tapped into his business accounts, but Everett's grandfather was an accountant at the cannery before he became an ordained minister. He suspected things were "fishy" and made a duplicate set of ledgers and hid them away. Preston has been working on them, with Durward's help, because everything was in code. Before they shut down, Durward made sure he recorded the figures for the employee's pension money."

"You're answering so many questions for me. There was a huge amount used to start Burrows Real Estate Organization. I'll bet my busted-up Lexus that that was the initial start-up money."

Ryder burst out laughing, never feeling more lighthearted, since he'd tossed away the rock of guilt he'd been carrying around all these years. Jilly knew, and things were going to be all right. "That would mean the former employees were investors in a multimillion-dollar corporation.

"I can't believe you and I are openly discussing the secrets I've been keeping from you all these years. All of us, The Association, had been shielding all this horror from the women we love and our families. How come you're not angry with me?"

"I'm not because I love you and recognize the sacrifices you've made for me, for us, all these years. I'm part of this now and want to help your investigation."

"First thing you're going to do is get well, and that means taking things easy for a while. Winnie will be keeping an eye on you."

They both looked up when the nurse walked in, carrying towels and a fresh hospital gown. "Sorry to interrupt, but Jillianne's due for a bath and meds."

"I'll take Watson for a short walk, but we'll be right back." He pressed an easy kiss to her lips, and Jillianne's mouth softened in return. Before he could pull away, she sank her teeth lightly into his bottom lip.

"Be careful, my love."

He stepped into the hall and nodded at Charlie McCarthy sitting on a chair right outside the door. He wore a light blue knit shirt with the word *Police* above the pocket. His badge was clipped to the belt of his black trousers, and his off-duty weapon was holstered high on his hip. The former police detective had volunteered, along with a number of patrolmen, to stand guard outside Jillianne's door. Ryder hadn't told Jillianne that the driver who normally drove the salt truck had been found in the county maintenance yard tied up and gagged. He hadn't been able to offer a description, and the only fingerprints they'd found belonged to the regular driver.

"Thanks for helping out, Mack."

"Glad to help since I know what's going on. The trolley rides have shut down for the season because of the cold weather. I needed something to do, so my old partner hired me as a school crossing guard. Rather than go home, I don't mind spending my time here watching the pretty nurses before I go for my afternoon assignment."

"I really appreciate you working with my dad, going through your old reports from the Holcombe murder. I just found out Margie Holcombe wrote in her personal journals that her brother was murdered. No one believed her because she was in the deep stages of dementia when she wrote everything down."

"When we interviewed her, she never indicted her brother was murdered. Can you get the journals?"

"I plan to as soon as possible. I'm going to take Watson for a walk, and I have to make a few phone calls, so I'll be a few minutes. Can I bring you a cup of coffee?"

"Thanks, no. I'm good. I'm familiar with the faces of the people going in and out of her room, so take your time."

Stepping out into the cold mid-November air felt refreshingly good. His father had brought him a topcoat and gloves. They walked, no, the dog pulled him to the wooded area at the back of the parking lot used by doctors and employees. Watson hated being on a leash, but Ryder couldn't let him run free. A couple of squirrels were rummaging for acorns under the fallen leaves. Under different circumstances, he'd let the dog have some much-needed fun, but he tugged on the leash. "By my side, Watson." The dog responded to the familiar command and sat by Ryder's leg. His eyes followed the teasing squirrels' every move.

Ryder was still blown away that Jillianne knew about the murder and what had been going on all these years. The other scary part was, Burrows had gone after her because of the knowledge she had in her head about his accounts. Unfortunately, hearsay knowledge wouldn't be admissible in court.

He sent out a general text to The Association. *Change of plans this evening. Jillianne finally said yes, and we are officially engaged. We're now having an engagement party, with a few changes and additional guests. Between the six of you, I hope you can make this happen..."*

He followed up with a call to his father, who was delighted to hear about the engagement and the party. He and Pollyanna would be there with bells on. Ryder asked his father to bring him another change of clothes. Jeans and a long-sleeved knit shirt wouldn't be appropriate.

When he got back to Jillianne's room, Mack said he hadn't seen anyone suspicious. Kaitlyn Griffin would be reporting at three. Ryder thanked him again and extended an invitation to the party. Jillianne was napping, so he made himself comfortable in the padded chair next to the bed and closed his eyes.

An hour later, Watson jumped up from his bed in the corner of the room at the soft knock at the door. Ryder quickly opened his eyes, on alert before he realized where he was. He stretched on his way to the door.

"Sorry to bother you, Lieutenant, but there's a Dr. Parisi and his fiancée requesting to see you."

Ryder stepped into the hall and greeted the couple. Sydney looked so different without her animal-print smock. Navy jeans were tucked into Ugg boots, and she'd opened the zipper on her black quilted jacket to reveal a deep-aqua sweater. He still couldn't recall where he'd seen that lovely face before he'd met her at the vet's office.

He offered the vet an apologetic smile. "Sorry, we're checking all visitors. The same individual that tried to pin the murder on Watson, tried to kill my fiancée earlier this week."

"We heard about the accident, but didn't hear someone intentionally wanted to harm her," Rogan said. "How's she doing?"

"Very well, considering. Nothing broken, but she has a lot of discomfort from being tossed around. She should be going home in a day or so."

Sydney stepped away from the arm Rogan had around her waist. "We came to see if she would be able to speak to us and hopefully answer some questions for me."

"Sydney, like I said this before, this is another wild-goose chase. The woman is just recovering from an accident."

She ignored Rogan's reasonable plea. "I found her picture in the high school yearbook. It's her!"

"Sorry, Ryder, when she gets an idea in her head, there's no changing her mind."

"Sounds like my Jillianne."

Sydney put a hand to Ryder's arm and pleaded, "I really need to speak to her."

"Can you tell me why it's so important?"

"I think she's my mother."

Chapter 13

This was certainly a day for surprises, but Ryder tried to let Sydney down gently. "I'm sorry to disappoint you, Sydney, but Jillianne never had any children. How old are you?"

"Thirty-one. I'll be thirty-two in February."

"I know for a fact that thirty-one years ago she wasn't even in the United States. She was in France."

Hazel eyes, the same color as Jillianne's, widened. "That's where I was born! When you mentioned that my face looked familiar, I asked around and found out you went to high school in Beacon Pointe. I went to the library and spoke to this sweet lady, Elsie Trent. She knew the year you graduated because you're best friends with her nephew, and she directed me to the high school yearbooks. I found a picture of the students in the drama club. You were standing next to a girl with strawberry-blond hair, and I swore I was looking into my own face when I was in high school."

He shook his head. *No, impossible. It couldn't be. Is that why she looks so familiar? If Jillianne had a baby, surely she would've told me. Who was the father?*

"Please, please!"

This was going against his better judgment, but he, too, needed some answers. "Okay, but if Jillianne starts to get upset, you'll have to leave."

Ryder entered the room first. His love was awake, and Watson had his feet up on the bed, and she was running her hand over his head.

The moment Watson saw the vet tech, he switched loyalties and ran over to Sydney as she got down on her knees and held out her arms. "You look pretty good for a jailbird," she teased and reached into her pocket for a homemade dog treat.

"Sweetheart, Dr. Parisi and Sydney, his vet tech and fiancée, came to see how you're doing. We owe them for helping prove Watson's innocence.

He stopped in the middle of the room. The look of astonishment on Jillianne's face answered the question Sydney didn't have to ask. "Are you my mother?"

Jillianne's heart rate increased, and the digital number on the monitor spiked, though not enough to indicate it was life threatening. *She has my face! My hair! My eyes!* Jillianne put her hand to her mouth. Words of wonderment were locked in her throat.

Ryder approached the bed and took Jillianne's hand. "Sydney thinks there's a good chance you're her mother. I told her that was impossible because you've never had a baby."

Her eyes shifted away from the beautiful woman, feeling her eagerness, her pain, and settled on the man she loved. She prayed he'd forgive her. "Ryder, please, please forgive me for not saying anything to you. I did have a baby, and I loved the baby from the moment the doctor told me I was pregnant. My world was torn apart by my father's arrest, but more so because I had to leave you. Life as I knew it was changed forever. I had seven months of bliss before my world was shattered once again." Choking tears ran down her cheeks. "The baby was premature, and they told me she died within hours of being born."

Ryder backed away from her. "You had a baby and didn't tell me?"

Hurt filled his voice, and she held out her right hand, and the bed gown slipped from her shoulder. "I'm sorry, love, for keeping my secret from you."

Sydney gasped, and they both turned to see that her eyes were focused on Jillianne's upper arm.

"I have a birthmark, too!" Tears of happiness escaped her eyes.

Rogan was grinning and stepped close to his fiancée so he could wipe away the tears running down her face. "I can't believe this is really happening. Her dream has always been to find her birth parents."

Mother and daughter stared at each other for a long, tender moment, before Jillianne patted the bed beside her leg. When Sydney moved closer, the similarities in their looks were even more obvious. Like a blind person who'd just been given the miracle of sight, Jillianne brushed the tip of her finger down her daughter's wet cheek, across her arched brow and the length of her similar strawberry blond hair. Her voice lodged in her throat when she tried to speak. "I'm shocked that you're here, in the flesh. I never knew about you. They told me you died." She ran her finger down the bridge of a very familiar nose. "Just like your father."

"I'm kind of numb at finding out you're a mother." The impatience in Ryder's voice drew her attention. "But as your fiancé, I think I have the right to know who fathered your daughter."

The jealousy and resentment in his voice were obvious. She offered up a silent prayer to the man upstairs, taking out extra insurance Ryder wouldn't hate her when she revealed the truth. Her lips spread in a tense smile. "Remember that I love you, Sherlock. Congratulations, Dad."

"What? You were pregnant and never told me? How could you? I had a right to know I was going to be a father!"

The number and beeps spiked on the heart monitor, and Sydney moved off the bed. "You told me not to upset *my mother* and you're doing that right now, *Dad*," she lightly scolded with a tearful smile.

"She's got some of me in her. Fight for the rights of others," Jillianne teased and watched him pour her a glass of cold water from the pitcher on the bedside tray and pass it to her. Inside she was furious and couldn't understand why she'd been lied to. Who decided to tell her the baby died? Someone had stolen their baby! For now, she needed to marshal those feelings in front of their daughter.

"Jilly, I'm having a hard time comprehending that we have a thirty-one-year-old daughter I never knew about. Why didn't you write and tell me you were pregnant? I would've moved heaven and earth to bring you back to the States."

"This is getting very personal. Are you sure you want to talk about this in front of us?" Rogan asked Ryder.

"This affects you two just as much, since you're the family we never knew about, so pull up a chair."

Jillianne urged Ryder to sit next to her so she could hold his hand.

"You know my mother took me away when my father was arrested. Soon after we went to California to stay with my grandmother, I discovered I was pregnant. I was so happy and wanted to tell you, but my mother was mortified, having suffered the humiliation of my father and now an unmarried, pregnant daughter. She poured on the guilt and said I'd be casting more embarrassment on your family."

"Jilly, I swear if you'd told me you were pregnant, I would've married you."

"I guess you don't remember how much you professed, even as a teenager, not wanting to get married because you were going to be a cop. That's why we always played the silly cat and mouse game. Now I understand why, especially with what happened to you as a teenager.

"She sent me to France to stay with distant relatives on my grandmother's side who owned a vineyard. Once I was there, I learned they were having financial difficulties and my grandmother gave them money to let me live with them."

"Were they mean to you?" Sydney asked.

"Not exactly. I overheard them saying they needed a lot more money to save their property and were going to approach my grandmother for additional funds. There was no internet, and I didn't have a phone. They left me to myself, and that was okay."

Jillianne placed a kiss on his palm. "I was sick most of the time, but I was happy because a part of you was growing inside me. My mother mentioned putting the baby up for adoption, but I said absolutely not. It was our baby."

Ryder shook his head. "I can't believe all this took place and you never said a word."

"I went into labor at seven months. They took me to the small local hospital, and the baby was in distress and I had to have a caesarean. I was totally out of it and didn't wake up until the following day. The couple told me I suffered internal injuries and the baby didn't survive. I never dreamed that they were lying to me."

Tears anew ran down her cheeks, and she drew Ryder's head to her shoulder. "I wanted to die, because I loved our baby so much. A month later, I returned to California. My mother was upset for me and said life had to go on. I thank God every day that you still loved me when I returned home."

Jillianne looked at their daughter. "Tell me about the couple who adopted you."

"Before I start, I'm so happy you two love each other so much. They were an older couple who couldn't have any children. I had a good life with them, but they didn't share the loving warmth that is so obvious in you two. I also didn't look like either of them. In my heart I knew there was something missing. When I was a teenager, I accidentally found my adoption paperwork in a Bible. My adoptive mother told me I was born in France and that they adopted me through a private agency. She did say that my mother and father were American teenagers. My adoptive parents both passed away when I was a freshman in college.

"I met Rogan in my junior year, and we've been together ever since. When his uncle offered him the chance to take over his vet practice, we were thrilled." She looked at Ryder. "When you came into the office last week and said I looked familiar, it got me to thinking."

A watery film covered Ryder's eyes when he announced, "We have a daughter!" He moved away from the bed and approached Sydney. "I never thought I'd ever say this, but how about a hug for your dad?"

Watching Ryder hug their daughter brought Jillianne so much happiness. "Rogan, I don't want you to feel left out. Welcome to the family."

"Thank God she's found her parents! Now we can get married and make our little boy legitimate."

"Are you saying we have a grandchild?" Jillianne asked, not knowing if she could take any more earth-shattering news.

"We have a five-year-old little boy named Oliver," Sydney said. "I told Rogan that my dream was to have my real father walk me down the aisle. So, Dad, will you do the honors?"

Ryder laughed out loud. "I'd be delighted, but I'm going to do one better. Your mother has finally agreed to marry me, and we're having a small engagement party this evening. Come around six, and please bring Oliver."

"We'd love to meet our grandson," Jillianne added and couldn't stop smiling. "Ryder, you better pinch me so I know I'm not dreaming."

"Jeez, how am I going to tell my father he's both a grandfather and a great-grandfather?" Ryder asked.

"I have a grandfather?"

"You sure do, along with a number of adoptive aunts and uncles," Ryder said. "I won't go into explanation now, but be prepared to be overwhelmed with lots of love. I hate to break up this family reunion, but your mother needs to rest up for our engagement party."

"Why aren't you waiting until she's home and feeling better?" Sydney asked.

"You don't know our friends," Jillianne quickly answered. "Believe me, this kind of party I welcome. They're bringing pizza and champagne." She glanced at Ryder with a loving smile. "It's been a long time coming."

"If the room gets too crowded, we'll move the party to the large family waiting room at the end of the hall, which reminds me. Sweetheart, I want to speak to the head nurse, and then I'll take Watson out for some fresh air."

"You will be back this evening?" Jillianne asked their daughter and future son-in-law.

"Mom, we wouldn't miss it for the world."

Ryder hooked the leash to Watson's harness as soon as they stepped into the hall. Kaitlyn Griffin, dressed in full regulation winter blues, was leaning against the wall, but her eyes were following the movements of doctors, nurses and patients. The moment she saw him, she stood up straight and tall. "Lieutenant."

"Thanks for putting in the time, Kaitlyn."

"Hi, Dr. Parisi, Sydney. Marshmallow is doing much better."

"Marshmallow?" Ryder questioned.

"Since I moved into my new condo, I got lonely, so the doc hooked me up with a rescue kitten. She's totally white and real soft."

"How long will you be staying?"

"Till eleven. I'm working the day shift tomorrow."

"I'll fill you in on what's happening later this evening after I take Watson out for a breath of fresh air."

He walked his daughter and Rogan to their car. *His daughter*. The two words blew his mind. It was going to take some getting used to. Everett had suffered a similar surprise, so he would be a good person to approach for some advice.

Sydney popped out a question before he offered a much-needed explanation as to why there was a cop stationed at her mother's hospital-room door.

"Is my mother in that much danger that she needs a cop outside the door?"

"Yes and no. I can't go into it, but we're dealing with a ruthless individual, and I'm not taking any chances with your mother's life. I'm a bit paranoid. You'll soon find out that having a father who's a cop is a lot different than having a regular dad."

He pressed a fatherly kiss on Sydney's temple. "As for this evening, there is a slight change of plans because the number of people invited will definitely not fit in her hospital room, and the menu has changed." He looked at Rogan. "I have your personal cell phone number and will let you know where we're meeting."

"You have no idea how happy I am." Sydney gave Ryder a quick hug. "See you later, Dad."

Despite the happiness he was enjoying, learning he and Jillianne were parents and grandparents, he was deeply troubled about the circumstances behind their daughter's adoption. He had questions for Jillianne, but didn't want to do anything to mar her happiness, especially today. Once he got her home, they needed to have a full meeting of The Association. That would be the perfect time to bring up the discussion, because it was going to get her upset.

He and Watson walked down a row between the cars, and the dog's eagerness to get to the wooded area came to an abrupt halt. The hairs on his back stood straight up, and a growl rumbled in his throat. Ryder's cop sense went on alert, and he slowly scanned the surrounding cars. The lot was full, and there were so many white cars they all began to look alike.

Watson tugged on the leash, and Ryder didn't bother to reel him in. "What do you see, boy?" A quick movement out of the corner of his eye drew his attention to a gray car three rows over, and he asked himself why the driver had the window open on such a cold day. It was then that he saw what appeared to be the long lens of a camera. "Okay, boy, do your job," Ryder ordered, releasing the hook on Watson's harness. The dog took off like a speeding bullet in the direction of the gray car.

The window was down but he couldn't get a clear view of the driver because the camera was in the way. Watson was five cars away when he started barking. Ryder picked up his pace, pulling out his cell phone at the same time. He couldn't take a picture of the driver, but he was able to get one of the car and license plate.

The driver immediately withdrew the camera and pulled out of his parking spot, but purposely aimed the car at Ryder. His leather-soled boots dug into the blacktop as he sought safety between two cars. Watson headed for the now vacant parking spot and started sniffing around. It would be a wasted effort to run to his truck and try to chase down the car. Were they hanging around to see when Jillianne would be released, hoping to get a photo of her condition? Had they found out she was under guard and that they couldn't get near her?

He reviewed the pictures he'd taken of the license plate. Diplomatic designation. Then it hit him. Photographer. Gianna Knight was in town doing a photo shoot and maybe offered to do a favor for her boyfriend.

While Sherlock peed and chased squirrels, he called Captain Clark and filled him in on what had just gone down and sent him a photo of the plate number. They'd barely finished the conversation when Paul came back with an ID. This plate was registered to Fabio Magellan. Country of origin Columbia. *Gotcha!*

"I look like a fighter that refused to give up." Jillian stared into the mirror attached to the top of the drawer in her bedside table and turned her head a few times, trying to get a better view of the purple and green splotches mainly on the left side of her face. "Watson, I look terrible."

He moved off of his bed in the corner, put his feet on the mattress and whined in sympathy. "If you were a female, you'd understand. This uptown girl can't go to her engagement party looking like this. All the makeup in the world can't disguise these bruises. I need a miracle."

Three quick knocks preceded the door opening. "Did I hear you say you need a miracle?"

"Manny!"

"Hi, sweet love." Manny swallowed hard and shook his head, approaching the bed. "Dr. Manny has arrived in the nick of time. Whoever did this to your beautiful face should be horsewhipped."

She held still when he put his finger under her chin and did a closer inspection of her face. He gently lifted a strand of her hair and pursed his lips at the spot they'd shaved to put in the ten stitches covered by a row of butterfly bandages. "Butchers! Luckily, I came prepared. My face resembled yours ten months ago, only mine was more swollen, so I understand what you're going through."

"I feel like I've been beaten up and thrown away, but I'm grateful to be alive."

"We're going to fix you up so you look beautiful for your party. I've a couple of cases in the hall. Kaitlyn is watching over them for me. I just wanted to make sure you are up to a hospital makeover."

"Why is Kaitlyn outside my door?"

"Oops, maybe I shouldn't have spilled the beans. Ryder isn't taking any chances with your safety and has had guards outside your door ever since you've been here."

"God love him. He's such a cop."

"I'm sure he didn't want you to worry. The Association sure knows how to take care of their women. I've got an hour and a half to make you the belle of the ball."

And come prepared he did. His supplies included a small portable table on which he set his makeup, brushes and items she'd never seen before. Before starting, he removed the teal hip-length jacket that he'd worn over a black and white bodysuit. He donned a long black smock and zipped up the front.

"Where's your future husband?" He helped her slide forward so he could work on the back of her hair. His hands moved quickly with practiced precision, careful not to hurt her.

"He's been running in and out, just long enough to check on me, give me a quick kiss and a silly grin. This started out as a pizza party with champagne. When the hospital administration found out via Noreen that Everett Troy's best friend wanted to have an impromptu engagement party, they offered the director's staff meeting room."

Manny stood back, did a visual sweep of her hair and gave a formative nod. "Sweetie, I'm good. Now I want you to rest your head on the soft pillow and close your eyes, love. I'm going to perform a miracle."

"Manny, before I forget to tell you, thank you for being a friend to all of us. We love you so much and are so blessed to have you in our lives."

"Stop, you're going to make me cry," he sniffed. "You've all taken me into your hearts and accepted me for who I am. I also want to thank you for asking me to chair the children's toy drive. Honey, this will be the best show ever. We've got so many donations coming in we'll need three tractor-trailers to deliver the gifts. Now we both have to stop crying, because I need to see what I'm doing."

Whatever he was applying made her skin feel cool, then warm, but refreshing and wonderful. The door opened and Ryder popped his head in and said they were right on time and he'd be back with a wheelchair at six.

"Manny, he's making me crazy! This is just an engagement party!"

"Indulge the man. You've been through hell, and he wants and needs to do this for you."

Neither of them spoke as Manny hummed, crooned ooh-la-la and concluded with, "Miracle complete."

"Are you going to let me see?"

"You're not quite done." He pulled out his cell phone and punched in a quick text message. "Five minutes to total princess transformation."

Noreen rushed in, wearing a pretty yellow and white dress. Her makeup had been skillfully applied, and she wore a necklace of yellow amethyst stones. She was as beautiful as her movie-star father was handsome. "Special delivery for Manny Symonds from Philippe's, New York."

"No one gets a special delivery from that store in one day," Jillianne said. "You have to make an appointment with him just to purchase a dress. Wait a minute! You ordered me a dress? How do you know my size?"

"Oh, honey, he's my cousin, and I bankrolled the money for him to start that boutique twenty years ago because his family said he was too sweet and irresponsible. He'll do anything for me. I told him what I wanted, and he knows better than to disappoint me. Honey, I know your size just by looking at you."

Manny lifted the top off the box, and Noreen gasped at the beautiful long gown of ice blue. The material appeared to be made from a cloud. The crescent sweep of the neckline across the front barely caught at the shoulders and would leave her arms and shoulders exposed. The handkerchief bottom would gracefully sweep the floor. Under the top layer was a scattering of faux diamonds and blue sapphires.

"Oh, Manny, it's perfect and so beautiful."

"I told him you couldn't wear a bra and we couldn't put any pressure on your chest. I'm going to step outside, and Noreen can help you get dressed. Oh, before I forget."

Manny went over to the one case he hadn't opened yet and took out a delicate lace hairpiece shaped like a butterfly and decorated with stones that matched her dress. "Once you're dressed, we'll put this in your hair and you can look in the mirror."

Noreen, too, was gentle, helping her get out of the hospital gown. Manny had thought of everything, and the dress had an opening in the back so she didn't have to lift her arms. The lightheadedness was gone when she stood up beside the bed so Noreen could zip up the back. Her legs felt stiff, but it felt good to move around.

"Noreen, what's really going on? This is over the top for an engagement party."

"Sorry, Jillianne. I've been sworn by the Hippocratic oath and can't say a word.

"You're not a doctor."

"Time's up," Manny announced, coming back into the room. "Oh, my. Oh, my, Jillianne, you are exquisite. Your handsome prince's chin is going to hit the floor. Hairpiece next."

Jillianne's mouth dropped when Manny held up the round makeup mirror in front of her face. The bruises were gone, and her face had a flushed, peachy glow. Her eyes were wide with the subtle brush of blue and pearl eye shadow. He'd drawn her hair off her forehead, and it hung in soft spiral curls. The glittery hairpiece swept the side of her head, covering the shaved spot.

"Wow! Double wow!" Tears welled in her eyes, sending Manny into a tizzy.

"No, no, sweetie. You'll mess up all my work."

Ryder chose that moment to walk in and stopped halfway into the room. His eyes widened and just stared. "Welcome back, uptown girl." He grinned. "You look exquisite, but I also love Lady Underdog." He gently placed the flat of his hand over her chest. "Tell me she's still in here?"

"She's still in there and will come out when necessary. Why are you wearing your full dress uniform?"

"I asked my father to bring me my dress suit, and the only one I own is at the cleaners, so he brought the next best thing." He turned to Manny. "Thanks for all your help in getting this done so quickly. We're all set."

Noreen rolled in a wheelchair. "Come on, Cinderella. This is the best we could do for a chariot to take you to the ball."

When Ryder pushed the chair into the hall, nurses, doctors and patients stopped what they were doing and started clapping. Kaitlyn moved to stand beside the chair. "Lookin' good, Jillianne. We don't have four horsemen to accompany your chariot, so I'm it."

“Where are we going?” she asked when he rolled her to the elevator.

“The first floor. Don’t ask me any questions.”

She glanced at Noreen and then Kaitlyn, but both avoided looking at her. He was up to something. When the elevator stopped, Noreen and Kaitlyn exited and headed down the hall toward the administration offices. She started to worry when he stopped in the middle of the deserted hall and stood in front her.

“What’s wrong?”

Chapter 14

Never had a plan come together so quickly and efficiently. His father, Polly and their friends had worked miracles. Now he had to tell her what he'd done. He should feel guilty for taking advantage of her present condition. She wouldn't be able to run if she changed her mind.

He squatted in front of his beautiful fiancée and took her hand, lacing their fingers together. "As you've already surmised, the party has expanded. Our friends are waiting for us, not in an office, but in the hospital chapel, which is right in front of us. This morning, you said you'd marry me at that moment, so I took your statement to heart."

Her beautifully made-up eyes widened in surprise. "Sherlock, you didn't." Disbelief filled her voice.

"I did, and at first our friends thought I was out of my mind when I told them what I wanted to do. You know the Fabulous Four. Give your best friends a request and they run with it. Now all they need is the bride and the groom."

"What about a license?"

"Pollyanna pulled strings with the mayor, reiterating that you were almost killed. After the ceremony, we'll sign the official paperwork." Ryder brought her hand to his lips and placed a kiss in her warm palm. "Jilly, tell me you haven't changed your mind. I love you so much."

"I've been dreaming of this moment all my life. I'm trying not to cry because Manny will be pissed if I ruin my makeup. Let's make this happen."

Ryder stood up and pushed the wheelchair to the end of the hall. On cue, Mack and his father opened the double doors. All the seats in the small chapel were occupied, and everyone was staring at them, wearing huge smiles. Sitting in a wheelchair in front of the altar, looking dashing in his old-fashioned tuxedo, was Durward Holcombe, Everett's ninety-eight-year-old grandfather. Clutched in his aged hands was a Bible. Watson sat right next to him, wearing a black bow tie.

The Fabulous Four, dressed in deep-gold cocktail dresses, holding bouquets of autumn-colored mums, stood to the left, and The Association, wearing black suits, stood to the right.

Dexter moved to stand in front of Ryder and Jillianne and pulled a white handkerchief out of the breast pocket of his suit jacket and wiped his eyes. He took Jillianne's hand. "Welcome to the family, my dear. This is usually done by the bride's father, but I'd love to escort you down the aisle."

"Dexter, I'd love it if you walked me down the aisle, and be prepared for me to call you Dad." She turned her head and stared directly at Ryder. "No one is going to push me in this damn chair. Lady Underdog can make it."

"Don't worry, son, I'll hold on to my new daughter's arm."

"Okay, then," he said and nodded to Sydney, who was standing near the front row. A wide grin filled her lovely face as all eyes watched her walk up the aisle and present her mother with a single white orchid surrounded by baby's breath. She, too, looked stunning in a gown a little deeper blue than her mother's.

"Thank you for making my dream come true," she said softly with a teary-eyed smile and looked directly at Ryder. "Plan to switch places in a few weeks."

"Okay, let's do this, sweetheart," Ryder said, wondering what happened to Neil. He helped Jillianne stand, and Dexter kept a firm hold on her arm. Before she could move, Neil rushed in, a little out of breath.

"Sorry, Sis. My daughter insisted I had to wear a suit so I had to run out and buy one after the show this afternoon."

"'Bout time," Dexter scolded and passed him a white rose for his lapel.

"Like I just said, let's do this, sweetheart."

"I'm good and can make it fine with two handsome gentlemen escorting me down the aisle. Now join your friends and prepare to make an honest woman out of me."

Ryder hurried down the aisle and took his place beside his best friends, who'd always been there for him, no matter what. Watson moved to stand beside the groom.

"Thanks for helping me pull this off and being here for me and Jillianne," Ryder said to his friends.

"You don't look half as nervous as I expected," Jackson said and patted Ryder on the back.

"Get ready to put on the ball and chain," Mason teased.

"If you two numb-nuts will excuse me, I'm going to sing the bride down the aisle," Everett said and nodded to Paige, behind the altar, to start the background music.

Everett stood beside his grandfather and started to sing *Heaven*, the popular song by Bryan Adams. Ryder had specifically chosen the song because it was his and Jillianne's favorite. It had been playing the first time they'd confessed their love. His heart and eyes were filled with her beauty as she slowly made her way toward him.

At the conclusion of his romantic ballad, Everett moved to help Durward stand.

First Neil and then Dexter kissed Jillianne on the cheek and passed her hand to Ryder. "Love her with all your heart," they said together.

"I already do," he said and accepted Jillianne's hand into his own. "Are you okay?"

"I'm wonderful, and I love that you had Everett sing our song. If I need to sit down, I'll let you know."

There wasn't a dry eye in the Lord's house when Durward's distinctive voice echoed through the small chapel. When it was time to exchange rings, a look of panic widened Jilly's eyes.

"Rings?" she whispered.

"Not to worry, my love. Judy at Judy's Gems came through."

Durward nodded to the young boy sitting between Sydney and Rogan in the front pew. He wore a black bow tie with his long-sleeved white shirt and carried a small white pillow that held two plain gold wedding bands. Pastor Holcombe gave the little boy a job-well-done smile and removed the rings nestled in satin. The blond child went to return to his mother and father, but hesitated and held out his hand to Ryder and then Jillianne. "I'm Oliver. Nice to meet you."

"Oh, Ryder, you thought of everything," she said and had a hard time taking her eyes off their grandchild.

"It was Sydney's suggestion."

"Talk later, rings now," Durward ordered with an understanding nod. "I love my grandchildren, too."

Jillianne's voice shook when she repeated her vows and slid the ring on Ryder's finger. When it was his turn, he held up the ring in front of her tear-washed eyes. "You've hesitated marrying me because I'm a police officer. Thank God you changed your mind." That drew a chuckle from their guests.

"I had something special engraved in your wedding band. 'Love never dies.'" Love filled his voice when he repeated his vows and slid the ring on her finger.

As soon as Pastor Holcombe said, "I now pronounce you husband and wife. You may kiss the bride." Ryder had to remind himself not to squeeze her too tightly, but Jillianne clamped her arms around his neck and kissed him in earnest. Everyone started to clap, and a couple of their friends cheered. Watson woofed in agreement.

"Walk or ride down the aisle, Mrs. Wayne?"

"Hold on to me, Mr. Wayne, then you can drive my chariot to our party."

Jillianne was tempted to pinch herself to make sure this was real. She'd married Ryder. Her eyes fell upon the plain gold band, a symbol of their love, on her left hand. She was Mrs. Ryder Wayne.

It felt wonderful to have all their friends witness the ceremony and enjoy the celebration afterward. As soon as they got to the meeting room, Polly had them sign the official paperwork to make their marriage legal.

Jillianne sat at one of the round tables covered with white tablecloths. A centerpiece of fall flowers decorated the center and complemented the gold cloth napkins. Hannah Clark had catered the food in the large meeting room, and everyone helped themselves to the elaborate buffet.

Irene, Mollie's baker, had put together a small wedding cake, but also baked and decorated iced sugar cookies of a bride and groom. The Association had furnished bottles of champagne to toast the bride and groom. Neil and Paige were supplying the music, but kept the sound low.

The biggest surprise to all of the attendees was when Jillianne and Ryder introduced everyone to their daughter, future son-in-law and grandson. A few had already met the wonderful vet and his assistant because he took care of their pets.

She was happy that Marion, Chase and Matilda's three daughters took Oliver under their wing. Before he went off to play with his new friends, they promised Oliver a visit when she got out of the hospital. Winifred was doubly shocked, because she was one of the few people who'd known Jillianne had been pregnant and believed she'd lost the baby. She was already in love with the little boy.

The night had been absolutely perfect. "I can't believe you guys pulled this off," she said, looking at the Fabulous Four and their husbands, including her own.

"Do you know how much self-control we had to use not to call you?" Laura said. "You can thank Manny for the dresses.

One of his girls is a florist and was thrilled to supply the flowers. He's one of the performers in the holiday show."

"Jillianne, how do you feel, body-wise?" Tamie asked. Concern filled her dearest friend's voice.

"Like I've been beat up, but I couldn't be happier. I still can't believe our daughter survived. And to have a grandchild! Look at Dexter, a great-grandfather, in the middle of the kids doing magic tricks."

"Dexter and Polly are coming to our Thanksgiving feast, and I asked your kids to join us," Mollie said. "Sydney loves to cook, so we just have to let her know what to make."

"Do you realize what you just said? 'My kids.' Talk about life-changing moments. In one day, I became a wife, mother and grandmother."

Jillianne picked up her glass of ice water, trying to dislodge the lump in her throat. This evening had turned out so differently than she'd expected. She'd planned to tell her friends she knew their dark secret. She also wanted to talk to Ryder about the circumstances behind their daughter's adoption. But not now. Tonight was for fun, happiness, friendship and love. Tomorrow was another day.

She turned slightly in her chair and experienced a pinching pain in her ribs when she slipped a hand around her husband's neck. "Hey, husband, did you forget about me?"

He slowly drifted into her and murmured, "Does this feel like I've forgotten about you, Mrs. Wayne?" She was prepared for a light kiss, but he slanted his head and took full possession of her mouth. The kiss went on and on. A melting sensation seeped into her body, and she was lost and so in love. She brought her other arm around his neck, never wanting this beautiful moment to end.

"Way to go!" the Fabulous Four cheered together.

Ryder and Jillianne thanked everyone for coming, and he pushed her in the wheelchair back to her room a little after ten. Jillianne's nurse said she'd be right in to help her patient get changed, but Ryder said he was perfectly capable of taking care of his wife.

The nurse just smiled and said she'd be in to check on her patient in a little while. Kaitlyn volunteered to take the dog out for his walk and would bring him back to the room in a little while.

"Well, we did it." She smiled with a weary sigh.

"We sure did, Mrs. Wayne. I can see you're exhausted."

He slowly lowered the zipper on the back of the dress, and it formed a soft cloud around her feet. His male hormones shot to full alert at the sight of her beautiful naked back and white bikini briefs that hugged her slender hips. *Down, boy.*

He placed a soft kiss in the hollow of her back and moved around to the front of his beautiful wife, and the food he'd eaten seemed to congeal in his stomach. Whenever the doctors had come in to examine her, he'd excused himself, and this was the first time he'd seen the injuries on the front of her body.

The seat belt had burned a wide strip across her breasts, and blue and purple bruises streaked her rib cage. "Oh, you poor baby," he moaned and placed light kisses across her breasts.

Jillianne put her hands to the back of his head to press his cheek against her stomach. "I'm okay, really. It hurts like a bitch, but it will heal. We'll have to put our wedding night on hold for a week."

"I'm not going anyplace, my love. Let's get you into that ugly hospital gown and comfortable in the bed. Let me get changed, and I'll even help you remove all that makeup."

"Ah, the perfect husband. Manny left makeup-remover towelettes and moisturizer in the bathroom."

Ryder put on a pair of flannel sleep pants and a T-shirt before setting the supplies and a warm facecloth on the bedside table. Efficient Manny had numbered the plastic bags. "This is a first, so let me know if I'm doing something wrong. I'll try to be gentle."

"This uptown girl has removed her makeup many times, but I'm sure you'll do just fine."

"I think you'll like my methods. Now settle back and enjoy."

The hairpiece went first. Her eyes drifted close when he slowly ran a brush through her hair, careful to avoid the area where she had stitches.

"Eyes next. Keep them closed."

The towelette had a pleasant smell, and once again he was gentle and smoothed the pre-moistened cloth over her eyelids. His face was so close his warm breath swept her cheeks.

"Now don't move." The bed shifted under her hip when he moved closer. His tepid breath swept her eyelid, followed by a supple brush of his lips. He repeated the caress to her other eye. Her heartbeat quickened, and she was glad she was no longer attached to the heart monitor. A new ache started in another part of her body.

"Okay, towelette number two. Face." The gentleness continued as he moved the cloth over the bruises on her left cheek and the rest of her face. "Keep your eyes closed. Almost done."

She moaned softly at the feel of the heated, soft facecloth that he gently laid over her cheeks and eyes. When he lifted it away, he tended to each cheek with the brush of his lips. She couldn't move when his mouth closed over hers, and she trembled slightly. Like before, she was lost in the moment, in him. Every time they kissed, it was like the very first. Now they had a lifetime to look forward to, together.

"Oh, Sherlock, what are we doing?" she whispered while he nibbled on the edge of her jaw.

"Practicing for our wedding night."

"We've been practicing for years," she reminded him with a little laugh.

"Well, then, it will be perfect."

When the door opened and Watson rushed in, playtime was over. The night nurse followed and hooked Jillianne up to the monitors. When she announced her heartbeat was slightly elevated, Ryder burst out laughing. She also said the doctor would sign her release papers in the morning so she could go home.

The time on his watch read one a.m., and he tried to get comfortable in the chair.

"Sleep's not coming for me tonight either," Jillianne said from the bed right next to him. "The only way we're going to get any sleep is if you lay next to me."

"Sweetheart, I'd love to crawl in there with you, but I'm afraid to hurt you."

"If you hurt me, I'll kick you. Now get into bed with me. I just shifted over."

Ryder pulled back the sheet and slipped in beside her. To his delight, she'd turned on her side and was facing him. "Doesn't that hurt your ribs?"

"I'm full of pain medicine, but I'm very comfortable."

Ryder lifted his arm, and her head found a home on his shoulder. It was the sniffing and moisture on his T-shirt that told him something was wrong. "Hey, why the tears?"

"I've kept all these emotions bottled up inside me, and I need to talk to you. I'm so happy, scared, we're facing a whole new life together. We've got a daughter. A daughter! And a grandchild! How did that happen?"

"Jilly, you know how it happened," he added with a light chuckle.

"You know what I mean. Why was I told the baby died? Who made the arrangements to have her taken away from me? From us!"

"Those same questions have been in my head since Sydney told us who she is. Who knew you were pregnant? Do you know if the couple you were living with is still alive?"

"My mother, my grandmother, Winifred, the Fabulous Four, but I swore them to secrecy. I have no idea if those horrible people are still alive."

"Your mother had a lot of close friends at the country club. Did she tell any of them?"

"She was tight with Jackson's mother and Liam Thompson's wife. Now that I recall, I overheard her talking to Celia Thompson, pouring her heart out about the double embarrassment from her husband and pregnant daughter."

"She must have mentioned it to her husband."

"What would Liam Thompson have to do with taking our daughter away from us?"

Ryder felt sick at heart as things in his mind fell into place. He needed to call Jackson to get some names. Hopefully, he was wrong. This scenario was going to upset Jillianne even more.

"Let's table that part of our discussion for now, because I really don't have any answers. We never got around to telling our friends that you know what's going on. I thought about it, but that ugliness had no part at our wedding. When do you want to tell them?"

"How about Wednesday evening? I'd like to have them meet with us at the theater, kind of like my home turf."

"That shouldn't be any problem. We'll meet in the theater school room."

"I won't be going into the office for the next week or so. I can use my desktop computer in my home office to work on my Footlight Theater responsibilities. I also have to get a new laptop."

"I don't have to be into work until Monday, so I can start moving my things over to your house. Nothing like leaving home when your fifty years old. My father is going to propose to Polly, and she'll be moving in there. It's best I leave those lovebirds alone. Did you know that in addition to using massage oils, they play strip poker?"

Jillianne gasped when she tried to laugh. "Stop, that hurts." She yawned into his shoulder. "Get some sleep, husband. I love you."

"I love you, too, wife.

Since his father had hired Mack to pick up the second school crossing-guard position at the high school, Ryder reported to work at seven Monday morning. After signing off on a ton of reports and speaking to Captain Clark, Ryder sat at his desk and read over the information Jackson had just emailed. He followed up with a call to Nancy Jean Harrigan for further confirmation. The same dishonest lawyer who'd arranged the phony adoption of Maya Vance had had a hand in the illegal adoption of Sydney. The unsuspecting adopting couple had had no idea they were being conned.

Two hours earlier, he'd reached out to Hudson and explained the situation. The security man was going to call their chief tech in New York to try to locate the couple in France. Ryder had just gotten an email confirming that the couple was no longer of this world. He dreaded telling Jillianne what he'd learned, but he was done with keeping her in the dark.

He'd already sent out a 911 text to The Association. *The eyes have closed, they will see no more. Meet at Footlight in lower level, children's activity room. Wednesday, eight o'clock.* He'd added two additional words. *She knows.*

He also contacted his father and Mack. Everett got back to him and said Hudson and Manny would also be there.

He glanced over to the empty dog bed. Watson had refused to leave the house this morning. It wasn't a bad thing, because he could keep an eye on Jillianne. A quick knock on the molding beside the door drew his eyes away from his computer.

"Lieutenant, do you have a couple of minutes for me?" Kaitlyn asked. "Mind if I close the door?"

"No problem, Kaitlyn. Have a seat. How can I help you?"

"After my conversation with your wife the night she got hurt, I checked my old files for the report I did on the town's economy in regards to the cannery. I printed out a copy for you." She set the stapled report on his desk.

"Thanks. You know I'll read it."

"Lieutenant, I've asked you this question a number of times, but I'm going to ask it again. What the hell is going on? I've put pieces together and have figured out Burrows had someone kill Marshall Holcombe. My long-shot guess is you and your friends witnessed the murder. I also know what 'fishy money' means. Burrows is still washing dirty money, for whom, I don't know."

Ryder shook his head. "I've said it a number of times. You're too smart for your own good. Everything you've said is correct. Captain Clark and your parents also know what's been going on. You can't tell anyone."

"I get that. How can I help?"

"I don't have time to go into detail, but if you really want to help, I need you to keep an eye on Gianna Knight."

"What's she got to do with this?"

"She's dirty and is working with Fabio Magellan."

"The Magellan drug cartel? Jeez, this is big."

"Exactly. I'm not saying you should become her shadow, but we need something to connect her to Fabio or men working with him. Snap a picture with your phone. Could you do me a solid and go over to Matilda Hennypenny's and ask if we can borrow her grandmother's journals? Give her a receipt, since they'll be put into evidence. Bring them directly to me or Captain Clark when you come on shift tomorrow morning. No one else. Don't tell anyone you have them."

"Do you suspect we've a dirty cop in our midst?"

Ryder didn't give her a verbal answer, but just stared.

"Gotcha. And, Lieutenant, you can trust me."

"I know."

Ryder walked into his new home and was greeted by a happy Watson. He was looking forward to a warm welcome-home kiss from Jillianne and spending the evening with his bride and enjoying one of his favorite pipes. Winnie was at the stove, preparing mashed potatoes, and the table was already set for two. She also appeared frazzled and shook the wooden spoon at him. "You better do something about your wife! She's a crazy woman and not listening to me!"

Ryder took off his leather jacket and draped it over his arm. Getting a quick cup of coffee appeared to be out. "What's she done that's got you upset?"

"She was supposed to stay in bed and take it easy. She doesn't know the meaning of the word relax."

"Where is she?"

"In the bedroom. You'll see for yourself."

"I'll take care of it. What time is dinner? I want to take a shower."

"Dinner will be ready by six thirty."

"Come on, Watson, let's find out what your girlfriend is doing."

He walked into the fancy, feminine bedroom, and his eyes were drawn to the screen on her new laptop computer on her dresser where a cartoon of Mickey Mouse and Donald Duck played. The floor outside one of the two walk-in closets was littered with shoes, boots, purses and clothes—more clothes than one woman needed. He walked in a little farther and found Jillianne sitting in the middle of the floor with her head resting on her knees, crying.

"Hey, what's going on?" He knelt next to her and lifted her forehead off her knees.

"I'm a total failure as a wife, mother and grandmother." He backed up when she threw her arms wide and almost backhanded him across the face. "I've got all these goddamn designer shoes and dresses and I've been trying to make room for your clothes. This is your home, too, and I didn't want you to think you couldn't put your clothes away. The bedroom is too fussy, too girlie.

"We need a couple of comfortable chairs to put in front of the fireplace in the den so we can watch and snuggle by the fire together, like at your dad's house. There isn't a shelf for you to display your special pipes. I don't even have one of those big-ass televisions."

Ryder bit down on his tongue, rather than burst out laughing. "Jilly, you're rambling. We'll do everything you mentioned, but it will take time. I love your frilly underwear, especially when you're not wearing any."

Her arm came out again, and this time slammed him in the shoulder. "That's not all! I'm a mother and should know how to do mother-daughter things. Sydney likes to cook, and I watched three hours of cooking shows, and I didn't have a clue what the hell they were talking about. Sauté, brine, blanch. I've been watching cartoons. Cartoons! So I have something in common with our grandson. There's a cartoon character by the name of Ryder! I'm a total failure as a grandmother!"

She was getting hysterical, and Ryder couldn't take anymore. He slipped one arm under her knees and one behind her back and carefully lifted her from the floor, making his way over to the bed. "Did you take your pain medicine today?" She just nodded. "You're only hurting yourself more by what you're doing. Relax while I get you a cup of tea."

He wasn't an expert about these things, but he knew who was. While Winnie was fixing the tea, he put out an SOS to Laura, Mollie and Tamie. They'd be over after dinner.

They did enjoy a quiet meal, and she was embarrassed by her meltdown and apologized. Not going into the office had contributed to her a panic attack. Relief filled her eyes when he told her the Fabulous Four would be over for a little while after dinner.

When Laura, Mollie and Tamie arrived and greeted him, they offered sympathetic smiles. They'd take care of Jillianne and start guiding her through the rough waters of her three new professions.

He'd decided to go over to his father's house and pack more of his clothes when Winnie said Officer Griffin was at the door and needed to see him right away.

The first thought that came to mind was, *What now?*

Ryder was surprised to see her in uniform. "Working a double?"

"Two guys called out sick." She turned and indicated the police car parked by the curb. "My partner is waiting for me."

"How did you make out at Matilda Hennypenny's?"

"I didn't. Two hours before I got there, Matilda got a visit from Gianna Knight and said she was doing a follow-up story on the town and heard Margie Holcombe had written journals about the town."

"Tell me she didn't."

"She did."

"Son of a bitch!" Ryder couldn't remember when he'd been more pissed off and frustrated.

"There's more."

Chapter 15

"I was about to leave when Faith Hennypenny approached me with a question. She said the license plate on the car the lady was riding in was funny. I asked the eight-year-old if she remembered the plate number, and she said of course, because she remembers everything. The number she rattled off was DC 103A and it wasn't from New Jersey."

"You just made a connection I've been needing. A car with that plate number was in the hospital parking lot the other day, and the driver was taking pictures. Now we have to find out who Gianna plans to give the journals to."

"Oh, that's not the best part. Earlier, we got a disturbance call at the Plumb Beach Restaurant. Deakins was driving, so I was making notes for my official report and a couple walked out, quite chummy and laughing. The man's arm was around Gianna Knight, and he was holding the journals with his free hand. He put the books in his car and backed her into the driver's door. Things got hot and heavy. The diplomatic plates were the same. I took about a dozen pictures and will send them to your phone. I Googled a picture of Fabio Magellan, and that's the guy she was locking lips with."

"Kaitlyn, if I could promote you, I would."

"Didn't she just take your written proof that Burrows was responsible for killing Marshall Holcombe?"

"That's the way you and I, as cops, would think, but those journals were written by a woman suffering from dementia. A sharp lawyer would have them thrown right out. You're in this mess now, and we're getting close to bringing them down. They're getting desperate. Watch your back and keep an eye on your parents."

"I will. Do you want me to continue to keep an eye on Gianna Knight?"

"Don't go out of your way, but if you see something out of the ordinary, call me."

It was after eleven when he got home. Polly and his dad had helped him pack up half of his closet. She planned to start moving into his dad's by the end of the week. They were planning a Christmas wedding.

He unloaded everything in the garage, where it would stay until Jillianne's closet was organized. The house was quiet when he entered the kitchen and walked over to the table. Winnie had left a piece of apple pie on a plate, with a fork. The slice was covered with something that resembled a small shower cap. A sticky note was stuck to the placemat.

Sherlock, I made this pie with the girls' help. Lady Underdog is going to be the best damn wife, mother and grandmother.

He removed the stretch cover and took his first bite. His taste buds silently cheered. "You'll definitely make it, Lady Underdog." He saved a piece of the flaky crust and gave it to Watson.

Jilly was already in bed, so he undressed in the bathroom. The nightlight gave off enough light for him to see where he was going, but his eyes were drawn to the big paper arrow attached to one of the closet doors. Wondering what was going on, he slowly moved the sliding door, trying not to make any noise, and got the shock of his life. It was completely empty. She'd posted another sign on one of the shelves. *Sherlock's Place—it's a start.*

Those women had worked miracles, he determined, and slowly lifted the covers. Trying not to shake the bed, he slid as close to her as possible. To his surprise, she was on her side and quite naked.

"I'm awake. Make my world complete and spoon with me, but first, ditch the shorts. I want skin to skin."

"I don't need a second invitation. If I hurt you, tell me to back off."

Her sigh of relief filled his ears when he lightly draped his arm over her hips. His open hand covered her stomach, and it took all of his self-control not to slip his fingers lower. Instant heat saturated his body.

"This is perfect. Did you find the pie?"

He lightly nuzzled the smooth skin along her neck before seizing the tip of her ear with his lips. "It was delicious, but not as good as you taste. You're torturing me, Mrs. Wayne."

"I'm not doing it for selfish reasons. This is what we both need. I almost died, and being surrounded by you makes me feel alive."

"Me, too, love. Thanks for the closet space. I don't know if I have enough clothes to fill it. What did you do with all your clothes?" He swallowed back a groan when she shifted her hips in a way she knew would coax a hard-on. His fingers slipped closer to the spot between her legs that he knew would be already simmering with heat.

"Tamie will bring them to church for the Good Will donation. What did Kaitlyn want?"

"I'll tell you in the morning, and stop wiggling." She knew what she was doing.

"You could finish what you started on our wedding night. Lady Underdog can take it." She purposely raised her leg and draped it over his thigh, and he gasped when she brought his fingers to the throbbing morsel between her thighs.

"Sherlock, husband, love, work your magic," she moaned and thrust against his massaging fingers. She was so primed, it didn't take long for her silky cream to coat his fingers. She cried out her release, shuddering in the aftershocks.

"Your turn," she promised when she got her breath back and took him between her legs and tightened the silky smooth flesh of her thighs around him in a vise-like grip. She took her time and rode his hardness, all the while flicking her thumb over the swelling tip until he couldn't take it anymore and spent himself on her leg.

"I'm so sorry, love, I couldn't hold back."

She turned her head slightly to give him a slow, easy kiss. "I'm sorry, too, because I wanted you so much."

"Don't move. I'll get a warm facecloth, and we'll both get cleaned up. Lady Underdog, what more can a man ask for? I've got it all. An entire closet, a perfect apple pie and a gorgeous, sexy wife who can make me come with her thumb. Five stars in the wife department."

"Are you finished with your work? We need to be downstairs by eight."

Jillianne gave her wonderful husband a big smile when he walked into her office at the Footlight Theater. It felt good to be here, and these few hours out of the house had helped ease her apprehension about what they were facing. Tonight, she'd be attending her first meeting of The Association-plus. A great deal was riding on what they had to discuss, and the others were counting on what she knew about Burrows's accounts, though everything she had to tell them would be considered hearsay in court.

"I'm done. I just wanted to double-check the files that Burrows said I'd embezzled from the theater accounts. Everything checks out perfectly."

She stood up from her desk and reached for the heavy wool sweater she'd hung on the back of her chair. Going braless felt wonderful, but going out in public was totally different. She'd taken to wearing one of Ryder's soft white T-shirts and covering it with a flannel shirt. It was so un-Jillianne. She loved it, especially pairing the pink and navy plaid material with jeans and boots.

Ryder, too, had chosen to wear his new Black Watch plaid flannel shirt that she'd bought him. His closet was so empty, she'd had to do something.

"Come on, Watson. We can't keep the master waiting."

"I didn't mean to rush you, but we have a lot to discuss." Ryder took her hand after she closed and locked her office door. "Are you sure you're up to this?"

"Physically? I'm still messed up, but mentally, I need the challenge and we've got to get Burrows."

"I've been meaning to ask. When the girls were over the other night, did they bring up the subject we're going to talk about tonight?"

"I'd be lying if I said no. They were so relieved that I knew and that we could go over what was happening between us. They also apologized for keeping everything from me, but they said they were sworn to secrecy. I told them I understood."

"I'm glad you let them know you're not holding any grudges." He held the door open for her and Watson before they walked down the stairs to the basement level.

"Laura told me why Everett had to leave and why she couldn't tell him about Noreen. Mollie explained what Burrows tried to do to her and the threat against Mason. Tamie Elise explained Jackson's fear of pursuing a relationship with her and what the demons did to Jackson's wife and the phony lawyer used in the adoption."

They'd just stepped into the corridor that led to the activity room for the theater school when Jillianne stopped and turned to her husband as a horrible thought came to mind. "We need to find out more about Sydney's adoption. Thompson and Burrows have always been best pals. He could have told Burrows the baby I was carrying was yours." Then it all fell into place. "That merciless, cold-blooded crook!" Jillianne pounded on his chest. "He learned they needed more money to save their goddamn vineyard and offered money for our baby!"

Her crying shouts alerted Laura, Tamie and Mollie, who were just coming out of the ladies' room.

"Shush, love, don't get yourself upset," Ryder urged, drawing her into his arms. "I was going to tell you tonight. I looked into it a little further, and the couple who sold our baby was approached by the same crooked adoption agency that conned Jackson. The couple passed away a number of years ago, so we can't charge them with kidnapping. No matter what, we're going to get Burrows for everything he's done to us."

"What happened?" Laura asked, running a soothing hand along Jillianne's arm.

"She came to the same conclusion I've been trying to prove. Burrows used the same agency that arranged Maya's illegal adoption."

"I hate him. I hate him," Jillianne muttered, wiping her tear-stained cheeks on her husband's shirt.

"Come on, sweetheart. Let's get on with the meeting so we can devise a way to take these guys down."

"The demons are not only facing The Association, but Team Underdog," Mollie said, trying to make Jillianne smile.

"Like my wonderful husband said, let's go take them down!"

The room was filled with friendly faces, many of whom had attended their wedding. Unlike the last meeting of The Association, Ryder didn't feel alone, because Jillianne's presence completed him.

Mack sat next to Captain Clark. Ryder was pleased to see that Hudson and Manny could make the meeting. His father had been invited but apparently was running late.

When Ryder stood, all eyes in the room fell on him. "I'd like to thank you all for coming this evening. You're all aware of what happened to The Association all those years ago and how our lives have been almost destroyed by who we now call the demons. Because your lives, too, have been affected and almost destroyed, we wanted you to be a part of our final efforts to take them down." He smiled down at Jillianne, and she took his hand. "Their latest efforts almost killed my wife. All along, we've been saying, 'No more.' This time, we have to stop them."

He nodded at Mason, and he stood. "You're all aware that Gianna Knight works for my parents, and me indirectly, and the part she's played in helping the cartel. She tried to destroy my parents' media corporation by helping the cartel try to infiltrate it, but we were able to stop them because I have a very smart and clever wife. We've needed something to prove Gianna is involved with Fabio Magellan, and Officer Griffin has provided us with photos of them making out in the parking lot of the Plumb Beach Restaurant."

"That doesn't prove she's part of their money-laundering operation," Mack said.

Mollie spoke up. "No, but she'll be guilty by association. I want to destroy her career for what Mason suffered at the hands of the cartel in their prison."

"My grandfather couldn't be here tonight," Everett said, "because he's been asked to officiate at the weekly service in the chapel in the convalescent center. Laura and I visited with him this afternoon, and he gave us a copy of his notes, the same ones he provided Preston Reynolds. They reviewed every one of the ledgers." Everett held up a number of handwritten pages. "This is a list of every one of the employees who lost their pensions and the amounts due them at the time the cannery was shut down. Calculated this many years later, these people would be rich."

"Was Durward able to backtrack the money buried in fish and the subsequent drug sales?" Mack asked.

"No, and that's a pity," Everett said.

"Can I say something?" Hudson asked. "Just don't hate me, because I'm going to play devil's advocate. We're surmising—I didn't say assuming—Burrows and his son ordered the hit on Holcombe. Matilda just told me about Margie Holcombe's journals, and I agree the rambling of the poor woman wouldn't be admissible evidence. Said journals are in the hands of the cartel. Wash one."

He dipped his head toward Everett. "We know The Association witnessed the murder, but no one believed them, and they didn't see any faces. In all probability, the murderers are dead. Wash two. They supposedly killed Harvey, the maintenance supervisor at the plant, but there's no solid evidence. We have knowledge via a relative of this person that the cartel was using the cannery to ship money and drugs in blocks of frozen fish. Wash three and four. We don't have anything to connect Burrows to the Cartel. Wash five."

"What about them being responsible for killing the woman I was supposedly married to and Maya's phony adoption?" Jackson questioned.

"Dylan's father killed your supposed first wife, and we haven't been able to connect the murderer to Burrows's illegal operations. Wash six."

"So what you're saying is that no matter how hard we've tried to prove Burrows is behind all this, we don't have any solid proof?" Laura cried out. "I'd like to personally beat him up for forcing me to keep the knowledge from Everett that he was a father. That monster almost destroyed our lives!"

"I agree with you, but I'm not the bad guy here," Hudson said. "I'm just trying to make sense of the situation. You have tons of circumstantial evidence, painful moral issues that have hurt everyone, but we need solid proof to bring him and his organization down."

Jillianne was much too quiet, and Ryder watched her doodle on the pad in front of her. "Now you see what we're up against," he said to her. "We can't get him for murder or, as Hudson said, for all of the moral issues. We need to get him where it hurts, his pocketbook. You've been in his accounts."

"I've been listening to everything you've said, and like Hudson, I'm going to be the bearer of bad news. When I was in his accounts, I saw all the pension money and the amounts laundered from the cartel. I saw the blackmail money you've been paying to Burrows all these years. His accounts were in such disarray, two accountants and myself cleaned up everything just in case he ever got audited by the federal government. If they looked at him now, he would appear squeaky clean. Legally, I've been blocked out of his accounts."

"Sweetie, I'm not a numbers person," Manny said, "but one of my girls is a CPA, and she takes care of my oodles of money. I know for a fact that she contracts with a company that backs up my accounts, and they contact me every three months for a new password, and I give it to my accountant."

"Oh, Manny! Oh, Manny!" Jillianne cried, forgetting about her injured ribs, and hurried around to the other side of the table and kissed him smack on the lips. "Oh, you wonderful person!"

"Thank you, sweet love, for that spectacular kiss, but your husband carries a gun, and I don't want to get dead."

"Manny, you're one of the few people I'll let enjoy a kiss from my wife. How about telling us what's going on? But sit first," Ryder said and put a hand on his wife's shoulder so she'd stay in one place.

"I do have a service that backs up our work every twelve hours, but when I took on Burrows's account, I contracted a separate company to back up his initial files before we updated any of his current figures. I did this just in case we made an error along the line, so we could go back and check the files he gave us from the get-go. I'm the only one who has access."

She looked at Paul Clark. "Can you get ahold of the guy who is working on Burrows's accounts for the court?"

"It would have to wait until tomorrow during business hours."

Hudson spoke up. "We work for the same company, and we're friends. I've got his personal cell number. I know for a fact he's probably up. His wife just had a baby."

"Great. If you get him on the phone, I have a couple of questions to ask him."

"While we're waiting, how about we discuss the children's toy drive?" Laura said. "Everyone involved is in this room." She looked at Manny. "As our chairperson, you've already put many hours into this wonderful event."

"Don't discount yourself, sweet Laura. You've put in as many hours as I have since you're my co-chair. The kids in the after-school theater arts program have been working so hard. We're doing six fabulous musical numbers. Maya and her friends in Eva Morris's high school theater class are supporting the younger ones. My girls will be doing *Santa Baby*. In order to get in to see the show, everyone has to bring a toy valued at ten dollars or make a donation. Children will get in for free. You've seen the advertising flyers and drop-off boxes in the stores for people who can't attend the show."

"I've had a wonderful response from my customers at the Book and Brew and have replaced the donation box three times," Mollie reported. "Mason has been advertising the event in the online and print editions. Elsie and Fred are overseeing the toys and donations coming into the newspaper office, and Polly is handling contributions coming into the municipal office."

Paul Clark popped into the conversation. "Hannah said the people coming into the restaurant have been adding their donations into the food and drink bills. She'll be sending a check to Jillianne after the show."

"The director of child services for the town is ecstatic. We'll be able to help out so many of the needy children that are in their files," Tamie said.

Hudson interrupted and handed the phone to Jillianne. "You two are on speakerphone. Jillianne, meet Preston Reynolds."

"Hi, Preston. I'm sorry to interrupt your evening, and thanks for taking our call."

"So you're the genius behind these accounts. I've never seen a cleaner set of books in my life. I still haven't found any accounts that would reflect you stole all that money."

"That's because I didn't. When I was told an independent audit was being performed, I knew the accounts were clean. The pension money and blackmail money are now in accounts that are legitimate. I didn't do anything illegal, because the money has been in the accounts for so many years. He's still laundering money for the cartel by funneling it into short-sale real estate. He made his accusations before I could find out where the money is coming from. I'll bet he keeps it in offshore accounts."

"That's one of the things I did find. He's got dummy corporations, and the money comes into the real estate accounts at the time of property sales. I'm in the process of tracking the source."

"Damn, you're good. I'm about to make your day. How would you like to have the initial set of files I backed up when I took over his accounts? They'll show the pension money, the blackmail money, which is listed under donations.

"Jillianne, you just made my day and night. Hudson will give you my personal email, and I'll get started looking at the unclean accounts tomorrow."

"I believe the pension money was used as the initial start-up cash for Burrows Real Estate Corporation. If you can find the initial amount, isolate the funds. We need to find a way to return the money to the former workers and-or their families."

"I love to search accounts for money that people are sure we can't find. I have a general idea where it can be located. I've worked with Durward, and he is another smart cookie. If you think of anything else, let me know."

"Thanks so much!"

"Now I feel better." Jillianne grinned at her husband and punched the air. "Yes! We'll hit him in his pocketbook."

"I'll have to admit you're the key to helping bring him down," Captain Clark said, "but I wish we had a way to connect Burrows to the cartel and them smuggling money and drugs. It would prove there was a motive for him killing Marshall Holcombe, the murder that started this thing." Paul looked at Ryder. "What happened to your father? He said he would be here tonight."

"He told me the same thing when I saw him just before he reported to his school crossing-guard post."

"Now I'm worried. Maybe you should text him," Jillianne said.

The echo of a door closing down the hall announced his father's arrival. "He's here," Ryder said with much relief.

"Dad, we were getting worried about you." Jillianne accepted his kiss on the cheek before he sat down beside his old partner. "Why are you so late?"

"We two old birds may be retired, but we're still the best damned detectives since Mickey Spillane!" Dexter announced.

"This afternoon, I got a call from Harvey's widow," Mack started. "The wife of the maintenance supervisor Burrows had murdered is moving into a retirement home and started to clean out the attic. She found an old Hasselblad camera that belonged to her husband, and she knows my hobby is taking pictures and thought I'd like to have something from my friend. She mentioned there was film in it, but has no way to develop the pictures. My cop instinct came alive, and of course I said yes. I couldn't pick it up, but my pal went over to her house."

Dexter pursed his lips in annoyance. "Do you know it's almost impossible to get old film developed? Everything is goddamn digital. A friend and a retired CSI we used to work with developed black-and-white film on the job and still does as a hobby. I called Joe Kentrus, and he told me to bring the camera right over."

Mack opened the manila folder he'd been holding on to, and a dozen eight-by-ten black-and-white photographs slid out. "Thank you, Joe, for helping solve this case. Here's positive identification of the bad guys working together."

Ryder picked up the photo in front of him. "Hot damn! This shows the interior of the cannery where they were processing the blocks of frozen fish. You can clearly see the men removing the sealed packages from the fish."

"Ladies and gentlemen, here we have a picture of the Burrows devils, as I like to call them, inspecting one of the packages of drugs and money." Jillianne laughed with glee.

"No, this one is the clincher." Everett held up one of Burrows standing next to a table with another gentleman, whom they'd all seen pictures of in the media when the Magellan Cartel was taken down. Pietro Magellan and Cornelius Sr. were shaking hands.

"We've got all this proof, but what are we going to do with it? I mean, how do we let the public know what a dishonest beast he really is?" Tamie asked.

"Before my father-in-law brought us these wonderful pictures, I thought of a way to expose Burrows." Jillianne looked at Manny. "He's responsible for having you beaten, so I don't think you'll mind if we add a special attraction to the very end of the show. He's an expert at turning the tables on us, but we're going to pull one on him."

"Sweetie, I'm in. Tell me what you want me to do."

"Everyone knows he portrays himself as a philanthropist and gives money to the youth center. This can't come from us, but Sean Harrigan has just taken over the directorship of the youth center organization. The board is going to honor Burrows for all of his generosity. What better place to do it than at a show that will be attended by the children he has supported?"

"Jillianne, you're brilliant," Mollie said and looked at Hudson. "Make sure you invite your friends from ABC, because they'll want to ask Burrows about his part in planting illegal booze at Eighty Eights."

"We can't prove he ordered the hits years ago, but we're going to find proof he ordered the hit on the two Russian guys that were part of his own organization," Paul Clark said.

"We'll be sure to invite Gianna Knight, and I wouldn't be surprised if she brings Fabio Magellan. Hopefully, by the time we have the show, Preston will have solid proof against the cartel," Jillianne added.

"At the rate we're going, we'll be able to fill out a long bucket list of the crimes Burrows committed." Ryder turned to his wife. "Okay, my lovely wife, I mean, Lady Underdog, tell us the rest of your plan."

Chapter 16

Two weeks later, Ryder found himself sitting at another long table, but this time the occasion was a lot more happy and festive. Jackson and Tamie had gone all out to decorate their new family room for the Thanksgiving season. Captain Clark had changed the shift rotation and given Ryder time off so he could spend time with his new family. In other years, Ryder had volunteered to work so others could enjoy the holiday with their loved ones.

He was surrounded by happy voices and laughter from the children, especially his grandson, who he'd learned had a hearty laugh. Adults wore pilgrim hats, and the children represented the Native Americans with headbands and feathers. Elsie and Fred directed the kids to sit on the rug in front of the fireplace and were showing them how to play jacks and marbles. While the women put the finishing touches on Thanksgiving dinner, the men took the kids into the backyard to play chase the hoop.

It was the best Thanksgiving he'd ever had.

Dinner was over, and the ladies were removing the dinner plates and what was left of the variety of vegetables and side dishes served with the three turkeys required to feed all of the guests. Belvedere had prepared a turducken, and everyone praised Jackson for his very first deep-fried turkey. The Association didn't fail to mention the fire department hadn't been needed.

"Dad, are you finished? I'll take your plate."

Ryder gave Sydney a big smile. She'd gone all out and wore a long colonial-style dress with a prim white apron. "I'm done." He patted the vacant seat next to him. "Sit for a minute. Your mother is in the kitchen and won't be back for a few."

He reached for the hand that she rested on the table. "I need to say this before the kids and adults go outside for the scavenger hunt. Your mom and I have a lot to be thankful for this year, but you coming into our life is the best blessing of all." Tears ran down her beautiful face that was so much like Jillianne's, and he grabbed a napkin from the table and wiped her flushed cheeks.

"No, this is the best Thanksgiving for me, Rogan and Oliver. I have everything I've ever wished for. When we came over to your house for dinner the other night, Mom asked if she could help plan the wedding next month. Two brides isn't unusual, but it might be the first double wedding where the bride and groom share their wedding with her grandfather and his bride."

"I'm looking forward to walking you down the aisle, and your grandfather and Polly are overjoyed. We're thrilled Oliver wants to be a part of the children's holiday show next month, but there's more to the event, at the very end. It's the culmination of something that's affected your mother and me since we were teenagers."

"Dad, it's okay. Rogan and I figured out you and Mom are involved in something that's dangerous. She was almost killed, and they tried to pin a murder on poor Watson. You're also a decorated police officer, and we have every confidence you know what you're doing."

"Speaking of the troublemaker, I haven't seen Watson in a while."

"He's hanging out with Wilkins and Jake and Elwood on the dock, watching the mallards. If you need our help, let us know. Please be careful. I couldn't bear to lose you now. And Dad, the Fabulous Four have decided it's the ladies against the guys in the scavenger hunt. If the guys lose, and you will, you'll have to pay up."

"Sydney, do not get involved with those crazy women. They're ruthless when it comes to payback."

"Oh, I already know." She laughed as she walked away and began to hum the Helen Reddy song *I Am Woman.*

Jillianne removed the dishtowel she'd tucked into her jeans while she helped put the food away and adjusted her yellow and black flannel shirt into the waistband of her black jeans. She was slowly becoming aware of what actually happened in a kitchen. Up until a few weeks ago, it had been alien territory.

All of this craziness was so not her. Setting the table, cleaning up after a meal and discussing recipes. She'd made a pecan pie all by herself and participated in a scavenger hunt with overenthusiastic kids. The guys had won and were trying to come up with a payback.

She lifted her hand and inspected her unpainted nails. When was the last time she'd had a manicure and pedicure? She hadn't tried to hide the faint bruises on her face with makeup, and this morning she'd gathered her hair in a ponytail. It was still too painful to wear a bra, so she continued to wear her husband's white T-shirts under soft flannel shirts.

Lady Underdog had overtaken uptown girl. Life as she knew it had totally changed. She'd never been happier in her life.

Belvedere and Valerie, his fiancée, were setting cups and saucers on trays, getting ready to serve drinks with dessert. Winnie and Polly were arranging buckeyes, homemade fudge and decorated sugar cookies on trays. Laura, Mollie, Tamie and Sydney formed a brigade and carried pies and cakes into the den. There were enough treats to feed an army.

Jillianne turned her head and smiled at the giggling coming from the newest bathroom off the kitchen. The kids were taking turns washing their hands. Noreen and Matilda were supervising and cautioned them to stop splashing water on the floor.

She was just about to go into the den and jerked back against the counter to avoid getting hit by a stampede of children. Marion and Chase led the pack, and the Hennypenny girls, Clare and Oliver brought up the rear. Once her grandson had gotten over his initial shyness, he'd become a chatterbox, and she was glad she'd learned to converse in Disney. Watching hours of Mickey and Donald had paid off.

She was surprised when he left the pack and ran back to her. His cheeks were flushed, and she straightened the tall feather tucked into his headband.

"Oliver, are you having a good time?"

"This is the best Thanksgiving ever. Grandpop said we're going to shoot off fireworks! I told him I don't like the loud noise, so he said they'd set off quiet ones."

"Trust your grandfather to come up with something special."

"I love you, Grandma. You're so much fun." Oliver threw his arms around her waist and gave her a quick hug before running off.

Tears ran down her cheeks at the beauty of the moment, and then she sensed she was no longer alone. Her wonderful husband was standing in front of her, holding out his arms. "He gave me a hug, too."

Jillianne let herself be enfolded in his arms and rested her cheek on his chest. "I've just learned that all the money in the world can't buy what you and I just shared with Oliver. Next summer, we should take him to Disney World."

Ryder put a hand on her forehead. "Not sick. Who are you, really?"

"Very funny, Sherlock. Inside, I'm the same woman you've always loved. I want your honest opinion on the pie I made."

"I don't know if I can take this. Hot in the kitchen and in bed." He caressed the top of her head with his cheek. "Who knew making married love could be that much hotter? Are you sure you're not hurting this morning?"

Jillianne's arms tightened around him in remembrance. "You didn't hurt me at all. You wanted to take things slow and easy, but those smooth moves had the opposite effect. You stoked a shivering frenzy in my entire body, and I had no control of the scream that came out of my mouth when I peaked. Damn, you were good. I'm sorry for biting you."

"Love bites are permitted, and it was the best for me, too. I'm looking forward to a repeat this evening."

Jillianne lifted her head and brushed his lips with a love-filled kiss. "Me, too."

"This isn't the time for business, but we're going to need a meeting to discuss what's going to happen after the show next week. Mason suggested we meet at the Book and Brew Sunday morning for breakfast, just the eight of us, which will fit into our schedule. I'm off the rest of the weekend, and Winnie wants help pulling out the Christmas decorations tomorrow. We also volunteered to watch Oliver because Rogan and Sydney are seeing patients in the morning. I'm glad my father saved all my Hess trucks and that I brought them over to our house."

"Sounds like a plan. Sherlock, I have one question before we dive into dessert. How are you going to come up with fireworks that are not loud?"

"I've got an extra set of ear protectors in my truck, and Oliver will think he's hot stuff because they say Police on them."

"I should've known. Ryder to the rescue."

Ryder helped himself to the pitcher of cream next to the bowl of sugar packets on the table and added some to his fresh cup of coffee. Mollie had set up a round table in the back parlor for them to have their private meeting. Sunday mornings at the Book and Brew were a madhouse, and they couldn't risk being overheard. He reached for Jillianne's hand, kissed her fingers and settled their joined hands on his lap.

"I'm sitting here thinking how far we've all come," he began. "Where we were four, now we're eight and have married the women we've loved all our lives. We've been through hell and back, faced challenges no one deserves to suffer through, but our camaraderie and friendships have lasted and, I've no doubt, will continue for the rest of our lives. We've shared a common goal, but are about to take down an evil human being who has tossed challenges into our lives that we've somehow overcome."

"You might even say we owe Burrows." Everett held up his palm before the others could protest. "Hear me out. He forced me to leave town, but I came back to find a family I never knew I had. The trouble we've been facing forced me to admit I couldn't live without Laura."

Jackson nodded in agreement. "Burrows attempted to destroy my life and hurt our daughter. I had a hard time dealing with everything, and I turned to the woman who has always stood beside me and loved me forever. The result is now we have a beautiful family."

"Almost losing my Moll forced me to admit that my love for her was stronger than the threats I've had to live with on two fronts, Burrows being one." Mason rested his hand on Mollie's flat stomach. "In seven months, we'll have a beautiful baby, and we're depending on all of you to babysit."

"Jilly and I faced similar challenges, but when she was almost killed, all my reasons for not moving ahead to make a life with her were off the table. She, too, had her reasons for not wanting to marry me, but those things no longer mattered. Burrows tried to destroy her, but we fought back, together, and our love for each other is stronger than ever."

"That's what I meant when I said we owe Burrows, but he's dirty and responsible for killing people. Once we're done with him, he'll pay," Everett assured.

Laura opened a folder and took out a sheet of paper. "As for the show, there will now be six acts. "Manny will be the master of ceremonies. Opening scene will be *We Need a Little*

Christmas from *Mame.* Manny suggested the opening comedy scene from *Christmas Vacation* where the Griswold family is trudging through the snow. Dylan and Maya will play Clark and Ellen. Red and Aaliyah will play their kids. It will be followed by the choir scene from *Home Alone*, *My Christmas Tree.*

"Tell me they're not all going to fall off the risers," Tamie said.

"No, they're just going to lightly crumble and sit down. Scene four will be from *How the Grinch Stole Christmas.* Manny's ladies will steal the show with their rendition of *Santa Baby.* The show will end with the closing scene from *White Christmas*, and all the kids in the show will participate."

"That sounds amazing," Jillianne complimented.

Laura gave her husband a grateful smile. "Everett has had the patience of a saint working with the kids."

"Thank you, love. Laura, Manny and I decided the children in the audience shouldn't be there during the so-called award ceremony. Santa is going to invite all the children in the audience to go down to the activity center to have refreshments and take turns sitting on Santa's lap. One of Manny's girls is a professional photographer and will take the pictures. Maya, Dylan, Red and Aaliyah will be Santa's helpers."

"Who is going to play Santa?" Jackson asked Laura.

"Chris Duke. He and his wife, Cyndi, play Mr. and Mrs. Claus during the holidays. They always do a great job."

"I've been in touch with Preston, and we've come up with a plan to pay back the people who lost their money," Jillianne began. "Next week, I'm going back to work—only four days a week—and my assistant is going to send out personal invitations to everyone on Durward's list to attend the special Christmas performance at the Footlight Theater. We already know many of them have passed on, but they have living relatives. Everyone is going to receive a big-ass check."

Tamie burst out laughing. "I love it. Burrows will be surrounded by the people whose lives he ruined. Was Preston able to track down the money in Burrows's offshore accounts?"

"The man is a forensic accountant genius," Jillianne said with a great deal of admiration in her voice. "He had no problem tracing the offshore accounts, but for his coup de grace, he was able to uncover the shell companies owned by the Magellan Cartel, who are funneling their money to Burrows. He's laundering their dirty drug money by purchasing real estate. Preston has already dropped a dime on Burrows to the IRS and reached out to Nate Haines, his contact in the FBI, and knows a few people in the State Department."

Ryder drank a little more coffee before addressing Mason directly. "I got a call yesterday morning from the detective who is investigating the murder of the guy you woke up beside on the Steel Pier. Seems he got a tip and was told he'd find the murderers holed up in an apartment. They're from Colombia, and if they claim not to speak English, they're lying. The detective was told to call me regarding the dead guy's friend who was murdered on the beach by the Beacon Pointe Light.

"Along with the two guys, they hit the mother lode. They found the gun that was used to kill both victims, a laptop and a couple of old journals. The two guys bragged the Magellan family would provide a lawyer. After three days, no lawyer showed up, and the detective convinced one of the guys to make a statement. He admitted they'd killed the three men and broken into the cop's house. They got their orders from a guy who owns a lot of real estate in Atlantic City, but his boss gave him the journals."

"Too bad he didn't have the big guy's name," Hudson added.

"I kind of hinted at the name of Burrows," Ryder said. "Finding out who killed Holcombe and Harvey would be like trying to find a needle in a haystack, but we're going to hint that Burrows ordered the hits."

"I think we all know who provided the 'tip,' Mollie said and looked at Hudson. "Please tell TJ we said thank you."

"I spoke to Sean Harrigan about an honorarium, and he loved the idea. To make it appear genuine, he's having a plaque made up and will show it to everyone. He's not the least concerned about this backfiring on the center's reputation," Everett added. "I'm going to invite my grandfather because he should be there to see Burrows get his due. Noreen and our son-in- law will sit by Durward.

"I'm going to make a suggestion," Everett continued. "This is a setup, but we need to give Burrows the idea he's beaten us. He's a great man to be honored for his generosity. You all know what I mean."

"I agree," Jackson said. "Seeing any of us might tip him off. Out of sight, out of mind. So what can we do? He has to know we'll be involved with the event."

Devilry danced in Laura's eyes. "I know we conned you guys into getting dressed up as femme fatales, but would you consider dressing up as elves? You can wear a cute hat and add a pair of glasses, maybe a wig? I'm sure Manny can come up with something. It would be the perfect cover, and you could move around freely."

Jackson raised a brow. "Do we have to wear tights and funny shoes?"

"What are you worried about, my love?" Tamie wiggled her eyebrows. "You have great legs and a cute ass. The tunic will probably cover it anyway. Unless you'd rather be a Christmas tree."

"And what do you girls plan to wear?" Jackson questioned right back.

"We're dressing up as girl elves with short skirts and tights. Manny got us these sexy boots with heels. We'll be selling candy canes when the people come into the theater. One look at us, and the guys will want to open their wallets," Mollie said with a much-too-confident smile.

"You're a pregnant woman, Moll. No funny business."

"Santa doesn't mind if girl elves get pregnant. Where the hell do you think baby elves come from?"

"Manny's ladies will be dressed up as cute girl reindeer and will collect the toys and or money. We'll also be doing a fifty-fifty raffle, so they'll be selling tickets. Anyone have questions?" Laura asked everyone at the table.

"Too bad Santa doesn't have your organizational skills," Ryder said before getting serious. "It's crunch time, and this will be our last opportunity to get Burrows, Fabio and Gianna. Jackson had Blumberg fired, but his name will be on the list we're compiling with the DA. Polly is helping Jillianne put it together. As for Sergeant Thompson, there isn't proof that he's done anything wrong, but he'll be under close scrutiny from Captain Clark. Once this case is out of our hands, it will be the feds' problem to bring these guys down."

"I just remembered," Jillianne said. "Unbeknownst to Burrows, Preston Reynolds will be submitting his official report to Judge Taylor, clearing my name. His expertise as a forensic accountant is highly respected, and he'll highlight accounts with questionable transactions and hint toward money laundering."

"If you're all done giving us a heads-up, this calls for a toast." Mollie had already set out glasses of orange juice, and Mason opened a bottle of champagne and topped off each glass except for his wife.

Side by side, friends, lovers, husbands and wives, they raised their glasses high and professed together, "Here's to The Association."

You are cordially invited to attend a

Special Holiday Show at the Footlight Theater

to benefit needy children.

After the musical production, you're also invited to witness

The Association's

long-overdue roast of

Cornelius Burrows and his associates.

A week later, Jillianne's stomach was in knots as she waited impatiently behind the curtain. Manny had just made the announcement to invite the children to visit Santa and have refreshments. Parents were encouraged to stay with the children. They were waiting until the young theatergoers exited the house before the next part of their program commenced.

She'd changed out of her elf costume and dressed in a red, flowing Vera Wang gown. Around her neck was a graceful necklace of rubies and diamonds. Missi, her hair consultant, had done wonders to cover the healing gash on the side of her head. Tonight, she was facing the audience as Jillianne Bennett-Wayne, the new Director of the Footlight Theater.

She was honored that the others had asked her to be the spokeswoman to represent the group, since Burrows had attempted to destroy her business and personal reputation. This would be the perfect opportunity to hold her Lady Underdog head high. Neil and Paige had helped her put together the slide presentation that should take about fifteen minutes.

"There's my beautiful wife," Ryder said, walking onto the stage. "I wanted to see you before I go up to the projection booth with the rest of the guys. Hudson, Robyn and Kaitlyn have taken positions in the back of the theater." He took her hands and raised a brow at the touch of her cold skin.

"Are you ready for this?"

"Yes and no. Ryder, my love, I need a bit of comic relief. You are the cutest elf in Santa's workshop. The tights mold your cute butt cheeks, and all I want to do is squeeze them. When we go home, I plan to bite them, minus the tights, and then you can give me a full-body massage. I ordered a new oil, Silky, Spicy and Hot."

"Damn! Woman, you never want to turn a man on when he's wearing tights," he teased right back.

"Okay, enough sexy levity. Where's Watson?"

"He'll be here in a moment. Manny insisted the dog wear a red bow tie to match his Santa hat. Remember the command 'by my side.' He'll sit next to you the entire time you give your speech. If they try to leave, just say, 'Now.' Burrows won't make it out of the theater. Do you have your earpiece in so we can communicate with you?"

Jillianne lifted her hair away from her ear. "Where are the police stationed?"

"They're scattered about, but Elsie and Fred, Mack, Dexter and Polly are sitting directly behind Burrows and company.

"What were you thinking? They're all retired and geriatric."

"No one will suspect them. Mack and Dexter investigated Marshall's disappearance, and Fred worked for him. Think of the deceased having his own cheering team. According to Polly and Elsie, 'They don't need any kind of lethal weapon to stop the bad guys if they try to run.'"

"We have Watson. What do they have?"

"I've no idea, but don't underestimate them. The ladies are wearing necklaces with red and green bulbs that light up. If they overhear Burrows or any of them say, 'Let's get out of here,' the ladies are going to turn on their neckless, before taking out their secret weapon."

"This is so insane it just might work."

"I want to kiss you, but I don't want to mess up your lipstick."

"I'll let you eat it off later. Sherlock, please be careful. I love you."

"I love you, too, Lady Underdog. This is going to work."

They both turned their heads to see Watson running toward them. If you could say a dog could smile, he gave a great impression.

"Oh, my, you sweet boy. You look so handsome!" Jillianne said, before bending down to give him a hug around his neck.

Ryder adjusted the Santa hat and stared directly into his brown eyes. "Stay by Jillianne's side. Tonight, you're a cop." Then he faced his wife. "I know you thought it wasn't necessary to have Watson by your side, but I'm also sending a message to Burrows. His plan to charge our dog with murder didn't work. Just like you, he's free and can hold his head high. Now, the both of you can go out there and kick ass." He kissed her on the forehead and winked. "See you later, Lady Underdog. I'm looking forward to sharing that full-body massage."

Ryder had just made his exit when the audience clapped after Manny's "thank you for coming" speech ended. The curtain parted, and he looked so festive in a Christmas-green silk suit. The lapels were bordered in faux rhinestones, but the gems in the rings on his fingers were genuine. In his lapel was a red boutonniere that matched his silk shirt and tie.

"Sweetie, I can't believe this fantastic turnout. My girls said they want to do it again next year. They got a standing ovation for their *Santa Baby* dance routine. I met with Laura, and we made oodles and oodles of money on top of all the toys we collected.

"In a few minutes, Sean will make his little speech. You'll walk out on stage, and they'll lower the screen for your slide show presentation. The Fabulous Four went downstairs with the children, but they'll hear your speech since they're also wearing earbuds. The guys are up in the projection booth with Neil and Paige."

"I know. My personal elf was just here to cheer me on. Manny, we all know how much this children's toy drive has meant to you, but I hope you understand why we had to add this to your dream show. We need to end this now so the guys, us, you, can get on with our lives."

"Sweet love, I've lived through the horror you've all suffered, especially Everett and Laura. I support you one hundred percent. Now let's take these suckers down."

Her pulse quickened even more when she heard Sean Harrigan step up to the microphone and introduce himself.

"Along with our most successful children's toy drive, we chose this night to recognize a man who has supported the youth club with his generous donations for many years. I'm the new kid on the block and haven't had the pleasure of working with Cornelius Burrows for very long, so we asked one of the most upstanding citizens in the community to help make the presentation. She's put together a wonderful slide show.

"Ladies and gentlemen, Jillianne Bennett-Wayne, the new director of the Footlight Theater."

She patted Watson on the head. "Let's do this!"

"Don't look at him." Ryder calmly spoke in her ear. "Paste on your beautiful smile."

And smile she did, holding her head high and walking confidently onto the stage as the audience clapped in welcome. She stopped at the podium and adjusted the microphone when the screen came down to the side of her. Watson stole the show and woofed in greeting before sitting by her side.

"Good evening. I'm sure you all know Watson, Beacon Pointe's decorated police dog. Since he played in *Annie* this past summer, we can't get him off the stage. I convinced him not to sing this evening." Her comment brought the laughter she was hoping to draw to lighten the mood.

"Along with Sean, I want to thank you for supporting all our efforts to bring happiness to children in need, as well as for being a part of the Footlight Theater family. We're here tonight to recognize a man who, up until recently, was a member of the board of directors. You all know him as a generous philanthropist, but there's a little-known side to him that a number of us have known for many years."

She paused, and this time, stared directly at the man of the hour. "Cornelius Burrows, we dedicate the next part of the evening to you. I'm sure you'll enjoy my presentation." Jillianne closed her eyes momentarily when the blowhard had the nerve to puff out his chest and grin back at her.

"Sweetheart, nice touches," Ryder whispered in her ear.

"Slide one, please." Four individual pictures of Everett, Jackson, Mason and Ryder from their high school yearbook filled the screen.

"Back then, you all knew these handsome guys as The Association. Like you, I appreciated their entrepreneurial services selling soda and snacks from their high school lockers between classes."

A number of people laughed and shook their heads in acknowledgment.

"Today, they've succeeded in their chosen professions. Everett is a Tony and Oscar-award-winning actor. Jackson is our beloved high school principal. Mason is an award-winning investigative reporter and owner of the *Beacon Pointe Gazette*. Ryder is a decorated police lieutenant and my wonderful husband."

"You're nailing this, Jillianne," Everett complimented in her ear. "Now lay it on thick."

"What you don't know is, when those boys were sixteen, they witnessed a murder, and no one believed them because they'd been partying under the boardwalk. A week after the incident, they were warned to never talk about what they'd seen, or they and their families would suffer the same fate. Shortly before they graduated high school, they were sent reminders to keep their mouths shut. Two of them lost scholarships to Ivy League schools. One had his admittance into Juilliard music school rescinded and was viciously beaten. The other lost his chance to go into the FBI."

She ignored the low troubled murmurs that had already started and continued.

"Slide two, please. For those of you who don't know this handsome gentleman standing in front of the cannery, his name is Marshall Holcombe. He took over the business from his father many years ago. Unfortunately, he ran into financial trouble.

"Slide three, please. You all recognize Cornelius Burrows Sr. and Jr. These two were lifesavers for the company, but little did Marshall know he was going into business with backers who had questionable reputations.

"Slide four, please. That brings us to Fabio Magellan, a member of the Magellan drug cartel, who I'm told is sitting in the audience. He's accompanied by his longtime girlfriend, Gianna Knight, from Trent Media. While doing our research for tonight's special presentation, we learned she's very good friends with Mr. Burrows."

A spotlight suddenly zeroed in on the reporter. The move hadn't been planned, but had Jillianne's brother's name written all over it. Gianna waved and gave everyone a very nervous smile. Jillianne felt the woman's cold hard stare that promised revenge.

"For those of you who remember," Jillianne continued, "the cannery was shut down by the EPA because of falsified inspection reports. Rather than fix the problem, the Burrows family decided to cut their losses and impose a financial hardship on the town. The workers also lost their pensions."

The murmuring got louder, and a number of people nodded in agreement with her statement.

Jillianne hesitated when Ryder spoke in her ear. "Burrows is grumbling, and Gianna told him to sit still. Everything we have is hearsay."

"Ladies and gentlemen, over the years The Association has endured personal hardship and blackmail at the hands of these heartless individuals. Those boys, now men, needed to find out who they saw murdered and why. The man they saw murdered was Marshall Holcombe. We believe he was eliminated because he found out that his beloved plant was being used to smuggle drugs and fishy money into the country."

Gasps of outrage filled the audience before Burrows shoved up from his chair and shouted, "That's a damn lie! This is all unfounded speculation because you were charged with stealing money from my company! You should be in jail! That damn dog should've been put down for killing Liam Thompson."

More grumbling filled the room, but Jillian wasn't the least bit fazed. "For your information, Dr. Parisi, the new veterinarian and my future my son-in-law, arranged to have the bite marks inspected by a forensic odontologist. Watson has been cleared of all charges." Watson woofed three times, confirming her announcement. "Oh, I've also been cleared of embezzlement charges. Now, if I may continue. Slide five, please. Mr. Burrows, take a look at this photo and tell me who you see."

A wave of discord filled the house when the audience saw the fish, money and drugs on the tables. No one had to guess at the identity of the men in the photos.

Gianna stood up and patted Cornelius on the shoulder. "Those photos have been doctored," she said to Jillianne. "You're scraping the bottom of the barrel in an effort to destroy Cornelius's reputation."

"Sorry to burst your bubble, Gianna, but those photos were developed by Sergeant Joe Kentrus, a retired police officer and CSI. He's prepared to testify in court. As for scraping the bottom of the barrel, we've just started.

"Mr. Magellan you'll be happy to know the forensic accountant who has been helping with the investigation also uncovered your shell companies and money-laundering scheme. The FBI and State Department have been notified."

He went to stand up, but Gianna pulled him down and patted him on the shoulder, just like she'd done to Cornelius.

"I've a bit of good news for the men and women and their families who had their pensions stolen," Jillianne went on. "You'll be receiving a hefty check from Burrows Real Estate Organization since it was your pension money that was stolen to start their corporation. It might take a while, because he'll try to fight it, but he'll be too busy facing charges of murder, kidnapping and embezzlement, along with a number of other charges."

"I've had enough of these false accusations!" Burrows yelled. "You and the others will hear from my attorney."

"And you'll be hearing from ours," she countered, smiling at Sean and Nancy Harrigan sitting in the front seat beside Sydney and Rogan. "Oh, one other thing, Cornelius. We won!"

"Wait for it…" Ryder said into her ear.

The row behind Burrows and his cohorts lit up like a Christmas tree.

"Sit down, you piece of shit!" Fred ordered. "Just so you know, I'm the one who called the EPA on you. I hope you rot in prison! Let 'em have it!"

The ladies had already opened plastic containers and dumped green and red slime on their heads. Gianna squealed in outrage and tried to pull the gooey substance off her head.

"Learned about this stuff from playing with the kids on Thanksgiving," Fred happily announced above the surrounding laughter.

"Ladies and gentlemen, that concludes our special presentation," Jillianne said. "I've been told there are still plenty of refreshments downstairs. Thank you all for coming."

Her legs weren't quite steady when she walked off the stage, but she was greeted by the most beautiful sight in the world. Her husband and friends were there to greet her, and she ran into Ryder's open arms. Laura, Tamie and Mollie were crying, and a watery film covered the eyes of each member of The Association. They'd all changed into street clothes and looked so wonderful and normal.

"You did it, Jilly," Ryder said. "It's over. With all the proof we've gathered, they won't see the light of day for a long time, if ever. Captain Clark is heading up the team taking them in. He loved the slime idea and said he would keep it in mind for the next time."

She nodded against his chest and swallowed, trying to dislodge the lump in her throat. Drawing on her Lady Underdog courage, she lifted her head and smiled at her friends. "I don't know about the rest of you, but I'm for a bit of celebrating and can use a cookie, but first we have to do this right, together. Has everyone left the house?"

Jackson walked out onstage. "All clear."

"Perfect. We're all going to the projection booth. Please don't ask any questions. You'll understand when we get there."

Her brother and niece had already left, but a dim light shone above the board that controlled the lights and sound system.

Tears continued to run down her face, but she forced the words out. "It all started here, and it should end here, but this isn't the end. It's the beginning." She gripped Ryder's hand. "We have so much more than when we started. Husbands, wives, children, grandchildren, and we can look forward to many more happy years together." Now came the hardest part, and she sighed deeply.

"I want us all to join hands," she said and smiled at Everett, who was standing closest to the control panel. She took his free hand to let it hover over the switch that controlled the house lights. "It all started with you, movie star, and you should have the honor of ending this final chapter."

The lights in the Footlight Theater went dark.

The End

Author's Note

I hope you enjoyed this four-book series as much as I enjoyed telling The Association's story. When I wrote the last line, I cried, having lived with these wonderful characters for over a year. I reached out to family members and dear friends who helped me put these books together. There are too many to list, but I will be forever grateful.

I love my fictitious town of Beacon Pointe so you'll be revisiting the shore town sometime in the future. Matilda and Hudson are already whispering in my ear because they want everyone to be there for the opening of the Bessandra Troy Museum. You'll also meet her two cousins, Irene and Vinny.

Before we do that, there is a character that deserves of his own book, Treig John Taylor so we'll be heading back to Laurel Heights. "*A Kiss at Sunset*" March, 2018. Have I got a love for him, Cameron McGregor. She'll be giving him a run for his money. It will be the first book in my new "Laurel Heights Inn" series.

You'll revisit friends from Laurel Heights, Lincoln and Jessie, Sallie Mae, and also meet Cindi and Preston's baby, from *The Wedding Gift* and Samantha and Luke O'Ryan's baby from *Tea in Time.*

Happy Reading,

Judy

OTHER GREAT READS BY

JUDY KENTRUS

ELUSIVE OBSESSION

MAID TO ORDER

ARREST OF THE HEART

Laurel Heights - Book 1

WINNER TAKES ALL – (Part One)

Laurel Heights Book 2

THE WEDDING GIFT – (Part Two)

Laurel Heights Book 3

TEA IN TIME

Laurel Heights Book 4

THE ASSOCIATION

Footlight Theater Series

Everett – Book 1

Jackson – Book 2

Mason – Book 3

Ryder – Book 4

Coming March, 2018

A Kiss at Sunset

Book 1 in the new Laurel Heights Inn series.

Kindle World Books

LOVE ON TAP

UNERCOVER HEART

LOVE LOST, LOVE FOUND

Coming July, 2018

"For Sale, Billionaire"

(Slightly Used)

Roxanne St. Claire's Barefoot Bay Kindle World

92275750R00128

Made in the USA
Columbia, SC
27 March 2018